Cracklin' Rosie
A Sweet Quirky Romantic Escapade
Jennifer Lynn Cary

Tandem Services Press

What Readers Are Saying

The Crockett Chronicles trilogy

"I love historical novels and this one did not disappoint. I was caught up from the first sentence and completely in love with the Crocketts by the end. Can't wait to follow along their next journey. Well done!" –Virginia Denise

"I love this book! The story is soooooo engaging! I can hardly put it down!"—DeNage

Tales of the Hob Nob Annex Café

"This is a well written book that hooks you on the first page. It's a very enjoyable read that makes you forget about all your troubles and step back in time. I loved this book and look forward to what this author writes next." –Ann Ferri

"I loved reading this book! It had me intrigued from the first page, and as the stories began, I could hardly wait to turn the page to see what happened next! Love the mix of true facts mixed with some good, clean, fun fiction! Easy, quick read. I highly recommend this book!" –CatSmit

The Relentless Series

"I lost my heart in this book, caught up in the lives of each character. I remember these times, which made it more real to me. I had tears of joy, tears of sorrow, grief, and smiles in the unexpected. Great story and hard to put down. Keep reading.... You won't regret it."—Novabelle

"I enjoyed another book by Jennifer Cary! As with all her books the story held your attention from the beginning to the end and I look forward to reading all her future books!"—Mary Rima

"I live in Indiana so I know of the places this book talks about. I so absolutely LOVED this story. It's the first one in this series I've read. I'm glad because I feel it should be the first book as it tells of the 2 families & how they connect. It so touched my heart that at times I cried. I couldn't put it down after starting it so anxious to know how things would turn out with all the difficulties Val & Jimmy had. I'm sure the other books in this series are equally as great."—Pat

The Traveling Prayer Shawl

"When her sister's inheritance depends on it, Cami must do the thing she resolved she'd never do, the thing which will break her heart as well as add one more tough task to her already overstuffed calendar. She must fulfill her grandmother's last request - and what's more, there's a deadline that puts in jeopardy her major project at work. As she begins working on the request, she finds even more complications. The inheritance may raise a conflict of interests. How Cami negotiates these and other potential pitfalls made for an interesting and warmhearted story.

Recommended to those who enjoy Christian Women's Fiction and readers who enjoy Debbie Macomber's stories."—Dana McNeely

"I loved this book so much I hated for it to end!"—Cindy

The Weather Girls trilogy

"I just finished all three of the Weather Girls books on my Kindle Fire! I found that once I started, I couldn't stop - and went from one to two to three - in a matter of 4 days! I work so had to leave my evenings to reading - but oh I hated to quit and go to bed! And then I'd run the story through in my mind again!" —Novabelle

"What a fun series! I'm loving spending time in the past with this family and learning more about the girls and their unique personalities." —Erin S

The Forgotten Gratitude Journal

"This incredible book is written in split time. I don't want to give any more away about the story. It's so enjoyable and I couldn't put it down, needing to know what happened to Molly and RJ!"—Annmarie K

"Jennifer Lynn Cary has written a beautiful split time story about love, love lost and love found again! Throw a mystery villain in the mix and you have a romance with suspense and drama! Such a good read for any romance lover!"—Anita Stafford

Cheryl's Going Home

"This book will touch your heart and soul. Cheryl and Aaron's heart-warming story is full of emotions, and you can feel every one of them. This book will make you laugh, cry and feel every emotion in between. I loved it and highly recommend this book and the entire series." —Ann Ferri

"The book is Christian fiction, but it is not heavy handed and fits the characters and the early 1970ties. The book is Cheryl's story, but also her estranged husband, Aaron's story as well. Their two stories, expertly wo-

ven together, share the experience of the rebuilding of their relationship from each of their POVs. It's a lovely journey evoking the time and place with musical and celebrity references from the era." —MLRumph
The Weather Girls Wedding Shoppe and Venue Series

"Wow. I usually don't read strictly romance but this book captured my attention from the back cover and did not disappoint." —Cheri Swalwell

"I love how this author can transport readers back to the 1970's and brings the past to life." —Connie Hill

"*Sylvia's Mother* of *The Weather Girls Wedding Shoppe and Venue* series will take you on a journey like no other and transporting you in the 1970s and showing you the lessons of God's Redemption, overcoming major obstacles, and showing what it means to be a Child of God." —lesliejune

"I was captivated by the storyline from the very first page." —familymgrkendra

"It's a book(*Runaround Sue*) you don't want to miss." —Jodie A. Wolfe

"*Runaround Sue* is such a sweet romance story." —Erin S.

In Memory of

Dr. Emil Larsen, DC

and

Dedicated to

my childhood friend

Linda Larsen, DC

who shared her memories of her father.

Thank you.

And he that searcheth the hearts knoweth what is the mind of the Spirit,

because he maketh intercession for the saints according to the will of God.

And we know that all things work together for good to them that love God,

to them who are the called according to his purpose.

~ Romans 8:27-28

Contents

The Cardinal in the Sycamore

Once upon a time, a legend grew from the native people living in Central Indiana.

If a couple really loved each other and they kissed beneath a certain sycamore tree *and* a cardinal landed on the branch above them, they would have a long life together.

In the late nineteenth century, a gas boom hit the sleepy farming town of Kokomo.

A family named Ferguson made their wealth with the event and built an impressive mansion on the grounds of the old sycamore tree. When they did, word of the legend came to them, and they passed it down their generations.

Finally, in 1970 the last member of the family sold Ferguson House to Sunny Day Whitcomb who, along with her sisters Stormy Day Crawford and Windy Day Norman, opened the *Weather Girls Wedding Shoppe and Venue* in the old mansion.

Now when couples come, they have their photos taken beneath the shade of the old sycamore and hope for a cardinal sighting to add spice to their kiss.

Welcome to the stories of the *Weather Girls Wedding Shoppe and Venue* series.

Cracklin' Rosie

A Sweet, Quirky, Romantic, Escapade

Book four of

The Weather Girls Wedding Shoppe and Venue Series

by

Jennifer Lynn Cary

Chapter 1
Monday, August 21, 1972, Kokomo, Indiana

R ose Crackinbush knew better.

However, the phone call came just before she tore out of the office, saying they would leave the sign on her front porch.

She ought to go straight to the meeting. Doc said this was an opportunity and would be exactly what she needed. That attending would give her another boost toward her goal.

Not that the gathering wasn't important to her, but this sign was the first tangible piece of the puzzle to go into place, touting that her dream might really come true.

So whether Doc approved or not, she made the detour. Good grief, it was basically a matter of crossing the street since she could see the VFW from her front window.

Rose had left Doctor Carlsen alone at the office while she was supposed to attend a Veterans of Foreign Wars meeting, one that Doc insisted would move her dream closer to reality. That was the plan. It's what she'd intended to do until that last-minute phone call came through.

But now she had to stop by her new residence and soon-to-be-office to see the sign in person, if only for a moment. Just to touch it.

Okay, maybe that wasn't quite the truth, but that's how it felt. Besides, it would only take a couple minutes and she'd be on her way with no one the wiser. And she wouldn't have to drive across town. Her house was within walking distance of the VFW.

On top of that, Doc had worked solo out of his office for years before Rose came on the scene. And she'd moved patients around so that it should be fairly slow while she was gone. Another few minutes added on wouldn't hurt him. She repeated that thought to herself to stifle any feelings of guilt.

She couldn't wait until this evening to come home and check out the sign. She just couldn't.

No matter what her watch said.

Oh, she was cutting it close.

Rose parked in front of her aging Victorian and raced from her car up the old concrete steps to her open wrap-around porch. There, leaning against the house behind her swing, sat the package.

It was heavier than she expected, so she balanced it on a white railing as she removed a portion of the covering, then gasped.

Dr. Rose Anna Crackinbush, DC

This was real.

Of course, she had been treating patients with Doc for a few months now, and she even had returnees who requested her. This is what the two of them were aiming for—to get her set up so she'd finally be able to open her own practice here, in her very own location.

Staring at the sign that would hopefully soon grace the front of her house caused her tunnel vision. Everything else blurred away. Time screeched to a halt.

This carved-out instant was the best. Ever.

She'd read about people falling in love and imagined that it must be sort of like this. There was no way it could be better. In fact, she couldn't conceive of anything surpassing this magic moment.

"Miss? Yoo-hoo, Miss!"

The world rushed back along with the realization that she needed to skedaddle. A glance at her watch told her she still might make it. Maybe.

"Hey, there. Are you alright?"

Rose turned to the voice to find an elderly lady waving a hankie and calling from the porch next door. "Oh, sorry. How can I help you?" *Please don't need me.*

"I was wondering if you've seen my cat. Her name is Miss Kitty, and she's an indoor little girl." The concern came through loud and clear. "I've searched inside the house and just know something awful's going to happen if I don't find her."

Rose glanced around her porch and then over the railings, finally spotting an orange, fluffy-looking mound. "I think I see her." She returned the sign to where the messenger had left it and tiptoed down her front steps to the azalea bush. "Here, Miss Kitty. That's a nice girl. Come to me now."

Pfft! The cat shot out her paw.

Rose narrowly got her hand out of the way in time. Little monster. Another peek had her amending her thought. Big, fat monster.

"She's here, but she doesn't seem to like me." Rose straightened.

"Oh, that's just how she plays. Nothing to worry about. Miss Kitty is as sweet as her namesake." The neighbor didn't move toward them. Why didn't she come rescue her own cat?

Neighbors should get along with each other, and Rose wanted amicable relations with hers. But she also needed to be at that meeting. With her hands on her hips and an ill-disguised huff, she took another gander behind the bush. Where was Matt Dillon when she needed him?

Miss Kitty comfortably groomed her tail.

She'd probably get nailed and end up walking into the meeting with deep scratches, but she had to put a stop to this now. Okay, once more, with fortitude. Rose stooped and this time she reached in quick.

Ow!

"Bad Miss Kitty." Rose held on tight. So did the cat. *Ow, ow, ow, ow, ow!*

The neighbor met her at the top of her porch steps. "Oh, thank you so much. You can bring her inside for me."

"Sorry, but I'm in a hurry. Can't you just take her?" She didn't want to be lured into the house, tricked into being company for a lonely old woman. Rose had places to go, things to do, a meeting she shouldn't be late for. Besides, Miss Kitty's nails were taking up residence in her forearms.

"She slips out of my arms these days. Guess I just don't have the strength I used to."

Sounded like someone who could use Rose's services. However, not this minute. She carried the cat to the door and the woman held it open.

"Will you be able to keep her inside if I set her down?"

"Follow me. You can put her in her carrier." Rose's neighbor led her to the back of the house where the wire cage sat on the kitchen table. After unloading and locking the naughty Miss Kitty in her jail, Rose turned to go.

"Oh, my, I didn't think she'd get you so bad. Let me find some Merthiolate for you."

"No, no, thank you." Just the thought burned worse than the scratches. Besides, now she wasn't going to make the first part of the meeting. "Since Miss Kitty is where she belongs, I really ought to scoot. I'm running late."

"Oh, and I've kept you. I'm so sorry." The neighbor walked Rose to her front door. "Please stop by any time, and thank you for rescuing Miss Kitty."

"That's okay. It was nice meeting you." Rose got as far as the sidewalk.

"But I didn't give you my name, and I don't know yours."

She turned and forced a smile. "Sorry. I just moved in not that long ago. I'm Dr. Crackinbush."

"Oh, a doctor, and I've held you up. Probably from an emergency. Just tell them Amelia Whitehead is to blame. You must be fresh out of medical school."

Rose shook her head, wiggled her fingers in a quick wave, and hustled to her car before she let the comment drudge up unintended offense.

While gripping her Pontiac Fury's passenger door handle, she got a good look at her arms and hands. Deep red furrows had appeared and traveled down her forearms. Although blood didn't pour out, it oozed somewhat. Now she'd have to stop at a restroom to rinse off and hope that would be enough. She needed to remember to keep a first aid kit in her glove box, or at least Band-Aids in her purse. She was a medical professional, for goodness sakes. Rose grabbed her bag and locked her car.

The VFW building sat across the street and down about three houses on the corner. Not far, but since she was already late, she didn't want to add to it.

After walking halfway around the old building, she found the entrance. By now, her feet were screaming at her from her pretty, strappy wedges.

This was so not her plan for the day as she got ready this morning. The sigh spilled out.

Still, these were the shoes she needed. Any device to help add height to her petite frame kept men from looking down on her.

As long as she didn't break her ankle, sprinting like an Olympian, of course.

Turned out the restroom was just inside the door, and she made a beeline there to try to remedy Miss Kitty's damage. Once she'd run water over them, her wounds didn't look quite so raw. She patted them down with a paper towel, thankful this place was more hygienic and not sporting one of those fabric loops for drying hands. They must not have a lot of women on the premises, because with its shiny white porcelain and pink hued walls the ladies' room looked almost new.

She'd done the best she could. Now to get in there. Rose dropped the paper towel in the trash.

Signs pointed toward a conference room on the other side of the foyer. She made her way, opening the door as quietly as possible, and slipped into the first vacant seat.

The man beside her flashed a smile.

Why, of course, he did.

Pause a minute, girl. Maybe he was merely being friendly. Nah, even if that were true, she'd been through enough to not trust a male right off the bat, no matter how affable his grin. Or how much he resembled Chad Everett.

He handed her a program.

Rose missed seeing any on her way in and nodded her thanks.

As she scanned the plan for today's meeting, she noted the special presentation. There was the reason Doc encouraged her to come. Very interesting. And she hadn't missed it.

A new speaker arose at the podium. "I too, want to welcome you. Could we take a moment and have a show of hands for those who are here for the first time?"

About four others raised their arms, along with Rose and the man next to her.

He leaned closer, his voice dropped to a whisper. "I had a feeling."

Now he held out his palm. "Brett Shoffner. You?"

Rose glanced to the front. Was anyone looking their way? No. She shook the man's hand, her firm I-mean-business grip. "Dr. Crackinbush. Nice to meet you."

"Doctor? I am too. What's your specialty?" His twinkling blue eyes were the same shade as his azure tie against his pale blue dress shirt.

"Let's talk after." She nodded toward the man up front.

"Okay." He turned back, but not before she caught the smirk.

Well, yeah, he'd been smiling before, but she could tell the difference. Even heard his thoughts. *A woman doctor. Right.*

The speaker continued. "... and with this bequeath, we are to interview several of you in the medical field. You do not have to be a veteran to be eligible, but having a heart for our vets would go a long way. The plan is to put together a varied team of specialists to form a group to monitor and treat our members. We're building an expansion here where you would have offices. Now we realize that you all have your own practices, but depending on how many of you we select to be a part of this, we'll divide this bequest between you, allowing you to set up a schedule and donate time so that our guys here have medical personnel who'll oversee the program. There is also a chunk of money that can provide for materials and supplies for each one chosen to be part of this co-op. If this piques your curiosity, please come see me afterward. Thank you."

The speaker stepped away and the first man returned.

Rose half listened to him as she entertained the thought of claiming a position on that medical team. Doc had been right. This could help in a lot of ways, and she should be part of it. She had a growing practice—slow growing, but still. And helping the vets wasn't such a bad idea. It would open opportunities for her to meet others who might become patients.

"... so we are looking for volunteers to aid in this fact-finding project."

This was her chance, a moment to prove she cared. Rose shot her hand up.

So did the guy next to her. Brett.

The speaker looked their way. "Great! You two were first, so come see me after the meeting, and I'll get you the particulars. Thank you. And now, feel free to grab a cup of coffee and a cookie donated by Puckett's."

He stepped away and the low rumble of voices in conversation filled the void.

"We'd better go find him. By the way, what happened to your hands and arms? Looks like Elsa the lioness attacked you." Brett sang "Born Free," until Rose put up her hand. Andy Williams he wasn't.

"My neighbor's cat got out, but it's okay."

"Happy to examine your wounds if you want. Remember, I'm also a doctor, a general practitioner. By the way, you never told me your specialty."

Here we go. Rose opened her mouth, but before she could utter a sound, the speaker hailed them. "Thank you for volunteering, and right out of the gate, so to speak. I'm Frank Brown, and my law group is overseeing this whole venture. It's such a large bequest and the stipulations are stringent." He reached out to shake hands.

She grabbed ahold first. "Dr. Rose Crackinbush."

That touch of smirk teased Brett's lips again as he shook Frank's hand. "I'm Dr. Brett Shoffner. Glad to be here. You said this is a fact-finding project?"

"Yes. Not every veteran in town is a current member of the VFW, though they may qualify. We want to investigate if there are more vets who would benefit from having medical assistance here on site."

Rose buzzed to jump at the chance. It was more than something to build her business. Veterans, like her grampa had been, were dear to her heart. "How do you see us doing that?"

"Here's the idea we came up with. We have a list of various citizens who've served in the military but currently aren't members. If you check in with them, request they do a quick verbal survey with you—the questions are on the back of the page—then record their answers and return it to me. That's it. Maybe start by phoning for an appointment, but assure them that your inquiries are brief. We would just like to know if this would interest them and what has kept them from joining."

"Oh, I see. How do you suggest we divvy up the work?" Rose was all for splitting the names. Divide and conquer. At least she wouldn't have to spend as much time with this nosy Joe Gannon wannabe. Kokomo was not L.A., and though the hospitals here were good ones, they didn't compare to TV's *Medical Center*.

"Actually, we really liked that you two chose to work together. We figure that a team approach would be better, and having it be a man and woman, making it feel more like family—and that's how we hope the vets feel here, like family—might help them decide to join."

Being chosen for her gender was almost as bad as being blocked because of it. Rose's blood pressure kicked up another ten points. "So you want us to work together. With each one?"

Brett shrugged. "That won't be so hard. We can do it. When do you need the data?"

Frank looked past them and raised a finger. "I have to speak with someone, but here's the list." He glanced at the paper, a last-minute scan. "Just get it back to me in two weeks? I know you both have your own practices, but I'm hopeful this will go quick."

Rose knew that look. The guy assumed Brett would be in charge.

"It's been nice meeting you. Good luck." He threw the last two words over his shoulder as he shoved the list into Brett's hand.

So Mr. Frank Brown wasn't as enlightened as he pretended. She should've known.

"Well, Dr. Crackinbush, would you like to go with me to figure this out? Or do you trust me to manage things?" The corner of Brett's mouth twitched as if the whole thing were a giant joke.

"I think we need to plan this together. Or I'm happy to be in charge." She smiled sweetly.

"Well then, maybe we could grab a cup of coffee and come up with something?" Brett's smile finally appeared more genuine, friendly.

Rose supposed she'd have to, since he didn't like the idea of her taking the lead. Might as well get it over with. As long as this counted toward her winning a place on the team. "Kresge's isn't far."

"Kresge's it is." He opened the door for her, pausing until she walked through.

Okay. Two could play this game. Rose made it to the exit doors first, holding one out for him.

And waited to see if he'd walk through.

Boy, oh, boy could he pick 'em.

Brett shook his head before motioning Dr. Crackinbush through the door. If he'd heard it once, he'd heard it a million times. Ladies first. And this women's libber wasn't about to change all the work his mother had poured into making him a gentleman.

"I've got it. You can go on." Her determined green eyes flashed a dare.

Brett needed to get along with the lady. So he swallowed his pride, hoped no one he knew saw him, and exited the building, making sure that he was on the outside of the sidewalk while they walked to the lunch counter at the small department store.

Was everything going to be a challenge? Oh, man, he hoped not. He needed to find some kind of neutral ground. "You mentioned your first name is Rose. May I call you that?"

She pressed her lips tighter, but then nodded. "I guess. You probably want me to call you Brett then?"

"That or Omar Sharif. That would work just as well." He dazzled her with a smile—or attempted to.

Her persimmon expression told him he hadn't succeeded.

He cleared his throat. "Sure, Brett is fine. So, have you always lived in Kokomo?"

"No. My family is from Lafayette." No elaborating, no pleasant reciprocal questions.

"I grew up near here. Ever hear of Russiaville? For those who pronounce it like it's written, Russia Ville, I'm here to set the record straight. *Roosh*-a-ville."

"Lafayette isn't that far away. I know about Russiaville. Especially about eight years ago when that tornado hit." She never looked at him, just continued ahead, her pace keeping him moving.

Rose would never understand what her words had done to his gut, twisting it into knots. She'd mentioned the tornado as if it were merely another storm. Only he remembered. Far too well.

Now she glanced at him. Was that concern in her gaze? Guess he'd been too quiet.

They'd arrived at their destination, and he wasn't about to let her hold this door for him. Brett reached around her to grab the handle.

Rose shot him a glare. Or maybe he read more into it because she also said, "Thank you," before heading into the store and making a hard right toward the lunch counter.

Brett followed and took a seat next to her. "Two coffees, please." He held up two fingers before turning to Rose. "How do you like yours?"

"Paid for with my own money."

Geez Louise. He'd never met a woman so prickly. "I apologize. It was my idea. I invited you and wouldn't have done so if I didn't intend to pay. I'm not trying to buy your good will, just being polite."

Rose sighed and her expression softened. "You're right. Now, I apologize. I've had too many people—men—try to take over for me as if I haven't a brain. I can pay twenty cents for a cup of coffee, but I appreciate your kindness."

"Let's start over. I don't know how we ended up like a couple of porcupines, but certainly we can get along just fine, working together on this project." He stuck out his right palm. "Hello, I'm Brett Shoffner, a local general practitioner and fun guy—not fungi as in mushroom." He winked and hoped that would help.

She shook his hand, just as strong as the first time, and the corner of her mouth sort of twitched. She'd be very pretty if she really smiled. "I'm Rose Crackinbush, a local doctor of chiropractic—"

"Chiropractor? I thought you said you were a doctor." Oh, boy. That slipped from his brain and out his mouth way too fast to stop it.

From the storm clouds filling her eyes, he should have tried harder.

The room grew silent as she smoothed out her tan linen skirt. He could imagine she counted to ten in her mind before she dropped her voice to just above a whisper. "The regulatory bodies have been overseeing chiropractic for over fifty years and consider it a long-accepted practice. Before I received my license, I had to meet rigorous educational and competency standards set forth by the National Board of Chiropractic Examiners and the state of Indiana. My training after finishing my undergraduate degree was as lengthy as your medical school training. I'll have you know I *earned* my title of doctor, at the top of my class, mind you, and no one, especially some joke-telling MD, will treat me as if I am a quack. I don't even possess sugar pills."

The lightning sure flashed in those gorgeous green eyes of hers. It was almost worth her ire to see the storm surge. He could even overlook her less-than-stellar view of his humor. "Again, I apologize. My aim was not to attack your intelligence. But you can understand how cracking someone's back ... Cracking." He stared and knew, just as sure as the coyote would fall prey to his plans for the roadrunner, he was about to get into more trouble. A whole lot of trouble.

But he couldn't help himself.

"You really are Cracklin' Rosie."

Rose dug in her purse and slapped two dimes on the counter before spinning off the stool and marching for the exit. Spine straight, shoulders back.

He probably shouldn't have said that.

You don't say? Brett's mother's voice whispered in his head that he should run after her and apologize for the third time. Three's the charm, right? But Rose was too hot to handle at this point.

He'd call her this evening and try groveling again. Maybe.

But a chiropractor? Come on. What did she think he would say? And with that profession and a name like Rose Crackinbush, what was he *supposed* to say?

You were supposed to keep that giant mouth of yours shut and those silly thoughts locked up in your brain.

Thanks, Alma. As if he couldn't figure that out already. It was bad enough hearing his mom correct him. Why did he need his big sister in his head too?

It wasn't the first time his mouth had gotten the rest of him in trouble. You'd think he'd have learned by now. But seriously. Rose Crackinbush, Chiropractor. Didn't that just scream Cracklin' Rosie to everyone? Someone? Anyone?

He drained his coffee and left a good tip along with payment before beating a path out of there.

Even though his stalwart receptionist/secretary/every-thing-that-the-office-needed-besides-a-nurse (or doctor) Belinda had cleared his afternoon in order for him to take the VFW meeting, he had scads of work waiting for him. He might as well head there and use the quiet of the afternoon to finish up paperwork.

Brett retrieved his car from where he'd parked and headed toward his office off South LaFountain.

It still sounded weird to call it his office. It had been Dr. Eilert's for as long as he could recall, even back when he was a little kid getting his shots and vaccinations for elementary school.

Oskar. That's what the good doctor wanted to be called these days. Brett needed to remember they were colleagues now. Peers. Sort of. Dr. Eilert would always be his mentor and the man who saved his life. Nothing about taking over the established practice changed that.

He pulled into the office lot and parked in his designated spot. Belinda's white 1966 Ford Custom was still there. That woman was a workhorse, and Brett learned more each day why he was blessed she'd stayed on. He'd given Pam, his nurse, the afternoon off since he wasn't sure what time the meeting might get out. Now he wished he hadn't. There might be an emergency. But his colleague, Dr. Forrester, agreed to handle anything urgent that came up this afternoon, so it should be quiet. As long as no one noticed his Buick Wildcat in its space.

"Hey Boss, how was it?" Belinda's original smiling face, surrounded by photos of her kids and grandkids sporting the same toothy grin, welcomed him back.

"The meeting itself wasn't bad but ..."

"But what? Something happen?" Now she was all concern with two furrows sprouting between her shapely eyebrows. She tucked her salt and pepper hair behind her ears, a sure sign she was worried and ready to do battle for him.

Should he tell her? Why not? Get an unbiased opinion. "What comes to mind when you hear the name Rose Crackinbush, DC?"

"Oh, she's a chiropractor?"

"Yeah, but doesn't that remind you of something?" He leaned in a little, his hand moving as if to pull the correct answer from his audience.

Belinda shrugged. "Should it?"

"Neil Diamond's 'Cracklin' Rosie.'"

She peered back.

"Don't you get it?"

Now her cheeks lost color. "Please tell me you didn't say that out loud." She stared at him, and he knew she read the answer in his eyes without him forming a word. "You did." Belinda groaned while covering her face with her fingers.

"What is so horrible about that?"

"Boss, I need to tell you something, and promise me you won't fire me for it." She took his hand and patted it, just like his mother would. "You are not as funny as you think you are."

He tried to pull his hand back and defend himself, but she held on and overrode him. "Now those of us who love you can find some things humorous, but I'm betting this was your first conversation with this Rose person. Am I right? Please hear me. You've gotta know your audience, or one of these days I'll be visiting you in the ER because you said the wrong thing at the wrong time."

"You're fired."

Belinda gasped, then chuckled and smacked his arm. "You couldn't function without me."

"Oh, if only that weren't true. Fine. But don't speak to me unless it's an emergency. I need to suffer in my office. Not funny? That was harsh, Belinda." He shook his head but couldn't help the tiny smile. She only confirmed what he knew all along. Rose was not the type of person to tease like that.

But not funny? He'd show her funny. Just wait and see.

He started through his stack of to-do work—some he'd left for himself, and some Belinda had added because it required his signature or attention. Usually there weren't enough minutes during the day to get at this. He really ought to hire an office manager who could manage the medical things Belinda couldn't.

Pam had the qualifications, just not the time. Nor the inclination, for that matter. She was a working mom with school-aged kids. Staying to deal with paperwork deprived her family of their only parent. Belinda was in a similar situation—employed here because she had to be—though her offspring were now grown with little ones of their own.

That got Brett to thinking. Why did Rose feel like she had to work? Wouldn't she prefer to stay home with her children when she and her spouse started their family? True, he hadn't noticed a ring on her finger, but most women wanted that, right? A husband, a house, and a bunch of kids in the white-picket surrounded yard?

Okay, maybe that was presumptive of him. But it shouldn't lessen a woman's intelligence to care for the next generation. Didn't children deserve moms at home to be there for them when they needed a parent?

Brett knew before he voiced any of this not to do it in front of a female. Today's women were sure they could do it all, and without a man. Yeah, right. There were a few things that still required the male of the species, so he didn't think his gender would become extinct like the Dodo, but he could envision a poster touting scarcity of the obsolete gentleman.

The train of his thinking made him depressed. Somewhere out there, there had to exist an old-fashioned girl who would love to marry a funny—

You're not funny. Belinda's voice invaded his musings.

What were the women in his life doing? Having a coffee klatch in his brain?

He tried again. Somewhere out there existed an old-fashioned woman who would succumb to his charms and want to build a home together. It had worked for his parents. Even when his dad was stationed overseas.

It wasn't a matter of a female being weak or brainless. His mother was neither. But she found satisfaction and happiness in raising her family and creating a loving haven for them all.

He needed an old-fashioned girl, like his mother.

Was that too much to ask?

Chapter 2

Rose dropped her purse into the bottom drawer of the spare desk Doc let her use, then kicked it closed a wee bit harder than intended.

"How did it go?"

She should have anticipated his wanting to know right away. "Fine." But she didn't sound fine, even to her own ears. Rose plopped into her seat.

"What happened?" Doc pushed out his desk chair and swiveled around to face her, apparently ready to offer his sage advice. Okay, he usually did have great advice. That point Rose was willing to concede.

But before she could pour out how she'd been wronged, and by a male chauvinist MD at that, he was on his feet, examining her arms.

"I repeat, what happened?" Doc's stare bored into her as if to cut off any attempt at lying.

"I helped someone capture her cat, and the feline wasn't as grateful." Rose took another gander at her war wounds. At least they weren't as ugly as when it first happened.

"Where was this?"

Great, now she had to fess up about her tiny—itty-bitty really—detour. "I ran by my house on the way—I mean it's practically across the street—and the lady next door saw me and was all in a dither about her cat. I did the neighborly thing and found it, quickly, but to make a long story short, the cat didn't like my returning her to her owner. I still made it to the VFW, though I stopped to wash my arms before going in."

Doc had pulled out a salve and applied it to her scratches. "Go on."

"I went to the meeting."

"And?" He returned to his desk, finding a spot for the salve jar in a drawer.

Rose leaned her head against the chair back. "I ended up next to a guy who must idolize George Carlin. It was one joke after another. And that was before he learned I was a chiropractor. They placed us on a committee together, and when I told him I was a DC, he busted a gut calling me Cracklin' Rosie."

Doc snorted, then wiped his hand over his face, removing the grin that fought to be seen.

"Not you too, Doc?"

"I'm sorry. But of all the nasty things I've been called over the years, that doesn't even come close. If that's the worst anyone ever says, then you're doing all right." He moved a page to a different stack on his over-flowing desk. "So, other than that, do you think this opportunity is a good fit for you?"

Rose paused to consider. "Yes, I do. The vets put me in mind of my grandfather, and you know I wouldn't be here without him. So if I can do anything to help them and honor him, I'm all in."

"Good. I have to finish my notes on Mrs. Brookwood and then we'll close up for the day. No other appointments. Run on home now if you want." He paused and caught her gaze. "Oh, why did you need to stop by your house on the way to the meeting?"

Rose knew he'd get around to asking that. "I had a phone call right before I left here. It was from Bell Signs, and they said they'd delivered mine and left it on my porch. I just wanted to take a peek." Her face heated as she confessed. "It was only supposed to be a minute, but that stupid cat …" She swiped her bangs away from her forehead, wishing she could do the same with her choice. Her laser-focused determination was a source of pride to her. It helped her through the tough curriculum at Ball State and Palmer College of Chiropractic. But today she let her zeal for her future make a snap decision. Being impulsive rather than decisive, that wasn't her. But it's what she'd done. She deserved a good talking to.

"How does it look?" Doc's grin returned.

"Beautiful." It did.

"Okay, then get yourself home to your sign, and I'll see you tomorrow. Mr. Abernathy is coming in early before work."

"Gotcha. Have a good evening, Doc."

"You, too." He was already back to working through the stacks on his desk.

Rose headed for her car and made it to her house in less than five minutes. Doc's place wasn't all that far from hers, though between August's heat and her chosen footwear, that moderate stroll would turn into big, fat blisters on her heels and long days of misery.

The package was where she'd left it, so she brought it in, unwrapped it again, and set it on her sofa so she could admire it some more. It really was breath-taking, for a sign. More than that, it was a symbol of her dream coming to fruition. Grampa would be proud.

She wiped a tear from her eye and climbed the stairs to her bedroom to change into something more comfortable. One shoe off later, her telephone rang.

Few people had her number—her mom, her brother, Doc, her best friend Teri. She hobbled to her blue princess slimline on her nightstand and answered. "Hello?"

"That's a fine way for a doctor to answer her phone."

She knew that voice. Brett, the jokester. Rose also knew if she slammed down the receiver, he'd probably call again. She pinched the bridge of her nose. "Dr. Shoffner. How did you get my home number?"

Something about using his surname niggled at her. She'd figure it out after she hung up.

"There's this little thing called information. You dial 4-1-1, and they tell you all sorts of things."

"Oh, right." Rose slapped her forehead. Not as satisfying as slapping him, but it was her own stupid mistake. "What do you need?"

"First, I want to apologize. We got off, for the second time, on the wrong foot, and it is all my fault."

He was right about that. "And?"

"Um, I hoped we could try once more so we could plan how to take care of the survey."

The survey. She'd forgotten about that in all the rest of her tumultuous misadventures. "You still want to do it together?"

"That's how they said they wanted it done. Do you have a day off or a half day in your schedule? Maybe we can figure out a way to coordinate." He sounded so normal and nice. Not even cracking any jokes. This guy couldn't be trusted.

She sat on the edge of her bed to keep from standing on uneven feet. "I work late on Mondays, come in after lunch on Wednesdays, and only schedule on Saturday mornings. The rest is my normal eight to five with an hour lunch." She and Doc made their lunches overlap in the middle to share notes and compare cases yet still have some solo time to eat. Doc would probably let her adjust around Brett's schedule if need be, but she didn't want to take advantage. Or give the guy a hint that it was remotely a thought.

"Wednesday mornings are a possibility for me. I have a standing appointment on Saturday afternoon. The list isn't that long. Would you like to divide forces to make the appointments? One of us can phone the families and make the dates for this week and then the other do it for the next week."

"Since today is Monday and you already have the list, why don't you set up the first round? I'll get the rest of the names from you Wednesday when we go to the houses." She sighed, not looking forward to this.

He still sounded chipper though. "Sounds like a plan. I'll call you tomorrow after I have everything penciled in. Once I give you the schedule, you can let me know where to pick you up." This guy presumed too much.

"I'll drive myself."

"Rose. Listen to reason. There's no need to bring two cars."

Reason, huh? "Then why don't I swing by and get you?"

She could almost hear him gnashing his teeth.

"Tell you what. How about I handle the driving this week and you chauffeur me next week. We'll take turns. Then no one can say I'm treating you subserviently."

Okay, maybe she was being ridiculous. However, she needed those boundaries set and immovable. "You promise you'll hold up your end of this bargain? You won't suddenly need to drive when it's my turn?"

"I know you can't see me, but I'm crossing my heart and holding up the Boy Scout hand signal. By the way, I'm an eagle scout, so technically, my promise is binding."

That brought a teeny smile to her, but she smacked it away. "Okay. I'll expect your call sometime tomorrow evening."

"Talk to you then. Goodnight, Rose." His grin filtered through the phone lines. It was a nice grin, but she didn't want to like it.

"G'night, Brett." She disconnected so there'd be no mistake about her playing some childish you-hang-up-first game and plopped back on her bed.

In time for the blamed thing to ring again. "What now?"

"Rose, are you okay?" Teri. Of course.

"Yes, I just got off from talking with... never mind. Let's say someone who managed to drain my well of patience dry. How's everything coming for your engagement party?" Teri was so head-in-the-clouds in love that it became sickening at times. However, enjoying her friend's happiness allowed her to vicariously experience this slice of life. Most likely that would be the only way Rose would ever get close to it.

"It's going to be wonderful. We've rented the back room at *Il Ristorante Italiano,* and my parents have hired a dance band. I'm making sure you'll be there, won't you?"

"Of course. Just because I can't see me ever getting engaged doesn't mean I'm not happy for you. I am. I know this is what you've wanted. I'll be driving up after my last patient on Friday. Be done by five. Give me a few minutes to get cleaned up and an hour to drive there and—"

"Dinner is at seven, so barring any traffic problems you'll be fine."

They chatted, or rather Teri chattered while Rose listened. She didn't begrudge her friend. In fact, she appreciated that Teri enjoyed her life, saw things in a positive light, and was excited for her future.

However, it was getting a little old hearing "Bart did this" and "Bart did that." One would think Teri's fiancé was about to be canonized with the verbal resume she shared.

But something Teri said when she sang Bart's praises made Rose stammer the accolades to a halt. "Wait, wait a minute, Teri. I just thought of... I need to ask... What is Bart's last name again?"

Muffled sounds whispered through the mouthpiece on Teri's end, and Rose could hear unintelligible voices. More than one. "Sorry Rose, I have to go. Mom's calling me. I'll see you Friday." *Click.*

Rose had a bad feeling. Teri had mentioned Bart's last name once upon a time, but Rose hadn't paid enough attention. Normally she would have filed it away in her mind, but she'd been half asleep when Teri called. That was right after Rose had stayed up nearly all night setting up her office space and then worked all the next day. She was so exhausted she couldn't remember her own last name by the time Teri called.

Was Bart's surname Shoffner? No, it couldn't be. Brett and Bart Shoffner? No way. It was something similar. Sure. Schaefer, possibly?

Besides, Teri had never mentioned that Bart had a brother. The guy was a lawyer. And Bart was supposed to be a saint in an Adonis suit.

That didn't describe Brett at all.

Okay, maybe he was sort of Adonis-like with that tall, muscular build and blue eyes and almost irresistible grin.

But that sense of humor ruined the whole effect.

What were the odds that out of all the males in their mid-to-late twenties living in Indiana, she would have a run-in with her best friend's fiancé's brother? Moreover, Brett was from Russiaville, and Bart lived in Lafayette.

Had he always lived in Lafayette?

It was a small city. There was no way Rose could have met every single male who lived there while she was growing up. So it was possible Bart was from her hometown and they'd simply never crossed paths.

It was just a coincidence. She was searching for problems where there weren't any. Rose tugged off her other wedge and dropped it to the rug.

But then again...

No. She was musing on this too much and would make herself crazy.

She could simply ask Brett on Wednesday. But then, would he take that as her showing an interest in him?

"Brett, do you have a brother who is a stand-in for a Greek god?"

Right.

"Brett, what are your plans for next Friday night?"

Oh, that was the perfect opening for him, and she wasn't about to give him one.

Nope. Rose would keep her mouth shut, go to Lafayette on Friday after work, and pray the whole way that this ugly twist in her stomach was the flu and not an omen.

Tuesday, August 22, 1972

"C'mon, sweetheart, just say *ah*." Brett stood poised with the tongue depressor fixed at the adorable-looking three-year-old's lips that were clamped tighter than Fort Knox. She shook her head, blonde curls swinging in his face for good measure.

"Angela, open your mouth for Dr. Shoffner." Mrs. Harshner's voice had picked up a tired edge.

"No! If I do—*augh*!"

Brett managed to slip the flat wooden stick between the child's teeth while her outcry had the same effect as an *ah*.

A quick glance at Nurse Pam, and he caught her wink.

Angela suddenly bit down hard and barely missed the tip of his fingernail.

"Hey, there's a good girl. I just need to check your ears now and then you can pick out something from the prize box while I speak with Mommy. Okay?"

Angela covered her ears, shaking her head again.

Mom was done and pulled her daughter's tiny hands away while the patient screamed.

Brett couldn't blame the mother. He had a feeling the little girl behaved the same way at home. Mrs. Harshner worked at the phone company, which meant Angela had a babysitter. Too bad. A full-time mother might have made the situation different.

He used the moment to check for possible ear infections and noted redness and a slight swelling of the right eardrum. "All done, princess.

The treasure box is ready for you to pick something." Pam showed her where they kept it in the cabinet. He still hoped to win the little one over.

"Can I have two?"

Brett started to shake his head, but the shrug from Pam coupled with the pleading look from the mom helped him give in. "Okay."

Little Snook'ms grabbed three things, and he thought wide-eyed Mrs. Harshner would lose it. "Angela Marie, he agreed to two and he didn't have to allow you the second. In fact, with your behavior, you shouldn't even have any. Now put one back."

The little girl's face crumbled as tears streamed her cheeks. She couldn't feel all that great with her ear like that. He was about to give in and say keep them all when Angela handed him a pink rubber ball.

"Thank you." He flashed his grin and hoped it at least worked on three-year-olds.

She blinked, rubbed her face with her fists that clenched the two remaining bits of swag, and smiled up at him. "T'ank you, Dockor Shoffer."

He stooped to her eye level. "You are welcome, sweetie. How about you play with your prizes now while I talk with Mommy, okay?"

Angela nodded and wandered to the little table and chairs in the corner.

Pam cleaned up and watched for his signal.

"Mrs. Harshner—"

"Oh, Doctor Shoffner, I'm so embarrassed. I'd hoped she'd outgrown the tantrums now that she was past the terrible twos but... " Like her daughter, she shook her head.

"Don't be. My mother always said the terrible twos were followed by the traumatic threes."

"Really?"

Brett dropped his voice to keep Angela from overhearing. "Yes. And couple that with the way her right ear must be hurting, it's normal. I'm hoping we can head this off before her eardrum bursts. She needs an antibiotic before you leave, but I wanted to explain that to you first. If she spikes a fever or complains of an earache, call me at once. I'll also write a prescription." He picked up the file folder on the exam table and glanced at it again. "I didn't note any allergies on her chart. Has she had penicillin?"

"Yes, she has, there's no problem."

"Good. Then if you will hold her facing you, we'll get the shot taken care of."

Only Angela must have heard the hated word and shrieked to her mother. "No, Mommy, no shot!"

Mrs. Harshner scooped her daughter up and hugged her close, speaking soothing words and gently bouncing her. Pam got the injection ready.

The child's mother raised her eyebrows and Brett nodded.

The bouncing slowed to a stop. Brett injected the penicillin into the child's upper thigh.

They had to have heard the caterwaul through the whole building. It was enough that Brett wondered about his own eardrums.

Pam put a colorful Band-Aid on the injection site and gently patted the boo-boo. "There you go, princess. All done. You're going to get better real fast."

"Thank you, Doctor Shoffner." Mrs. Harshner wiggled her hand free for him to shake.

Which he did. "Not a problem. Just get that prescription filled and call me if things don't improve in forty-eight hours." He held the door and escorted them toward Belinda to finish.

On to his next patient. No lunch today. Apparently everyone decided to save their woes for him rather than going to a strange doctor yesterday while he was out. Brett ought to take it as a compliment, and maybe he would once he had a moment to breathe.

He opened exam room two's door. "How are you doing today, Mrs. Jones?"

The fifty-six-year-old woman sat on the examination table, her left foot extended. "I just don't know why my big toe is so sore, doctor. Hurts like the dickens."

Brett had a good idea but probed for confirmation.

Mrs. Jones's yelp was all he needed.

"I'm afraid you've got a case of gout. What have you been eating lately?" It wasn't the first time he'd discussed dietary choices with the woman.

She blew out her breath. "I had roast beef last night for dinner. Sunday, I had the family over for beef Stroganoff with asparagus tips."

"What about your breakfasts and lunches?"

"Oh, I'm trying to lose weight like we talked about, so I just have a cup of coffee for breakfast and a glass of diet Pepsi for lunch."

Brett wanted to shake her but remained in control. "Are you drinking any water?"

"I try not to. Don't want to build up water weight gain, you know."

He set his folder of notes on the counter, took her hand to check her pulse in her wrist, and mentally came up with a way to break the news to her that she had some big changes headed her direction.

"Mrs. Jones, how much do you know about gout?"

"Benjamin Franklin had it?"

Brett nodded. "Yes, you're right. And luckily for you, we've learned a lot about it since. Gout is actually a type of arthritis that happens when uric acid gets trapped in soft tissue of joints, like your toe. When it does, it is in the form of tiny needle-like crystals, which is why it is so painful. I'm going to give you some meal changes that you will need to implement, or this won't be going away. In fact, it can become chronic and a whole lot worse. You don't want that, do you?"

Her eyes were big and round as she shook her head. He'd scared her. Good.

"First, you need to be drinking at least eight cups of water per day. Let's start there and increase up to twelve by next week."

She started to balk, but he raised his hand and continued. "I also want you to stay away from red meat starting now through September. After that, you can reintroduce it back into your diet in small doses, and not two days in a row. Maybe twice a week. Also, watch out for mushrooms and asparagus. They are both stinkers when it comes to causing gout. Stick with carrots and peas." He winked at her.

"Anything else, doctor?" She shuddered before she finished the last syllable.

"Let's start with this. Good ol' H_2O is what will give you the best relief. And if you cut out the pop, you won't retain the water. It's the sodium in the soda that does it."

"Why not just shoot me now?"

"Oh, come on, Mrs. Jones. Do you want to feel better? I know gout is very painful. I also have seen what happens when the lifestyle changes aren't made, and it's not pretty." He hoped that got through to her, though he had his doubts.

"Is there anything you can give me immediately to deal with the pain?"

"Take Excedrin and apply ice to the toe. Also, increase your water intake right away. That's the fastest help. Trust me on this." He offered a smile and his hand to assist her from the exam table. "The best part is that you are in charge. You get to make the decisions that will help you heal faster."

She slipped her black thongs between her toes. Those foam rubber sandals couldn't be any good for her pain. "Okay, Doctor Shoffner. I'll try."

He opened the door for her. "I know you can do it."

"That makes one of us." She followed up with a giggle while she limped alongside him to Belinda's window.

He patted her hand as he left her there before heading back to the first exam room. This would be the tenth patient today, and it was only eleven in the morning. Without Pam reading his mind half the time and Belinda keeping everything running smoothly, he'd never have made it this far.

Four hours later, lunch was still a no show, but Brett finally caught a chance to breathe. He hadn't seen a day like this since that outbreak last month. Every doctor in town had more business than they needed during that little mess. However, today was just extra busy, making up for being gone yesterday afternoon. He collapsed into his office chair.

"Hey, boss, would you like a sandwich?"

He raised his head to spot Belinda standing in his doorway.

"Sure, whatcha got?"

"Nothing special, but I have peanut butter and strawberry jelly and a loaf of Dietzen's." She winced as though it was a pitiful offering.

"Sounds wonderful." And it did. His stomach would be happy for any attention. "Will you cut it into triangles without the crust? Pretty plu-eese?" He gave her his best pleading look with his bottom lip thrust out.

"Oh, you. Anything for a laugh. So, do you really want one?"

"Yes, please. And thank you."

She left, and he started on his paperwork, only to have the list from the VFW stare back at him. Right. He needed to get the appointments made and let Rose know.

Rose. Rosie. That fit her better. With her pretty blonde hair and flashing green eyes, she seemed more like a Rosie than a Rose, though her thorny temper wanted to argue with him.

He sighed and drew the phone closer. There were ten names total. If they took care of five this week and five next, that balanced it. Where were these people located?

Brett pulled out a map of Kokomo and plotted the addresses. If they could meet with the ones on the west side tomorrow, they could manage the east end next Wednesday. That would work. He set to dialing, still trying to put his intro together as the first number on the list answered.

"Hello, this is Brett Shoffner. May I speak to Master Sergeant Ira Brown?"

Someone covered the receiver to muffle the yell. It took a minute, but then an older, mellower voice came on the line. "This is Ira Brown. What can I do for you?"

Brett introduced himself again before continuing. "I'm calling in regard to the VFW. I was wondering if we might come by tomorrow morning and speak with you?"

"Who's we? You gonna bring the whole kit and caboodle around?"

Brett chuckled, trying to diffuse any problem. "No, sir. Just a friend and myself. We were hoping we could ask you a couple of questions. I promise we won't take up much of your time."

"Time's the thing I got plenty of. Until I don't. Sure. About when?"

After making a quick note, Brett suggested nine in the morning and thanked the man before saying goodbye.

One down. Four more to go. If they were all as easy as Ira Brown, this would be a cinch.

Belinda showed up with the sandwich on a paper towel. He had to laugh when he noticed the crust trimmed away and it cut into four small triangles.

"As you wish, your majesty." She tossed him a wink and returned to her desk up front.

He knew she was kidding, but was he really that hard to get along with? Brett made it a practice to be friendly and personable. Another reason he enjoyed humor. Happy people were easier to get along with. But lately, the laughter seemed to be missing. Were his jokes so out there that no one else thought them entertaining?

Great. Now Belinda had him questioning his best quality. He *was* funny. In fact, he was downright a hoot 'n' a half.

So why did he suddenly feel like he was walking on eggshells with a certain petite blonde?

Brett dialed the next number, still no closer to an answer.

Chapter 3
Wednesday, August 23, 1972

Rose stood in front of her dresser, gazing in the mirror to check her hair and makeup, all the while balancing on one foot as she pulled the heel strap of her jute platform wedge into place on the other. For the umpteenth time, she told herself she needed to make a good impression on the people. That's why she chose this white sundress with the big pink flowers. It had nothing to do with proving to a certain general practitioner that she was a professional.

She stuck her tongue out at herself, blaming her reflection for insinuating that she had any interest about how Brett viewed her. She couldn't care less. Rose even repeated the thought aloud. "I could not care less." *So there.*

Someone knocked at her front door.

Rose peeked at her bedside alarm clock. It read 7:45. Brett wasn't due for another fifteen minutes. Could it be her neighbor?

No. Rose shook her head. Mrs. Whitehead wasn't able to make it down her own steps by herself, let alone climb the ones leading to Rose's porch, so it wasn't her. She glanced out her bedroom window that faced the street to view a seafoam green car with a black vinyl roof parked at the curb in front of her house.

Oh, he wouldn't. He couldn't. Not fifteen minutes early. A buzz pinged her stomach.

Fortunately Rose was ready, but she'd wanted to be waiting on her porch swing to keep from letting him into her home. She could still prevent his entering, but it was going to seem rude, and she didn't want to start off that way. Their history revealed they could not be in close proximity without some form of argument. All she wanted was to prove it wasn't her fault. Besides, it might be nice for him to realize she wasn't purposefully looking for disagreements.

So long to that idea.

Rose shouldered her purse strap and headed downstairs.

Brett was peeking through a lace panel that covered the sidelight windows. What a Nosy Ned!

Or didn't he trust her to give him the correct address?

Ouch. That thought was a tad barbed. Nicked her conscience.

She pulled the door open and stepped through, blocking any attempt at entrance and making sure he knew he was not coming in. "All ready, even though it's only fourteen minutes before you were supposed to be here."

He grinned. "Sorry. It's a family trait. Shoffners are always early or they're not on time." And he looked good in his white button-down shirt, open at the collar, the cuffs rolled to the middle of his forearms. Just the right blend of casual and professional for their assignment.

Stop noticing.

"Sounds like a generational curse that needs breaking." Ooh. That was harsh even to her own ears. She turned away to lock her door. Why did he have to bring out the worst in her, especially when she was trying hard to be on her best behavior?

"One day I'll find someone who appreciates that quirk. Anyway, let's make like a banana and split." He walked beside her down the steps to his car before holding the door for her.

"Thanks." Despite her gritted teeth, she remembered her manners. At least he hadn't tried to buckle her in. Was there a seatbelt?

Brett climbed in on his side, started the ignition, then handed her a list of names and addresses before pulling onto the street. "I checked to see what residences were closest to each other so we could make the most of our time. These all tend to be over on the northwestern part of town."

"That makes sense." Good to know he used his brain for more than coming up with stupid remarks. "Then Ira Brown is our first stop?"

He nodded. "Seemed like a nice man. I'm wondering if one reason the people on our list haven't joined the VFW has to do with lack of transportation. I mean, I know there's always a taxi, but what if the budget can't accommodate? I didn't notice anything on the questions addressing that."

"I guess it's possible. Maybe someone figured it would be insulting to inquire about income?" She would get hot under the collar if some stranger probed into her finances, that's for sure.

Conversation quieted. Unlike most people, Brett hadn't switched on his car radio, which made the silence between them loud. Disturbingly so. Rose fidgeted with her scalloped hem.

"How was work yesterday?"

Startled by his voice, Rose turned to stare.

Brett just grinned while keeping his eyes on the road.

"You really want to know?"

"Sure. I have no idea what goes on in the life of a chiropractor. So tell me about your day." This time he glanced her way for a moment before expertly braking at a stoplight.

Well, he asked. She managed to keep from shrugging. "It was busy. Ever since Doc, Dr. Carlson, took me on, business has picked up. That's the plan so that I can eventually take my patients with me when I set up practice at my home."

"Oh, so it's like a residency?"

Rose thought for a moment. "Yes, you could say that. I'm learning things from Doc that are beyond anything I could acquire from classroom or practical learning at the school. He's been doing this a long time, so he has great advice."

"What's been the hardest part in all this?"

Rose couldn't help but think he should be able to answer that himself. "Convincing patients to give me a chance. Some are used to Doc, some look down on me for being a woman in a man's field. Others just see my size and are sure I can't do it. But all I need is that one opportunity to prove myself and convince them. The funny thing is, I expected the men to have doubts, but it's often the women who distrust me."

"Wonder why that is?"

Rose shook her head. "Couldn't tell you. How was your day yesterday?" She might as well keep the polite conversation going.

"It was long. And busy. Finally got a quick bite of lunch around three thirty. Tuesdays aren't normally that crazy, but I have a feeling that people waited to see me rather than go on Monday to the doctor I had covering while I was at the meeting. But it was one thing after another—two ear infections, four rashes, one hernia, a case of chicken pox. Oh, and one case of gout. There were more, but that's off the top of my head."

"I see." What else was there to say? "Do you have a nurse?"

"Yes, her name is Pam. She's great, but as a single mom, she needs to work when the kids are in school and get home to them as soon as she can. My receptionist, Belinda, is amazing. You'd like her. She doesn't think I'm funny either, though she still appreciates me." His grin was back.

"I believe I would. Like her, that is." She giggled when he glanced her way. "I mean anyone who agrees with me about your humor and is bold enough to tell you must be pretty intelligent."

His left fist clutched at his chest. "You wound me, Rosie."

"What did you call me?"

"Rosie?"

"Yeah, that. No."

"Why? I think it fits you. And I'm not even teasing like with Cracklin' Rosie. I just mean... Oh, I don't know how to say it but, you are more Rosie than Rose. At least, that's how I see it. Besides, Rosie is one of my favorite names."

"It is?" Great, he was sucking her into this craziness. Her name was Rose. Ever since Mom remarried and Grampa died. "You only met me the day before yesterday." She paused, trying hard to mount a firm decree. "I'd prefer... Fine. Just don't call me that when anyone else can hear you. I know I can't talk you out of it anyway." What a wimp she was. Rose glanced at him and caught his smile, like he'd just won something. Too late now to put her foot down.

"I'll abide by that. Rosie only when we're alone."

Hold it. She didn't plan on spending that much solo time in his presence. She rested her head in her hands, realizing he *had* won something. The unspoken agreement to spend time alone with him.

Fortunately Brett pulled his car to the curb and parked in front of a single-level home that had seen better days. Her clarifying pronouncement would have to wait.

Rose managed to get her door open and was halfway out when he showed up to lend a hand. She didn't want to take it, but honestly her wedges were tall enough that they made getting out of cars and certain positions more difficult.

"Why do you wear those silly things?" He stared at her feet.

She let go of his hand and used the door frame to pull herself out. "You try being five-foot-one in a medical professional world. The bit of added height makes a huge difference."

"I'd think that once people got to know you, those few inches wouldn't matter."

"And you'd be wrong. Let's get up there."

Fortunately he let it go, taking charge and knocking on the screen door. The guy was so steeped in chauvinism that he just didn't see it.

A thin man, probably in his seventies, cracked the door. "How can I help you?"

"Mr. Brown, I'm Brett Shoffner and this is my friend Rose Crackinbush. You and I spoke on the phone yesterday afternoon?"

"I remember. You wanted to ask me some questions. Sure. C'mon in, young feller."

Brett allowed her in front of him, and she followed Mr. Brown through a small screened-in porch and into a cozy, well-worn living room.

The man motioned toward the green nubby couch that had seen better days. "Have a seat. Can I get you something to drink? Got coffee or water."

"No, thank you." Rose displayed her smile, realizing those were the first words she'd had in the conversation. Hopefully Brett wouldn't commandeer the visit, like he was apt to do.

"Nothing for me either, Mr. Brown. We don't want to take up too much of your time."

The older man shrugged and took a seat in a deep mahogany-tone leather Morris chair to face them. "So, what sort of questions do you have for me?"

Brett handed her a folded paper and a pen from his breast pocket. Now she understood his plan. He'd do the asking and expected her to play secretary, noting every answer. It was too late to put him in his place here with Mr. Brown, though she was going to set this Neanderthal straight. Dr. Rose Crackinbush was no one's girl Friday.

She sent him a glare that should have made him fear for his life before turning a sweet smile on the elderly gentleman, waiting for them to get started.

Twenty minutes later, they'd covered everything they were supposed to, or rather, Brett had. She'd merely transcribed what Mr. Brown related. The good news was that he'd just never thought much about joining the VFW and now considered it.

If the rest of their meetings this morning went as well, that would be great.

Rose waited until they were back in the car—she'd made sure she was the one to close her door—before she nailed him with both barrels. "You are not living in the fantasy world where I take notes while you interview, I hope, because if that's how you saw this going down, you are sorely mistaken, buster."

Brett turned to her, his mouth opened and his eyes blinking. "What?"

"Did you think I wouldn't notice how you waited until the last second to foist that menial task on me? I assure you that I am happy to share interviewing duties with you, but I will not follow you around like a puppy excited to take down every word you spout." Rose crossed her arms and *hmph*ed back into her seat.

"Rose, I had no idea you felt this way."

"Of course you didn't. You simply assumed that since I'm the woman, I'd be happy to oversee the notetaking while big, intelligent you asked the questions and interacted with the... " What in the world should she call the people they were visiting? Certainly not the patient. "The client. But now you know. So what are you going to do about it, pal?"

"Rose, I'm sorry. I simply realized we needed to take down Mr. Brown's answers, and I've got atrocious penmanship." Brett started the ignition and pulled from the curb. "Maybe back before college it was legible, but med school and residency destroyed all that. Seriously, when someone looks up the term 'doctor writing' in the encyclopedia, there's a sample of my handwriting." Did he have to question every move he made to make sure he didn't insult her womanhood?

"And what makes you figure mine is any better?"

Okay, she got him there. He assumed as a female, her notes would at least be readable where his would be questionable. "You know what, you're right. I took for granted you'd have the more legible handwriting. I'm sorry. It wasn't me trying to take over, I assure you." He needed to keep his eyes on the road as they headed for their next stop, but he also wanted to see just how angry Rose was. He sneaked a peak.

Oops, she was hot, and not in a good way. Well, she was in a good way too, but that wasn't what he meant. He could have easily imagined steam coming from her ears.

He tried once more. "Tell me how you see us completing this survey job." At least give him some directions so he could stop ending up with his size eleven loafer in his mouth.

The quiet grew so loud, Brett almost pulled to the curb in order to focus on her face-to-face.

But then she let a sigh escape. "Okay, maybe I overreacted. I know someone has to take notes, and maybe if we'd discussed this ahead of time… " From the corner of his eye he watched her fold her hands in her lap and stare at them. He heard her intake of breath and the soft whooshing release and knew she had something to say. "How about we take turns? I'll question the next person while you play scribe—and I'm sure you'll find a way to transcribe legibly. We'll just switch back and forth. Perhaps we can learn something from each other's style of interacting with the, uh… "

"Client?" He flashed her a grin, hoping she'd finally cooled down.

"Right, client. Will that work for you?"

"Sure. But don't go squawking that you can't read my chicken scratches. Just sayin', Rosie." Once again, the words were out before he thought. Would she take offense at squawking?

Rose shook her head. "Your foot sort of likes to hide in your mouth, doesn't it?" At least she didn't yell.

"Yeah, I've got a knack for that. Do you want to read through the questions a few times to practice?" Brett turned onto the street where the next vet lived and parked in front of the house.

"I can manage them, especially after having you run through them for me with Mr. Brown." She gazed out her window. "Who lives here? Do you know anything about them?"

"This is Mr. Zeke Hoopengarner. He's a veteran of World War II and had been a career man, enlisting back in 1928 out of high school. I enjoyed our brief chat when I called. You'll like him." At least Brett hoped she would. He opened his car door.

"Okay then. I'll do the talking. You can take notes and look pretty."

Brett froze mid exit. "Ooh, so that's how this is going down? I see. Should I flash a little leg?"

"Hey, you're the one who said you enjoyed your chat with him. I have no idea where it went after you got his address." But she grinned and shocked him by winking.

"My goodness gracious. Miss Rosie has a sense of humor. Who'd a thunk?"

"When it's funny I do. Now let's get up there." She did that whole grabbing the door to pull herself out bit.

He should have hustled around to help her, but as Rosie was quick to point out, she was perfectly capable. Suddenly, Brett could feel his mother's disapproval. "Sorry, Mom."

"Did you say something?" Rose squinted at him.

There was no explaining. "Nope." He shook his head and waited for her to join him on the sidewalk.

Twenty minutes later, they were back on said sidewalk, heading for his Buick Wildcat. Brett wanted to shake his head but was afraid Rosie might see and interpret it as a critique of her leadership. Maybe that's what it was.

She had taken charge and plowed through to get her answers like a steamroller, smashing all the innuendos Mr. Hoopengarner made. *Such a little thing to be a professional. Were the two of them an item?* At least she hadn't reacted with offense, though Brett was sure he'd hear about it in the car.

And what did Brett do while all this was going on? He wrote. Scribbled, really. Kept his head down as if he were in his foxhole, dug in, pen to the paper. Not that anyone could interpret his marks, not even him. Which was a bad thing, because when Rosie decided to try to decipher it, she'd be asking him all sorts of questions, and he'd have to make something up. Or admit that he couldn't read his own writing.

He opened the door for her out of habit before climbing in on his own side.

Seriously, this notetaking was not a male/female thing. This was pure practicality. His handwriting was abysmal. Especially compared to Rosie's that was clear and precise. How did she do that?

"So, where to next? By the way, I think I'm okay with taking notes now."

Brett practically gave himself whiplash, snapping his neck around to face her. "What did you say?"

"Oh, stop. All these men are of that older generation. There's no retraining them to see me as a professional. If all I'm going to get are questions about why we're not a couple or why I can't wait to be tied down with babies, then I'll do the writing so we can finish. Picking a fight won't help the VFW's cause." She shrugged.

"Rosie, you are wise. And when you see my notes, you'll be doubly glad about your choice."

"Oh, I saw. You weren't kidding about the chicken scratches." She tossed him a tiny grin for good measure.

"I only hope you remember the answers to the questions he gave, because I can't read that mess either."

That made them both laugh. And all at once, there was a tiny chink in the barricade between them. This Rosie he could enjoy spending time with. She might have to learn to appreciate his humor, but at least she was fun.

The next stop was to see Mr. Victor Meadows. He was another World War II veteran but slightly younger than Mr. Hoopengarner. His wife joined in the conversation, and she and Rosie seemed to hit it off.

When they'd finished with all on the list, they had very positive news to report and a little extra time, so Brett suggested they get a bite at Scottie's Drive-In. Things were going so well, he was hesitant to say anything, but maybe they could hold a conversation without a flare-up.

Rosie paused and seemed to be studying his profile while he drove toward her house, which was just this side of the drive-in. "Okay. But I pay my way."

"Absolutely. I've learned my lesson. You are woman, and I hear your roar." He flashed a wink and a grin only to be met with a stoic expression.

"Wasn't it your receptionist who said you weren't funny? Maybe you need to listen to her."

"I'll run it past Belinda, but I'm telling you, you're missing out on some real gems." Okay, so she didn't get all fiery or try to exit his moving vehicle. Check. For progress.

"I have my doubts. What time do you need to be at your office?"

Brett peeked at his watch again. "Not until one. You?"

"My first appointment is at one, but I'd like to be there a bit before-hand to catch up with Doc about anything that happened while I was gone." She paused. "Should we get our order to go?"

He shook his head. "Nah. We've got time. Besides, school's still out, so we don't have to stand in line between half of the KHS Wild Kats."

"Very true. I hadn't thought of that." She settled into watching out the window.

Where had the fun gone? They'd found an easy banter after the second stop. Even had a couple of one-liners with the people they visited.

Now she only stared while the world passed by. Had he done something wrong? Again?

"What do you like to do for fun, Rosie?"

Her sigh told him she'd heard the way he spoke her name, but she kept to her agreement. That was fine because he was determined to convince her she was more of a Rosie than a Rose.

"I really haven't had a lot of time for fun in a while. I've focused everything on getting through school and setting up my practice." She paused. "I read whenever I get the chance."

"Who is your favorite author?"

"That's easy. Agatha Christie. Her Miss Marple is so underestimated and yet so brilliant. I think Ms. Christie is the same way."

"Hmm. I like her books too, though I'm more of a fan of her Hercule Poirot. He's got style." They had something in common. Sort of.

"I'll give you that, but Miss Marple is an undercover feminist, and everyone who dismisses her ends up with egg on their face."

So in other words, do not, under any circumstance, underestimate Rosie. Note taken. This hint he'd have no trouble deciphering.

He pulled into the parking lot, and they headed inside. Even without the high schoolers, there were plenty of people choosing Scottie's for lunch. "If you want to grab us a table, I'll order."

Rosie glanced around the place, her eyes revealing her decision-making process. "Fine." She dug in her purse and pulled out two singles and handed them over. "Just bring me back the change."

"I can do that, but it might help to know what you want." He added a smile to soften his words.

"Oh, right. A cheeseburger, small fries, and a medium Sprite." Then, with a nod, she turned away to find a table and hold it for them.

She gave him two dollars. Two dollars? The cheeseburger was thirty-three cents, the fries were twenty-six. And the drink? A dime and a nickel. Good grief. Was she testing his honesty?

Then another thought hit him. She was trying to buy his lunch.

Nope, no way. That wasn't going to happen. No woman paid for his meal. And Ms.—or rather Doctor—Crackinbush would have to learn that lesson. He had his pride too.

Tucking one of her bills into his pocket, he explained he had two separate orders, but added they could all go on a single tray and gave Rosie's first to the beleaguered kid behind the counter, who seemed to be counting the days until school started and his summer job was done.

Once he'd paid for Rosie's order, he made his own, making sure her change went in one pocket and his in the other. Even though the meals were virtually the same—he went with Coke rather than Sprite—the whole thing came to less than a buck and a half, plus tax. But someone just had to pay for her own. Good grief.

It didn't take long before his tray was ready, and he wove his way around other customers to find the table Rosie reserved for them. Before sitting, he grabbed her change and extra bill and slapped them down. There. Now she'd understand he had strong feelings about this too.

"Why are you upset?"

"I'm not upset." He gave a little shrug as he slid into his side of the booth. "What makes you think I'm upset?"

"Oh, I don't know. Maybe how you practically threw my money at me? And why did I have so much change?"

Brett drew in a breath as he scrutinized her face for the truth. "Were you trying to pay for my meal?"

Rosie's cheeks pinked. "I just thought it would be a nice gesture since you did all the driving today."

"But you didn't say anything."

"Well, I wasn't sure how you would take it. I wasn't even sure you'd figure it out."

"What if I had and let you do it? Would you have accused me of stealing?"

The shock radiating from her eyes as her face paled only proved what his brain told him the second the words left his mouth. Bad idea.

"I never... The thought didn't... How could you believe that?"

"What else am I to think? You made sure to tell me to give you the change and then handed over more than twice what you needed."

Rosie stared at the table. "I'm sorry. That was not my intent. I thought I was paying for both of us."

"Why? I'm just as capable of buying my lunch as you are yours."

"You're right. I should have considered that. But now you know how I felt when you took over the other day." She paused. "And I get how you felt when I pitched a hissy fit, like my mom would call it. I'm truly sorry."

Brett realized he'd made a bigger deal of it than he should have. In fact, he never ought to have brought up the whole mess. "I'm sorry, too. Look, can we start again? For the... How many times have we tried this do-over?" He smiled and caught a twitch at the corner of her lips.

"I don't know. But yes, let's give it another go. If three's the charm, this many, however many, should be golden."

They each unwrapped their cheeseburgers, but then Brett caught Rosie glancing his way. There was something there. He wasn't sure what it was, or if it was worth the headache of exploring, but there was definitely something.

And he was going to find out what.

Chapter 4
Friday, August 25, 1972

"There you go, Mrs. Krantz. You certainly were ready for this adjustment." Rose helped the grandmother from her table. "Let's not wait as long between appointments if you can help it. I know you had extenuating circumstances this time, but we'll be able to get your alignment to stay longer if we don't allow it to fall into bad habits between procedures." Rose stepped off the platform that raised her up enough to work on patients, hating how her work shoes made her look so short and immature.

"Oh, Doctor Crackinbush, I really couldn't help it."

Rose patted the woman's hand as she led her out where Doc's wife, Mildred, would oversee the billing. "I know. But you're through all that now, so let's see if we can get you in next Tuesday."

"Okay. Thank you, doctor. I do feel better."

"Good, that's what we want. You have a nice weekend." Rose smiled, not just to be friendly, but because Mrs. Krantz was her final patient for the day. Now she'd race home, clean up, and hit the road for Lafayette.

Somehow in all the conversation last Wednesday, she never got around to broaching the subject of Brett possibly being related to her best friend's fiancé. If she were honest, maybe because she really didn't want to know. If he said yes, she'd be searching for reasons to back out, and that would be a rotten thing to do to Teri. Of course, he might've replied no. And then she'd be stuck answering a bunch of questions. But since she wasn't sure, she would choose whatever outcome she wanted. So there.

Until she had to face reality.

Which she would be doing in less than two hours. It was enough to make her want to scream.

She did a quick physical assessment. Fever? Nope. Stomach? Jumbly, but nerves explained that. Drat. What about...? She sniffled. Even her sinuses were clear. Where was a summer allergy when she needed it? Rose couldn't come up with a single reason to miss that would be reasonably valid with her best friend. Double drat.

All she could do was go home and get ready.

Slap on a smile and some lipstick for Teri and her party.

If Brett showed up, she would make nice. She'd proved it possible on Wednesday. He was still alive, wasn't he? So if she could demonstrate that much self-control once, she could do it again. Right? Of course, they'd collaborated as professionals.

Tonight would be a whole different story.

Oh, please, don't let Brett be there!

Yet...

He was fun to be with at times. And she liked how he interacted with the vets during the interviews. There was something caring about the guy. *No, don't let your thoughts meander in that direction.*

She rifled through her dresser drawer for a scarf to protect her hair on the drive. Brett was akin to someone singing off-key when it came to humor, but every once in a while, something tickled her funny bone. Not that she'd ever let him know that. Oh, heavens, no!

So if she arrived to find he was there, would that really be the end of the world? Maybe. Maybe not. She slammed the drawer closed harder than planned. She needed her *Calgon-take-me-away* moment, but there was no time.

No matter. It was Teri's night. Well, her and her fiancé's. That's where Rose's focus had to stay. Besides, she'd discussed this with God long enough. Whatever happened, it was in His ballpark. Rose pulled the band from her low-hanging ponytail and fluffed her hair, debating whether she had time to heat up her electric curlers. They'd been a Christmas gift from her mother, who said she needed to streamline things in order to accomplish all she had planned. Mom was right, but sometimes even using that convenience took longer than Rose allotted for.

She ran her brush through her Mary Tyler Moore-styled flip and called it good. One more check in her mirror, and she decided her new green sundress with the white flowers and pink ruched waist was a great choice for a spur-of-the-moment buy. And her lime-colored platforms went perfect. At this point, she had a dozen alternatives in her closet, but these proved the best. The only flats she kept in here were her slippers and a ratty old pair of Keds. Of course, her work shoes remained at Doc's.

With a shake of her head and a last glance to make sure she hadn't just messed up her hair, she tightened the scarf under her chin. Then Rose grabbed her pink clutch and headed for her car. She'd gassed it up at lunch, so that was one more thing off her plate.

Lafayette, ready or not, here I come.

She pulled from her drive, and after a couple blocks, switched on the radio for company. Wouldn't you know it. Carly Simon was singing "Anticipation." Somehow it spoke a little too personally to the flutters in her stomach.

Fortunately the next song was more to her liking, though she'd never admit it to anyone, even Teri, and she joined Sammy Davis, Jr. in an all-out duet about "The Candy Man." As she pulled to a stoplight, the guy in the car to her left glanced over, and Rose remembered her window was down. Now the face staring back from the rearview mirror was bright red. Tom Terrific.

She gunned it as the light changed and eventually settled in as Sycamore Road led her out of the city limits and on her way to her hometown.

Thoughts of growing up came unbidden, making her not want to drive so fast. Chances were her mom and stepfather would be in attendance, and that was never fun. Oh, Mom was fine. She always tried to make peace. But Rose reminded herself that Howard would be picking at her over every decision she'd made. It still frustrated him to no end that Gramps's bequest opened a way of escape for her. It even kept Howard from insisting she attend Purdue. She'd have had to live under his roof if she did, but Ball State got her out and away from his edicts and allowed her to try her wings. Though she'd never admit it to her stepfather, there were days being solo on that high wire of adulthood without his safety net that were plum scary.

Why had she been so concerned about Brett when she had Howard to look forward to?

It was enough to make her pull into the first gas station she saw, call Teri with an excuse, and turn around for Kokomo. At least she remembered Teri had invited her to spend the night at her parents' house, and she didn't have to go to Mom and Howard's for a never-ending helping of more criticism.

Teri needed her.

Okay, she needed Teri too. Working with Doc had left little time for making friends, and not too many of the patients who came through his doors were of Rose's age and mindset. Even Doc's wife, Mildred, nice as she was, didn't seem as interested in the women's movement. Or was that an assumption on Rose's part? She and Mildred had yet to have an in-depth conversation about anything aside from Doc, the practice, and the patients.

One more thing to stew about as Rose maneuvered through the familiar streets of Lafayette, Indiana. Despite what her stepfather claimed, she loved this place, named for the Marquis de La Fayette. A thriving college town with a rich history.

She found the restaurant, Il Ristorante Italiano, and pulled into the already-full parking lot. Though it was still light out, it would undoubtedly be dark when it was time to leave, and being at the back end of the last lane of cars didn't feel so safe, but if she kept circling in hopes of a better choice, she'd be late.

Maybe Teri and her fiancé would walk her out afterward. Or Brett, if he were there. Her breath hitched. Which was scarier—to leave by herself or accompanied by Dr. Shoffner?

Rose slipped her scarf off, locked up, and tucked her clutch beneath her arm while mentally preparing for the hike to the front of the restaurant. All the while, tiny prickles of perspiration started at her hairline. Just wonderful. Along with achy feet, she'd be sweaty too. Without the wind for cooling, it was definitely a hot August night.

She'd need to touch up her hair at the restroom. At least the scratches on her arms were fading, though to be honest, that added touch of makeup helped tone them down even more.

The hostess, most likely a coed, smiled and pointed her toward the ladies' room, adding the whereabouts of Teri's party for when she came out.

The large mirror hid no flaws. Rose fluffed her hair and touched up her lipstick. It was the best she was going to be. Unfortunately, Howard's critique sermon in her brain played even before running into him. *Lord, keep a tight rein on my mouth, and if You've got a moment, would You please help me understand what my mother sees in the man?*

That was as far as she could postpone the inevitable. Time to face the music, sour notes and all. *This is Teri's night. Smile.*

With that mental reminder, Rose donned a mask of friendliness and headed in the direction of the back room where the party was located.

Guests milled around what would be the dance floor after dinner, while waiters prepped the tables that encircled the perimeter. Before she could find Teri, Rose spotted Mom, dressed in a short sleeve yellow shift, who turned to see her and wave. And of course, Howard stood beside her. Oh, boy. She hoped God had heard her prayer and had a plan because she didn't have anything other than to try to make nice. Try really, *really* hard.

"Hi, honey, so glad you could make it. I wasn't sure if you'd be able to."

Rose dropped a kiss on her mother's cheek. "Teri's my best friend, Mom. I wouldn't miss it. Are you trying a new hair style? I like it. Hello, Howard."

"Wondered when you'd get around to acknowledging me. You need to call your mother more often." Did he actually jump right in that way? Even in the pastel-green leisure suit, he still looked ready to pounce.

"Howard, doesn't Rose look lovely tonight?" Yay, Mom, for trying to smooth things.

"Thanks, Mom."

"Well, if it isn't Dr. Crackinbush. Now this is a surprise."

Uh-oh. That voice. Right behind her. Still, he hadn't called her Rosie. And honestly, should she turn and hug him or slug him?

But at least she had her answer as her heart thudded in her throat.

Brett was here. Apparently the latest in white-knight evening wear included a navy suit with a vest, baby blue silk shirt with French cuffs, and a textured silk tie. Holey Moley.

"Dr. Shoffner. Good to see you. Have you met my mother, Millie Holtz?" Rose waited a beat while Brett and Mom shook hands, desperately trying to hide her own surprise. "And this is my stepfather, Dr. Howard Holtz."

Brett stuck out his hand, but Howard stared at it. "You're not a chiropractor too, are you?" There was no missing the condescension.

Brett pulled his hand away but kept the smile on his face. "No, I'm an MD. In Kokomo. What is your specialty?"

"I teach pediatrics through IU's School of Medicine at its Purdue location." Howard's ego voice softened a little. "Where did you get your degree?"

"Through IU at their Indianapolis campus. I'd love to talk more with you, sir, but they sent me on a mission to bring Rose over to Teri. Apparently the bride-to-be needs her." Brett tried another go at the handshake, and this time Howard cooperated. "It's nice to meet you both. Excuse us." Then he hooked Rose at her elbow and steered her away toward the far side of the room.

Rose dropped her voice and leaned close, his clean woodsy scent inhibiting her words just a little. "I can't thank you enough, though I am surprised to see you."

"Imagine how I felt to learn my brother is marrying your best friend."

That wasn't too difficult to visualize. If it hadn't been for her run-in with Howard, she might have been more perturbed, but it was hard to get shook up over Brett's presence when he'd just come to her rescue. "What's Teri's emergency?"

"Oh, she didn't have one."

"What?"

"Apparently your friend wasn't kidding about your stepfather. She sent me to run interference and get you away." He made a little bow as if he'd just rescued Nell Fenwick from Snidely Whiplash.

"Okay, Dudley Do-Right." She punched his arm. "But just remember, I'm no helpless damsel in distress. However, in this instance, I appreciate your good deed."

"I aim to please." He rubbed his bicep and paused. "Dudley Do-Right? Seriously?"

She schooled her face to display her serious women's lib expression before her true self emerged in an unladylike snort.

It made them both laugh.

Thankfully Howard was now across the room and couldn't add that to her list of infractions.

Her smile faded. Even in her head, her stepfather could snuff out the fun.

Brett bumped her shoulder. "You okay?"

Rose tossed off Howard's shadow. After all, Dudley Do-Right walked beside her. That had to count for something.

"Sure." But why in the world did she even care?

Whoa. So that was the famous Dr. Holtz. Brett had heard stories about him from med school colleagues who'd chosen the Indy campus to avoid the man. No wonder Rosie took offense so quickly last Monday.

Still, it was a surprise to see her here. A nice one he was beginning to enjoy.

"You're awfully quiet. What gives?" Rosie bumped his arm, bringing him back again. "Not miffed about the Dudley Do-Right comment, are you?"

Brett chuckled. "Nah. Besides, I guess I had it coming after the Cracklin' Rosie one."

They arrived at the table where Teri took possession of Rosie. "Yay, he saved you."

"I'd have eventually disentangled myself, but I'll admit Dudley here came in handy." Rose grinned and ducked her chin.

Oh, she was so going to get it. His lips itched to grin.

"Dudley, huh? As in Do-Right? Of the Canadian Mounties?" Bart slapped the table, utensils jumping. "That's perfect, little brother."

"You're one to talk." Alma gave his twin the evil eye. "There are some things I could share about you, you know." Brett could count on his big sister to put Bart in his place.

"Forget about all that. Sit, you two. Rose, it's been too long, and now I can finally introduce you to everyone." Teri pointed at Bart. "This is my Prince Charming, Bart Shoffner, who comes along with his sister, Alma, and twin brother, Brett, who you've apparently already met. Everyone, this is my bestest friend, who knows more dirt on me but I trust to keep it to herself or I'll get even, Rose Crackinbush." Teri wrapped Rosie in a major hug before allowing her to shake hands with the others.

Alma hopped her seat closer to Bart, making room for Brett to add a couple chairs. "So, how did you two meet?"

Before he answered, Rosie jumped in. "We met at a VFW meeting. They've received a large endowment that is earmarked for therapeutic and preventative help for the vets, so they invited members from the medical community to attend. He got us roped into a survey they need done and then proceeded to call me names."

"What?"

Every eye at the table drilled into Brett.

"Wait a minute. It wasn't mean, I just—"

"You were trying to be funny again, weren't you?" Alma didn't think he was funny? That was cold.

"It wasn't like that. She..." He glanced at Rose for verification on his retelling. "Rose introduced herself as a doctor. When we had a moment to talk, I asked about her specialty, and she told me chiropractic. Somehow cracking backs and Dr. Rose Crackinbush just made a connection in my head, and I verbalized it."

"What did you say?" Teri sounded a wee bit protective of her besty.

Would anyone get the joke? "I said... I said she really was Cracklin' Rosie."

The whole table groaned.

Could he please just slink out of the restaurant?

Alma patted his arm. "Okay, fair is fair. What song would you say, Rose, reminds you of our dear clueless brother?"

Rosie tapped her chin a moment. Then her eyes crinkled with her smile, and he became very afraid. "I've got it. Ready?" She waited until everyone leaned closer. "'Tears of a Clown'."

"You didn't just say that. Oh, Dr. Crackinbush, you have a cruel streak." Nothing like a double whammy.

Bart laughed the loudest, of course. "Perfect. She's got you there, bro. But what I don't get is why you didn't go for the obvious with Rose? I mean, she's a chiropractor, why not the chiropractor song?"

"What's that?" About everyone at the table joined that chorus.

But Bart merely speared Brett with a grin. "You know, 'Bend Me, Shape Me?'"

Now Rosie cracked up. More than the rest of them.

"That, you laugh at?" Brett shook his head.

"Can't help it. It's funny." She tossed him a look that he couldn't quite read. Either she felt sorry for him or was apologetic about laughing, though she still did.

"Just for that, after dinner I get your first dance." She might not think much of his sense of humor, but he needed her to believe he didn't hold a grudge. Besides, maybe he could dazzle her with his fancy footwork.

Rosie paused before grinning. "Sure."

The black-and-white-clad wait staff served the salads, starting with the guests-of-honor table. Talk eased but remained amicable with a touch of friendly sibling rivalry. Alma's husband, Ed, joined them, and so there were now three couples together enjoying the fun.

It was revealing to see Rosie interact with everyone. Her playful side had come out, and she surprised him with some great one-liners. Made Brett want to keep his mouth shut and just listen.

As they finished the main course of manicotti and meatballs, Alma got a strange look on her face and grabbed Ed's hand, placing it on her stomach. "Feel it?"

Ed's smile told the story. Their baby had moved, and he felt it.

"Oh, I just thought of something." Alma turned her gaze to Rosie. "My OB doctor recommended a couple pediatricians, and one's last name is Crackinbush. Is he any relation?"

"That's my brother." Rose's smile didn't reach her eyes, but because she quickly glanced down at her plate right after saying that, Brett was pretty sure he was the only one to notice.

The band started. Brett decided it was time to collect. "How about that dance, Dr. Crackinbush?" He held out his hand.

She took it and stood with a smile. "Let's go."

Only a few couples left their tables to join them, so the floor wasn't crowded at all. The song, "The First Time Ever I Saw Your Face," was slow and not what Brett expected to get people out to boogie down. Well, many continued to eat, so that might be the reason. Still, he wasn't looking the gift horse in the mouth as he spun Rosie into his arms. Taking all those cotillion dance lessons back in the day had been a pain, but Mom promised he'd eventually thank her. He'd make sure to compose that note as soon as he got home. Or he could just go tell her, since she was with Teri's parents.

Later.

Funny how the lines to the song made him recall glancing over at Rosie when she originally sat next to him in that meeting. He'd known there was something special about her, though her prickles caused him to doubt his intuition. Now, after getting to know her better, his first impression seemed the right one.

She didn't lean in too close, kept proper distance to withstand scrutiny, but just enough to where the wisp of her perfume softly hinted as he breathed in. Like a spring garden. He could get lost in that scent.

"You're awfully quiet tonight. Did I overstep?" Her eyes no longer laughed but instead searched his face.

"No, of course not. Sometimes I say things without thinking it through, and I decided to try harder this evening, for Teri and Bart's sakes."

"You're sure?"

"Very. It's also been a long week, but I wasn't about to miss my brother's engagement party." He dipped her before bringing her close. A little closer than before, as a new song began.

"I felt the same. There was no way I couldn't show up for Teri. We've been friends since we were four." She leaned her forehead against his shoulder, sending a thrill through his chest.

"That's how she knew to extricate you from your stepfather."

Rosie nodded but didn't look up.

"I'm really sorry. No wonder you took offense at my ineptitude. The way he asked me if I was a chiropractor, I can't imagine how he's reacted to you."

This time, she met his gaze. "Could we change topics? That's not one of my favorites."

"Sure. What would you like to talk about?" His lips were so near her ear, he barely had to whisper.

"So, Bart is your twin? Not identical though."

He should have known this was where she would go. Technically, he'd expected it sooner. "Yeah, no, not identical. He's three minutes older and uses that to his advantage every chance he gets."

"Is that why you went into medicine? To one-up him?"

Brett had never considered that. "No. Not really. I wasn't about to become a lawyer, that's for sure. But my goal was to continue our family tradition in the military." Now was not the time to go into it. Just saying that aloud had brought up flashes of memories.

Rosie tipped her head up to capture his gaze. "What happened?"

"Much too long of a story for now. Maybe someday I'll tell you about it. Let's just say that falling into medicine when I did turned out to be a gift."

She continued the eye contact a moment longer before lowering her chin and nodding into his chest. Even in those ridiculous shoes, he still towered over her. If he were to tell anyone all of it, Rosie would probably be the one. But this was one evening after less than one week. There was no rush.

The wait staff had begun clearing tables and bringing out plates of cannoli drizzled with white chocolate. As the song ended, Brett guided Rosie back to their seats.

"You two looked pretty good out there. Are you sure you haven't been practicing for tonight?" Teri's grin and wink didn't disguise her probe for possibly more to this... Whatever this was.

"No. We only met last Monday. But I'll give credit where credit is due. Brett is a great dancer." Rosie caught his gaze as she finished her statement.

His brother chimed in. "You can thank our mother for that. We had lessons throughout our freshman and sophomore years of high school. However, I think I got more practice and have better technique." Bart tossed out the challenge as he held his hand toward Teri.

She stood, a smile blooming on her face, and followed her fiancé to the dance floor.

"Is Bart always so competitive?" Rosie aimed her question Alma's way.

72

"I think it's a middle child thing. Just guessing here, but based on my Psych 101 class, it fits. Actually, it only seems to come out when the boys get together. No idea why."

"I see."

What did Rosie see? Brett knew she was intelligent. Had she figured out something that he'd missed all these years?

Ed scooted away from the table and held his hand out to Alma, and the two of them headed for the dance floor, leaving just Rosie and Brett.

"Not exactly how I saw tonight going." Rosie followed up with a sigh.

"Is that a good thing?"

She gnawed at her soft pink lip a moment. "I don't think it's a matter of good or bad. Merely different. And it's been pleasant, so yes, I guess it is a good thing. I just never expected you, or the sibling banter, or the way the evening has gone."

"I get that. I didn't expect you either. In fact, I'd barely learned of your presence when Teri asked me to rescue you."

"Did I thank you for that? If not, I do. Thank you."

"All in the line of duty for a true Mountie. Dudley Do-Right, at your service." He saluted with a grin. Just like the cartoon character.

"As long as you are on Mountie duty, when it's time to go, would you mind walking me to my car? I'm at the far side of the parking lot."

Brett saluted again. "My pleasure, dear lady. Happy to oblige."

They both grinned, and his heart skipped a beat. Okay, could be she did find him a little humorous. Maybe. For now, he'd settle for that.

Chapter 5

What had she done? Rose had refused to entertain that stupid inkling about asking Brett to walk her out, but somehow the words exited her lips. How could she gracefully renege?

"Want to dance?"

His voice snapped her back to the moment. He stood in front of her, his palm held out to her.

"Sure." Is that what she'd really wanted to say? It was what came out of her mouth. Why wouldn't her brain and her words come to an agreement? Rose slipped her hand in his and followed him to the dance floor.

It was another ballad, meaning he held her in his arms while he expertly led her around. The cover band did a great job serenading with the Stylistics's "Betcha by Golly, Wow," leaving Rose to wonder what were the odds of this evening turning out as it had. She hadn't even known of Brett's existence a week ago, and most of their encounters since their explosive introduction never pointed to the remote possibility of the two of them slow dancing to a romantic song. The whole night blew Rose's mind.

The tempo changed as the band segued into "Everybody Plays the Fool," and the irony was not lost on Rose. She peeked up at Brett as he adjusted to the beat. His eyes telegraphed the message that he got it too, while he swung her out for a faster pace. Oh, my. The man knew how to dance. More than that, he effortlessly led. She nearly felt tricked at being made to follow. Except that was what she was supposed to do. Still, it displayed shades of subservience, and that irked her.

"Let's sit." Rose still held his hand, pulling him back to the table.

"Are you okay?" Confusion clouded his eyes.

If she explained, they were headed for another blow up. And that couldn't happen at Teri's party, not with her stepfather in hearing distance. If Howard thought she was maligning a "real doctor," he'd join in the fray. "Just tired. This week is catching up with me." She paused, needing to justify herself, even though she technically told the truth. "It's only going to get busier from now on, what with hoping to become part of the VFW's team, setting up my practice, and still seeing patients on a regular basis. Guess I need to get used to this." Rose chuckled. "And to think I honestly believed life was going to slow down once I graduated. No more studying until I dropped and getting up early to double check myself before tests."

"Right." He chuckled too. "No more twenty-four-hour shifts and grabbing naps on a cot in the hospital storeroom."

Once they'd started, more memories of the days and nights and weeks and months and years of studying and doing everything necessary to earn that title, doctor, came flooding back. Seems they had a few similar stories, including being driven to do their best, not settling for anything less.

Rose had never really given thought to how hard Brett had worked. Rather, she'd not wanted anyone to imagine she'd slacked or that her studies hadn't been rigorous. But a glance at Dr. Shoffner, and she caught something in his steady gaze. Respect. That meant more than any words he could have uttered.

Maybe the guy wasn't all bad.

The other couples returned to the table. Ed picked up Alma's clutch and handed it to her. "We're going to scoot out now. You don't have the room that much longer, do you?"

Teri and Bart both looked at their watches and shook their heads. "The evening has flown. We'd better go around to the tables and thank everyone for coming."

Bart stopped Teri. "Why don't we just say something from the microphone?"

"We should do that first, but then we can make it personal. Come on." She tugged him toward the front, while he glanced back over his shoulder and mouthed *help*.

"Bart isn't big on doing the meet-and-greet stuff. He'd rather just get down to brass tacks. Going from table to table is going to make him crazy." Brett laughed and glanced at Alma. "I like Teri."

Alma giggled. "Me too. She's good for him. But we need to run. It was lovely meeting you, Rose." She kissed Brett's cheek and walked with Ed toward the exit.

"Will you be driving back tonight?" Brett repeated the question with his eyes.

The words caught Rose as she was following Teri and Bart with her gaze while they made their rounds. "Oh, no. I'm spending the night with Teri. She wants to talk wedding and then I'm going to leave early tomorrow so I'm back in time for my first patient."

"I see."

"What are your plans?" It was only polite to ask.

"I'm crashing at Bart's and leaving early too. If we'd only known, we could have shared a ride." The corner of his mouth twitched. "Wonder who would have driven?"

She laughed at that too. Oh, man. She hated to feed his humor ego. But it did crack her up. "So I guess we're both waiting for them to come back since they're our hosts."

"Yep."

Bart and Teri eventually returned and plopped in their chairs. "Whew! That was a whirlwind. Bart kept me moving from table to table." Teri turned on her fiancé. "You do know that your mother is not going to be pleased that we didn't stay and talk with her longer."

"I can handle Mom."

Brett snorted and everyone turned to him. "What?"

"If you've got something to say, little brother, spit it out."

"It's just that you have no idea how much our mother plays you. She even lets you believe you've got the upper hand when she's convinced you to do it her way." Brett crossed his arms and leaned back.

"Okay, hold on you two. There's time to discuss that later. Right now, since it's just us, Bart and I have a couple of questions for you." Teri glanced at Bart who winked and nodded before she focused on Rose. "You've been my best friend practically my whole life. Rose, would you please be my maid-of-honor?"

It hadn't been unexpected, but Rose never wanted to assume. "I'd be delighted. This will be fun." She hugged Teri.

"And, despite the fact you've been a pain my entire life, there's no one else I'd rather ask to be my best man than you, little brother. What do you say?"

Brett's grin got even bigger. "You got it, bro. I'm happy for you." The guys punched each other on the arm. "But, as for you, Teri, I hope you know what you're getting yourself in for with this crumb bum. You seem so intelligent. I'm just worried about you."

Bart slammed his twin a little harder, but Teri laughed. "I've got a good idea. He's pretty special." The couple shared a glance, and Rose could imagine they'd developed the art of communicating without words. "My dad said we didn't have to stay until the last person left. He and Mom have it covered, so if you all are ready, we can head out."

Brett peeked at Rose, and she felt her lips wanting to tip up at the ends. He was about to walk her to her car.

"I rode with Bart, so if you all want to meet at my place?" Teri's words pulled Rose from Brett. Her friend stared as if she were just discovering something.

No. That was not going to happen. Rose had plans, and there was no room for romance in them. But if there were... No. She shook off that rogue what-if and firmed up her resolve.

"We'll all meet up at Teri's then." Brett decided for them. That in itself should be enough to tamp out any stupid feelings. The guy just automatically assumed instead of allowing her the courtesy of answering for herself. That would drive her bonkers. No, there could never be anything between her and Dr. Brett Shoffner. She stood. "Let's go."

His light touch at her elbow as he guided her toward the exit caused her nerves to become Rice Krispies. It took every bit of willpower to keep from pulling away. But then, if she did, she'd miss the tingles that wanted to overpower her, something that had been lacking in her life until now. Like a sweet torture. It made it hard to concentrate, impossible to vocalize coherent sentences.

Rose was in dire trouble. That much her brain understood.

A light breeze teased at her hair, and she tried to keep the strands from her eyes. She'd been right about the far end of the parking lot being in the dark and felt that much more secure knowing Brett was at her side, despite there not being another soul in the vicinity. They reached her car, and he held the door after she unlocked and opened it.

Then a thought broke through. "Do you know where Teri lives?"

He shook his head and tucked a few stray wisps of her hair that dared to dance on her face behind her ear. "I'll just follow you."

His touch was so gentle and quick, she almost wondered if it really happened, or had she imagined it? But she needed to acknowledge what he said. What had he said? Oh right. "Guess you're lucky that's where I'm headed then."

She couldn't help the edge that crept into her voice, though honestly, it wasn't entirely directed at him. More at herself. She needed to get it together and act like someone with a fully functioning brain. Only the last few minutes had been an emotional roller coaster, plus his presumption to follow, logical though it may be, irritated her. Why couldn't he have simply asked?

Brett closed her door and took a step back as she rolled down the window. "Guess I am. I'll see you there."

"I'll try to make it easy. If we get separated, she's on North Court. Stay on South Street until you get to 30th Street, head north and you'll find it." It was the least she could do after getting snotty with him. Okay, maybe not snotty, but he could tell. *Wonder if he understood why?*

Brett saluted and headed toward his car, a few lanes closer to the building.

Why, oh, why did she always feel like she'd kicked a puppy with him when her plan was simply to stand her ground, not let him walk all over her? Now she wanted to kick herself.

She flipped on the radio. Gilbert O'Sullivan was bemoaning being "Alone Again (Naturally)." The guy didn't know how good he had it. With all the people in and out of one's life, the silence of being alone wasn't so bad. Maybe.

Even after other songs came through her speakers, that first one continued to tease at her like that was her destiny in life. All alone. Naturally, since she'd run everyone else off. This was not how she wanted to look at her life. True, a family wasn't in her future, but nowhere had she planned on being lonely.

Rose pulled up in front of Teri's apartment house and parked, leaving room for Brett to pull in behind her. Bart and Teri should already be there since they left first. She popped open her trunk and yanked out her overnight bag.

All at once, a hand snatched it from her.

Heart frozen mid-beat, Rose swung on the intruder, nailing him with her purse smack dab in the face.

"Rosie, it's me."

She gasped as her pulse went from racing to slowing, and her vision de-tunnelized. Oh, no, it was Brett. Trying to help her. "You scared ten years off my life."

"I think you gave me a black eye, so we're even. May I carry your bag?"

"I can't believe you still want to. Why didn't you just say something?"

Brett switched her luggage to his right hand, lowered the lid of her trunk closed, and then gingerly touched the fleshy part at the top of his cheek. "I was trying to avoid an argument. Thought if I just helped, you wouldn't try to debate it. Looks like I need another strategy."

Rose walked beside him to the door. "I think your best bet is to simply ask. I might have said yes. Or I could've pointed out that I can carry my own luggage. Either way though, I would have appreciated the offer."

"Good point. One I'll remember."

"Really?"

He winced as his fingers probed near his eye. "Oh, that's a definite yes. I'll absolutely remember that advice."

"I need ice." Rosie pushed past Brett and headed into the next room on a mission, making him wince at the spotlight suddenly highlighting his existence.

Teri jumped from her seat by his brother to take a closer gander at what he assumed was a growing purple welt at the top of his left cheek. "What did you do?"

Brett shrugged. "I forgot to ask."

"What?"

Rosie came around the corner about then with a dishtowel bulging with big lumps of something, most likely the ice of her errand. "I nailed him with my purse because I thought I was being accosted. Turns out he was only being a gentleman, attempting to carry my bag."

"You did that?" Bart's eyes were round, and his voice held so much incredulity, now Brett wanted a mirror to check out just how bad his shiner was.

Teri must have figured out his thoughts because she pointed down the hall.

Rosie followed him, holding the ice remedy at the ready. "Do you really need to look? I'm so sorry."

He'd made it to the mirror by then. "Wow. You are dangerous."

"You scared me."

Brett leaned in against the sink for a closer view. "I get that."

"I said I was sorry."

"I believe you."

"Oh." She grabbed his hand and plopped the cold package into his palm before turning and disappearing back to the living room.

What was he supposed to say? He told her he believed her. He understood he'd scared her.

You could have said you forgive her.

For what? Standing up for herself?

To let her know so she can forgive herself.

Oh. Was she really so bothered?

Yeah, all he had to do was consider her reactions and he would have figured it out right off. Instead, he was busy trying to see what kind of a black eye he'd be sprouting. He needed to go apologize to her.

When he returned to the living room, Teri had her arm around Rosie and Bart was giving him The Look. He knew what that meant. He and his twin had been perfecting that signal for as long as he could remember—a warning to tread carefully, that all was not right in their world.

"Hey, Rosi—Rose, don't worry about it. It was an accident and all my fault. If I'd just spoken, you'd have known not to go into attack mode."

"Attack mode?" Teri hadn't moved, but somehow her growl made her appear to grow as if to tower over him.

"He's right." Rosie reined in her protector. "That's what I did. I chose fight over flight. I'm so sorry, Brett."

"There's nothing to be sorry about. It's fine. Besides, it gives me a macho appearance. My patients will think I'm tough." He tried to wink but ended up wincing, which hurt just as much.

Rosie stood and took the now dripping dishtowel of ice from him. "At least get this on your eye so it can do some good." She pushed him onto a chair and gently lowered the cold pack to his cheek. "Hold it here while I find another cloth to soak up the melts."

Brett did as he was told. It was easier that way, despite the chilling drips tracing down his face to his neck. Besides, whether she believed him or not, the only person he was upset with was himself. It wasn't as if he were clueless. She was independent and would obviously try to defend herself against an attacker. That was simple logic he should have figured out after this past week.

He raised his gaze to his brother, who simply shook his head. "When do you want to leave?"

"I'd planned to stay awhile until you caused a scene."

"Thanks. I have my own wheels. Just no key to get into your place." Brett swiped some more at the cold water that trickled into his collar.

Rosie returned then with another towel and transferred the ice before handing the new cold pack back to him. "Are you sure you should drive? What if it has messed with your vision? Besides, you can't hold this on your face and steer a car at the same time."

Brett sighed and closed his eyes to consider everything. Morning would come early, and at this point, he was in no mood for joking around. Sleep was the best idea he had. "I'll be fine driving."

That's when Bart stood. "Then I'd better go too. Just to make sure he gets there without any more incidents."

Why was it suddenly dawning on Brett that he would never hear the end of this? "I can drive to your place. I'll wait in the car for you."

"He can't wait in the car. He's injured!" Teri now became protective of Brett. It almost made him smile. He liked Teri.

"It's not the first time he's waited in his car. He's a big boy. Tell her, bro."

"Tell her what?" Now this was funny. His brother needing Brett's help to keep his soon-to-be-wife from going all Super Girl. In a match, Brett's money would be on Teri. He smiled as sweetly as possible.

"You really are a pain, little brother." Still, Bart stood, leaning over to kiss Teri goodbye.

She rose too, wrapping her arms around Bart's neck, and now it was a bit awkward as the kiss deepened.

Rosie caught his glance. "Should we wait in the kitchen? Give you two some privacy?"

Teri jumped away from Bart, her cheeks growing pink. "Right. Okay. I'll walk you to the door."

It was a whole five steps.

But who was counting?

Rosie walked beside Brett. "I really am sorry."

"Please. I'm fine."

"You aren't fine—"

He held up his hand. "Honest. And if you need to hear it, I forgive you, even if there's nothing to forgive. This was all my fault. We're good. I promise." Brett handed over the ice pack to prove he was tough and held up the Boy Scout finger sign.

She studied his face a moment before nodding. "Okay. I'll have the list all set for next Wednesday. Call me tomorrow evening and give me your address."

Right. It was her turn to drive. "Good. I'll talk to you then." He almost gave her a peck on the cheek, but worried about her reaction. His eye throbbed enough. Instead, he let his fingers stroll down her arm to her hand and squeezed a little before slipping out the door past his brother and Teri, lip-locked again.

He knew it. He was going to have to wait in his car.

This was not at all on his radar when he left home this evening to come to Lafayette. But enough good had transpired that he couldn't say it was a total wash.

Brett rolled down his windows in time to catch Teri's words to Rose as they headed for the house. "You have to tell me all about meeting Brett. I think there's something there."

Rosie glanced his way about then, and the fear on her face gleamed in the porch light.

If he'd had any illusions about her experiencing the same pull he did, that halted them in their tracks. He scared her.

That didn't set well. Brett counted himself as harmless as his Hippocratic Oath commanded. Why would she be afraid of him?

She hadn't seemed all that frightened when they talked or danced. At least, not that he noticed.

Bart pulled from the curb, so Brett fell in to follow. His twin's apartment was less than five minutes away. Parking behind Bart, Brett trailed him into the small craftsman house, the sudden flip of the light switch nearly blinding him.

"Gee thanks, bro." Brett blinked to cool his retinas.

"You are such a baby."

Brett dropped his overnight bag. "You're just mad because Teri made you leave to make sure I was safe."

"That's right. The night of our engagement party, and I have to cut short any alone time with her because you got injured. How bad does it feel anyway? Need more ice?" Already, Bart headed to his kitchen.

"Sure. Couldn't hurt. It's gonna be pretty colorful tomorrow, and I have a meeting with Doc Eilert in the afternoon. He's bound to say something."

His brother came around the corner with another ice pack and handed it off. "Not to mention your patients. Or Belinda and Pam."

"Yeah, they're just the precursors. I have to go see Mom on Sunday. That's gonna be so fun."

Bart cracked up. "Get used to being made over by all the women in your life. And I'll bet you dollars to donuts that at least one won't buy the just-trying-to-help excuse and will want to know what you really did. What *did* you really do?"

"Nothing! Not a dog-gone thing but reach in to take her bag for her. I should have announced my presence but figured she'd argue with me. We've had numerous discussions to that effect, and I thought I was circumventing a problem."

His twin sucked in a breath through his teeth. "How'd that work out for you, bro? By the way, how well do you know Rose anyway?"

"Not well enough." Oops, that's not what he meant to say.

"Oh. So Teri's right. There's interest there."

"What's not to like? Rosie's smart, feisty, and very nice to look at. But I don't figure she's feeling the same." Brett lowered the ice pack that had already started to drip.

"I don't know. Teri seems to think that Rose... Did you call her Rosie?"

Brett took the ice pack to the kitchen to buy some time. He hadn't meant to let that slip, though that's how he thought of her. "She's more Rosie than Rose to me. Just don't tell her I called her that. She insists that I can only do that when we're by ourselves."

His brother's eyes widened. Great. Another thing he shouldn't have said. Couldn't he just keep his foot in his mouth so he wouldn't speak any more incriminating evidence?

"So you spend time alone with her?"

"I have to. We're doing that survey work for the VFW together. That's all we've had in common since last Monday until tonight. And I'd bet money she wants to keep things strictly business."

"I don't know about that. You should talk to Teri. She knows *Rosie*." Bart grinned as he spoke her special name. "They've been friends a long time, and she's pretty sure you've provoked some interest, although, according to Teri, Rose has sworn off men and plans to only focus on her career."

Could that be what frightened her? That maybe she *was* feeling that tug, the same one he felt, and didn't want to fall into that trap?

Was it a trap?

She definitely wasn't an old-fashioned girl who would prefer to stay home and raise a family and support him while he brought in the means of living. Could he deal with a working wife?

Wife?

He'd known her less than a week.

But if the attraction continued in this way, that was where it was most likely to lead. For Pete's sake, look at his brother. He and Teri started off attracted, followed that to its logical conclusion, and now they were getting married. That's how these things went.

Still, it was only a week. They argued more than they shared, and she was dead set against marriage. Besides that, his dreams of the future looked far different from hers.

They might be able to compromise some, but from the way this was shaping up, someone was going to surrender their dreams to make it work. From what he could tell, he was that someone.

And that, Brett wasn't ready to do.

Chapter 6
Saturday, August 26, 1972

Rose left the outskirts of Lafayette, passing corn fields appearing more golden than green here at the end of their season, topped with wispy clouds against a cerulean sky. She picked up speed on the highway, allowing the breeze through her open windows to cool her. A car with air conditioning was at the top of her needs list after setting up her business. Definitely. Another reason she used her work schedule to hit the road early—to avoid the day's heat as much as possible.

Doc had volunteered to give her Saturday off so she'd have the whole weekend. However, after the men left last night, Teri's interrogation only confirmed that two more days of cross examination over a misplaced notion of a budding romance would have driven Rose to homicide. It was best she left. For humanitarian reasons.

She loved Teri, who was absolutely the best friend anyone could have. However, the bride-to-be, after finding true love, wanted everyone to experience it, ignoring all the reasons Rose had given as to why it would never happen to her.

It couldn't. There was no room in the plan for it. Besides, what man was so enlightened that he'd be willing to forgo a family because of his wife's career? Or, if a child should end up part of the picture, would volunteer to stay home and care for the baby while his wife worked? Sure, that guy existed. In someone's fertile imagination maybe.

Okay, perhaps if there was a guy who viewed a woman as an equal and treated her as such, she'd *consider* discussing a plan. So far, though, he only materialized in her dreams.

Stoplight. Stoplight. *Stoplight*!

Uh oh.

Rose glanced in her rearview mirror. Lights flashed as the siren started. She pulled to the shoulder, berating herself before the state trooper even got close.

His looming shadow arrived at her window before he did, giving him a larger-than-life appearance. The big, giant hat didn't help, either. "License and registration, ma'am."

Rose dug in her purse. "I'm sorry, officer." She handed him her driver's license before undoing the registration from the steering column. "I realized too late." Maybe she shouldn't have admitted that.

"Get out of the car, please." He stepped back so she could open her door.

Out of her car? With a huff, Rose complied, hopeful Mr. Authority would see he was pushing his weight around for no good reason. Fortunately she wore her platform wedges so she wouldn't look like a grade schooler next to the man.

"Do you wear glasses or contacts?"

She shook her head. "No."

"Have you been drinking?"

"It's seven in the morning. Of course, I haven't been drinking." Keeping her temper in check was becoming more difficult by the second.

"Are you on any medications?"

"I am a Doctor of Chiropractic. I do not use medications."

Now a touch of mirth danced in his eyes. "A doctor?" He didn't believe her. What a chauvinist.

"Yes. And I am on my way to Kokomo to see my patient. Is there anything else?"

He smiled, one filled with condescension. "I hate to give pretty little... doctors, like you, a ticket on such a sunshiny morning, so I'll write you up a warning and let you be on your way."

"Wait a minute. You're giving me a warning instead because I'm a woman?" Of all the nerve!

"Yes, ma'am. Is there a problem with that?" The guy had gone from patronizing to flummoxed in microseconds.

Rose shoved a hand to her hip and stared up at him. "If I were a man, would you have given me a warning or a ticket?"

"Ma'am, I'm just trying to do you a favor."

"No strings attached?"

Now his face bloomed with color while his mouth hung open. Maybe she went too far.

"Write me the stupid ticket." There was no way the man would ever understand.

Officer Jansen, according to his name plate, whipped out his booklet, scribbled a moment, and tore a page out, obviously ready to get rid of the loony bird.

As he held it out to her, Rose glanced up in time to see a familiar seafoam green Buick drive past.

And slow.

And pull over to the shoulder in front of her car.

This isn't funny, God.

"Is there a problem here, officer?" Brett could move pretty fast when he wanted to.

Officer Jansen stared Brett to a stop. "None of your concern, sir. Go about your business."

Though not moving closer, Brett didn't turn around. "Rose, are you okay?"

"Yes. I'll tell you about it later." She swiped the ticket along with her license and registration from the big oaf. "Now I need to get to my patient. Thank you for treating me like a person and not a child. May I go?" Rose gave the officer a taste of his own medicine and stared him into submission. She even cocked her eyebrow for added measure.

He blushed again, nodded, and touched the brim of his hat.

With that, Rose climbed into her car.

Brett must have taken it as okay to check on her and leaned in at her window. "What happened? Do you need anything?"

She watched until the police cruiser pulled away.

"He was going to let me off with a warning."

"That monster. What did you do?" Brett's lips pressed tight, and she knew he was holding in a chuckle.

All at once, Rose saw this from another perspective. One with higher intelligence. "I, uh, demanded he treat me as he would a man."

"You made him give you a ticket?" Brett's eyes—even the eye with the magnificent shiner—grew round with incredulity. "You could have gotten off with a warning, but you demanded a ticket? How much?"

Money. Uh-oh. There was a monetary cost to all of this. She glanced at the paper still in her hand as it started to shake. Fifty dollars. Rose raised her gaze to meet his while just how idiotic she'd been tumbled over her. "It says fifty dollars."

He gently took the ticket from her and glanced over it. "Wow. It sure does. You talked yourself into a good one."

"Yeah. Hooray for me and my beeeeeg mouth. I suddenly feel like Ralph Cramden on the Honeymooners."

"Are you all right to drive, Rosie?"

That time, his pet name for her wrapped around her in a warm hug. There were no questions about how she ended up running a red light or judgment about her stupid pride. Just comfort and concern.

"Yes. I'm fine. However, I need to get back to Kokomo. To work." As if he didn't already know this. Somewhere she'd misplaced her ever-lovin' mind, but there wasn't time to look for it now. She could wallow in her embarrassment after she finished with her patients.

"Good." He straightened. "I think I'll follow you back though, just to make sure."

"There's no need."

"I know there isn't. Still. To put my overactive imagination at ease, I'll be behind you." He patted her open window frame and stepped away.

That was simply wonderful. The last thing she needed was for Brett to play knight in shining armor when she was trying to resurrect her self-esteem. She should gun it and leave him in the dust. Of course, then Officer Jansen was probably up ahead just itching to complete her citation set and give her a speeding ticket.

She'd tolerate her reverse escort.

Fortunately, Rose wore her work clothes and didn't need to stop by her house. That would save her time. She pulled into Doc's driveway forty-five minutes later.

Brett gave a little honk as he kept on going to wherever he was headed.

Funny, she'd not thought to ask him where his office was. Not that Kokomo was all that huge, but it was big enough that she hadn't learned where everything was located. Yet.

Once inside, she checked her watch. Five minutes to spare before Mrs. Gershrom arrived. Rose pulled on her white jacket and did a quick once over of her treatment room.

There was a tap at the door jamb before Doc came in. "So how was the party?"

Rose shook her head. "If I were scripting this for a TV show, they'd say it was too unbelievable."

"What happened?"

"Remember that MD from the VFW?"

Doc nodded.

"Teri is marrying his brother. His *twin* brother. Teri threw us together for the evening. He even rescued me from Howard, and then I rewarded him with a black eye."

Doc's stare grew in intensity.

"Oh, it gets worse. I was doing too much thinking on the way here this morning and ran a red light. A state trooper caught me and was going to let me off with a warning, only I had the feeling he was doing it because I'm a woman. So I demanded the ticket. In time for Dr. Shoffner to spot us as he drove past. And then stop to see if he could help."

"You've had a busy day already."

Rose sighed. "There's more."

"Somehow I'm not surprised. Go on."

"Just to ensure I stayed out of trouble, he followed me all the way to work. I almost decided to make a getaway, but I can't afford another ticket."

Doc snorted before busting into a guffaw. "There's never a dull moment with you, is there? Rose, you are one of the most talented doctors I've seen in this business. You've got a natural bent for it, and you are smart enough to get to the heart of situations. You have the makings of an outstanding DO. But don't let your pride cause you to stumble. Sometimes it's okay to accept the gift." He headed to the doorway before turning back. "If you were my son or daughter, I'd give the same advice." Then he left as Mildred showed Mrs. Gershrom to the therapy room.

The middle-aged secretary was the first of five patients on Rose's schedule for the day. That kept her out of her head, musing on the last twenty-four hours, until time to go home. A place Rose longed to be. The stillness and serenity of her own house never felt lonely. Instead, it was a respite, a place to recharge.

She so needed to recharge.

She also ought to go over that conversation she had with Teri last night, especially in light of how her morning played out. She needed a plan. Only a fair-haired doctor with twinkling baby blues kept interrupting her thoughts.

Having Brett care enough to see she got to Kokomo safely did irritate her self-sufficiency. However, though she'd never mention it aloud even to Doc, there was a teensy feeling of security having that seafoam-green vehicle behind her. Who knows, she might have had a flat tire or engine trouble leaving her stranded if not for Dr. Shoffner's stalwart, Dudley Do-Right presence.

Rose was no Nell Fenwick needing to be saved from Snidely Whiplash. But knowing Brett had her back today had confused her with a mixture of irritation and comfort. Was there any middle ground where she could take and give in a friendly, community-type atmosphere and not end up a needy, helpless woman tied to the railroad tracks in front of an on-coming train?

Howard sprouted in her imagination, doing his best villain cackle while twirling a long black handlebar mustache. She needed to tell Mom to never let her stepfather grow one. It was far too sinister.

Rose perused her fridge for a quick lunch and settled on some leftover chicken to make into an open-faced chicken salad sandwich. The lack of choices confirmed she needed a trip to the grocery and soon.

Settling in at her kitchen table, she went over everything from the time she'd left home yesterday through to when she had arrived at work. Then she figured it out. Sort of. Brett confused her. It was as if her heart thought him kind, but her brain refused to trust him.

Well, he *was* kind. Mom would call him the perfect gentleman. Probably would even say he was exactly who she'd been praying for to cross Rose's path. Her mother couldn't stand the thought of a solitary life for her only daughter. Had Mom and Teri been plotting behind her back?

Great. Now she was paranoid. Another lovely added quirk to an already-labeled strange personality. What would it take to get those two to accept Rose needed to remain single?

And there was no quibbling. It was a need.

Giving in to the pull of romance would destroy every one of Rose's dreams. All the work she'd put into making her goal a reality, tossed to the wayside. There was no room for love and marriage in the life of Doctor Rose Crackinbush, DO.

So why did her mind conjure Brett's smiling face?

More importantly, why did it just wink at her?

Brett stifled his yawn behind his palm, hoping Mrs. Tomlinson hadn't noticed.

"Didn't get your beauty sleep, Dr. Shoffner?"

She noticed.

"Actually, my brother is getting married, and we had his engagement party last evening." Why in the world had he shared that? Oh, right. He was tired and needed a nap.

"I see. Partied until dawn, did we? Looks like it got a little rough." It wasn't the first time today someone had hinted at wanting to know the story behind his black eye. However, the woman's patronizing quips irritated more than usual, due to him having tossed and turned on Bart's lumpy couch and his early escape this morning. If he hadn't stopped at that diner for a fast breakfast, he'd have missed seeing Rosie.

Who was the real reason sleep eluded him last night.

Changing the subject, Brett focused on the purpose for this visit. "Mrs. Tomlinson, have you been taking your blood pressure medication?"

She nodded.

"As directed?"

The woman gave a sheepish smile and shook her head. "I get busy and forget. And after that one time of trying to catch up and landing in the emergency room, I just skip it if I don't remember."

"Well, we don't want you back in the ER, but you'll be there if we can't get your blood pressure where it belongs. A heart attack or stroke will get you admitted for sure. Is there any way you can think of to remind yourself?" It would have to be her own suggestion, or she'd ignore it.

Mrs. Tomlinson's face clouded as what he'd just told her sank in. "It can't be that bad, doctor."

"I'm afraid it is, Mrs. Tomlinson. Now, what can you do to remember?"

"I'll put my pills next to my coffee cup and take it with my breakfast. Or better yet, if I set the table before I go to bed, I can put the bottle in my cereal bowl." The woman beamed at having solved the problem.

"Those are both good ideas. And to see what happens when you get consistent with taking it, let's have you come back in one month. I have a feeling your numbers will be better if you implement your plan." He helped her from the table. "I'll walk you out."

Belinda had already unlocked the front door by the time he'd arrived this morning, which meant a semi-full waiting room greeted him. Thank goodness Belinda anticipated his urgent need for coffee.

Right now, he could use another infusion. Or that nap. A snooze in his own bed sounded rather nice.

"Mrs. T. was our last patient for this morning. Anything you want me to do before I head out?" Belinda must have read his mind as she held out another steaming cup.

"You are amazing. If only you appreciated good comedy." He took a sip and sighed while Belinda giggled. "Nah, go on home and have some fun. Do you have any plans?"

"Thought I'd take the grandkids shopping for school clothes. It will help my daughter's budget, and I get the joy of those sweeties."

"Then you do that. I'm going to finish up a couple things and then head out myself. Be sure to lock the door on your way out." Brett gave her a finger wave before stepping into his office and attacking the paperwork that waited. The never-ending mound. He set the mug down and cracked his neck. Time to get to it.

An hour later, his phone rang.

It was his private line, so he answered. "Dr. Shoffner."

"Brett, my boy. Checking to make sure you remembered our appointment." The scratchy voice could only belong to one person. Dr. Oskar Eilert.

"Sir, you know I'd never forget. I'm about finished here. Do you still want to meet at Artie's?"

"Is there any place else?" The man chuckled and ended up in a phlegmy cough.

"Are you all right, sir?" Brett worried his mentor didn't take care of himself. Take care of others? In a snap. But he put himself at the bottom of that roll.

"Don't you go worrying about me, boy. It'll take more than some cough to keep me from a breaded tenderloin sandwich. I'll see you there in an hour." *Click.* Guess the conversation was over.

Brett rubbed his eyes and drained his coffee. There weren't a lot of people outside of his family that he'd forgo a nap for, but Doc Eilert was at the top of that list.

Twenty minutes later, he pulled into the gravel parking lot on South Main Street. There was still a robust crowd, despite it being just after lunch. The smells of all things breaded assailed Brett, putting a smile on his face. Even his stomach growled with approval. Hopefully the good doctor had grabbed them a table.

He had. The elderly man apparently had been watching the door and motioned him over to a booth in the corner.

They shook hands before Brett slid in across from him. "Did you order yet?"

"No, just got here and decided to wait for you."

The teen waiter showed up as if summoned.

They both ordered breaded tenderloin sandwich baskets and then went silent until the lanky teenager returned behind the counter.

"That's quite a shiner you got there, boy. Somebody objected to the engagement?" Even though his mentor chuckled, Brett knew he was waiting for a full explanation.

"No, I accidentally scared someone while I was trying to do a good deed, and she isn't one to run." Brett added a chuckle himself, hoping that was enough to satisfy the man's curiosity.

"A woman did that?"

"With her purse." Why did he feel the need to add that?

"I tell you, these women's libbers are dangerous. Only I didn't realize just how dangerous until now." Doc Eilert shook his head.

"It wasn't like that exactly. I was trying to be a gentleman and help the maid of honor get her bag out of her trunk. It was dark, and she didn't hear me come up beside her, and when I reached in, she... " Brett shrugged and pointed to his eye. "She also was extremely sorry and tried to take care of me, so it's hard to bear a grudge." There was no reason to go into any more detail since the man was getting more agitated with every word Brett added.

"She should have been begging your forgiveness. And she should not have gotten in the way of you being a well-mannered gentleman. What is with these females today? Thinking they can do it all, no need for a man." Doc Eilert's face grew florid.

"Let's change the subject. What have you been up to lately?" Brett did his best to steer the conversation into more peaceful waters.

The waiter returned with their meals. That was providential. Artie's breaded tenderloin sandwiches always conjured a smile for them both. There was nothing like them, and Brett couldn't help the soft moan that escaped with his first bite. Man, they were good.

But once the teen moved on, Doctor—Oskar—climbed back on that same old horse of controversy. "Women don't know their place today. I blame World War II. It was a necessary evil to have females doing men's work while the soldiers were away, but now they think they can take over the world."

Did Brett sound like that when he longed for an old-fashioned girl? He hoped not. However, disagreeing with his mentor would only make things worse. "Did you catch the Cubs game yesterday?" Maybe getting him to talk about his favorite team would help.

"Yes, I did, but you are changing the subject. Brett, you're a young man, a professional. Do you know how many women are out there stealing jobs from men like you? All these girls who think they can manage medical school. This could be a danger to your practice and cause irreparable harm to the community. Frank Brown told me some female doctor is applying to be part of that VFW endowment. You'll be cleaning up her messes. That is, if any of the members will let her near them."

Brett barely kept himself from choking. Setting his sandwich back in the basket, he marshaled the mobbing thoughts invading his brain into a semblance of order, reviewing each to determine the best response that would be truthful yet calm Oskar's rant. "I wouldn't worry about it. If she'd been told she couldn't apply, there'd be a lawsuit. But if she sees it's pretty much just older men, she might prefer to keep her practice out of the running."

"You're right. She'd probably sue. Who knew all that discrimination buzz would end up dealing with women? But I thought Frank told me you were working with her."

Now all those riotous thoughts were chanting in unison that Frank had a big mouth.

"We didn't hit it off, so she'll probably drop out." Brett crossed his fingers beneath the table despite technically telling the truth. To say Rosie and he hadn't gotten along was like saying Old Ben, the world's largest steer—on display less than two miles from here at Highland Park—was just another stuffed toy. They'd gotten off to an explosive start, that was for sure. But Rosie dropping out? That was never going to happen, and Brett knew that all too well.

"Were you able to show her the error of her ways?"

More like she showed him. "She has a temper, so I didn't try to sway her opinion on anything."

Oskar took another bite of his sandwich, giving Brett a respite to change the subject once again. "Belinda and Pam both said to say hello." Maybe if the man thought about the fact he'd hired women at his office, he might simmer down.

"Those two are the exception to the rule. They're in situations where they have to work, but they still put family first, and they don't try to take jobs from men. Give them my best." He paused. "Maybe I ought to stop by the office to say hello one of these days."

Brett would be honored under normal circumstances. But if the man were to go off on another of his tirades, especially when there were patients there to hear, it could be a disaster in the making. Pam and Belinda loved their former boss, but there were other people coming through those doors who might take offense at Oskar's opinions. "One of these days. The girls would be happy to see you. Maybe we could do an in-office lunch on a slow day." When the waiting room was empty.

"I sure miss the practice." With a sigh, Doctor Eilert shoved the rest of his food away. "I should have stayed longer."

A part of Brett wanted to take advantage of the moment and ask why he hadn't. Since Oskar encouraged him to pursue medicine after his military career was destroyed before it could even start, Brett had envisioned working together with his mentor for many years. Instead, Oskar had remained only long enough to certify Brett's residency in family medicine, and then he retired. However, considering how the conversation had run so far, the question of why didn't want to be asked. At least, not at this time. And Brett couldn't force the words out of his mouth even if he wanted to. Rather, he stuffed another bite of breaded tenderloin in his trap to keep that and other queries silent.

"You're pretty quiet today. Is everything all right with your family? Your mother?" Kindness filled Doctor Eilert's words. There was the mentor Brett had grown to respect and look up to.

"Everyone is fine, excited for Bart and his fiancée. Mom is over the moon, what with her first grandchild coming and adding another daughter to the family. It's just been hectic racing to Lafayette for the party last night after a full day and then back here to see patients this morning. Nothing that a nap won't cure." Brett added an awkward wink for good measure.

That seemed to work. And to make the timing perfect, the waiter brought their bills to the table at that moment. Doctor Eilert snatched them both up.

Brett never had a chance. "I thought it was my turn to pay."

"I don't accept charity, young man." Oskar slipped out of the booth, heading for the cash register before Brett could mount an argument.

Apparently the take-turns compromise that had worked so well with Rosie was all but forgotten here.

Should he still try to fight to at least pay for his own meal? Would he look like a freeloader if he didn't? Or would he come across as ungrateful for all the man had done for him over the years if he did? Brett followed him to the register. "Thank you. Next time it's on me."

"You'll have to be a lot faster. Now go get that nap."

They shook hands in the parking lot, and Brett headed for home.

He had one more thing to do before trying for a little shut eye. A phone call to a certain chiropractor who was messing with his head. But he'd promised to let her know his address. Besides, the thought of hearing her voice again sort of perked him up. He smiled in his rearview mirror.

Maybe he wouldn't need that nap after their conversation.

Chapter 7

The phone rang just as Rose slipped her washed plate into the drainer. She wiped her hands on the dishtowel tossed over her shoulder and grabbed the receiver. "Hello?"

"Hey, it's Brett." As if his voice hadn't given him away.

"I can't get away from you, huh?" She followed with a chuckle to prove she wasn't that mean-spirited.

"What can I say?" Then he went silent. Shouldn't he have another line? Some kind of flattery or at least a quip?

"I don't know. What *can* you say?"

"Well, I started to mention your incomparable beauty and magnetic personality, but figured you'd hang up on me."

"You're going with honesty then? Or is it fear?" Where had she come up with the chutzpa to say that? Now he'd add vanity to his list of her flaws along with stubborn and pig-headed. Oh, and over-sensitive. She snapped her jaw tight.

He coughed. "Guess you nailed me on that. May I start over?" Without waiting for her permission, he continued. "I thought we could get the particulars for Wednesday set up, and since we've both been busy, I wondered if you'd like to meet for dinner this evening. My treat or go

Dutch if you prefer. But going someplace neutral where we can plan and not end up rushed sort of sounds nice. What do you think?"

It did sound nice. Especially since she didn't want to go to the grocery today. But she'd need to if she planned to eat supper at her house... "Sure." But as the word left her lips, a question popped into her brain. "Wait, are you asking me on a date?" Her heart slammed in her chest.

"Do you want it to be?"

No, no, no, no, *no!* "Um, I don't date." Still, her empty pantry and fridge called to her. And she really didn't want to go shopping today. However, that meant she'd have to tomorrow for sure. And now she was rambling in her brain. Great. Back to her dinner dilemma. Now that she'd agreed, how did she take it back? Would he be insulted? He'd given her the choice, and she'd said no to dating. "I'm not averse to meeting up with friends. Friends who agree to go Dutch treat."

"Dutch treat it is. Does that mean you'll meet me at the restaurant? Because I have no problem picking you up. As a friend, of course." There was a touch of laughter in his voice. Maybe he wasn't all that insulted.

"I'll meet you, friend. Where are we going?" That might be an important thing to figure out.

"I was thinking Krieg's. I don't feel like getting too dressed up. No tie."

"Ah, I see. Krieg's works. And, promise you won't make a big deal of it, but I concur with the part about not wanting to dress up." She winced, waiting for his reaction.

"We agree on something? Wait, I'm putting this on my calendar. Holy cow! It'll become a state holiday." He didn't try to hide the chuckle.

"Okay, you got me. What time?" Rose crossed her fingers that he'd not want to go too soon. Let it cool down a little first.

"Is seven too late for you?"

"Nope. Sounds perfect, Brett. Oh, and bring the paperwork." Her smile insisted on gracing her face even though she tried to stop it. At least he couldn't see it.

"I'll make sure I do. Meet you at seven, Rosie."

"At seven." She took a breath and hung up. They'd come close enough to saying goodbye that he shouldn't consider it ill-mannered. Wait. Did he think she'd been rude? Had she been? Why was she worrying about whether Brett considered her social skills lacking? *Stop it.* Those games were for high school, and that was years ago.

Plus, this wasn't a date.

If she kept telling herself that, she might finally believe it.

A glance at her Timex told her she had four hours before she had to be at the restaurant. Four long hours to get something accomplished. Or 240 minutes to stew about any ulterior motives Brett had. Hold it. Did he want it to be a date but was trying to placate her? He wouldn't try to trick her, would he? How could she tell?

Oh, good grief! Rose smacked her forehead with the heel of her palm. It was time to get off this crazy train to Looneyville before the men in the white coats showed up and took her away to the funny farm. Ho, ho, hee, hee, ha, ha.

She decided to check her mail, crossing her fingers that there'd be a distraction from all this mind swamp invading her brain. The way things were going, she'd need hip boots to wade through her thoughts.

August still had strength to keep the air sizzling, and the clear azure sky hadn't a single scudded cloud. No cooling rain in the forecast. Rose wiped away a trickle of sweat that broke free, rolling in front of her ear, and scanned her neighborhood. Her feline-loving neighbor, Mrs. Whitehead, stood out on her porch, focused on something to the opposite side of Rose's house. What in the world?

Just as she started to call out and ask, the idea of where the conversation might lead presented itself. The woman would undoubtedly rope her into coming over and her excuse for leaving was three plus hours away, if she counted getting ready and driving, which Rose did.

Still, the matron appeared lonely, and when better to build neighborly good will? Besides, she really wasn't a bad sort. Just a little needy. Or lonely. What would it cost Rose to simply be polite?

"Mrs. Whitehead, is everything okay?"

The woman whipped around with her finger to her lips, then motioned for her to come over. Hmm?

The vibe got to Rose, and she caught herself doing a Nancy Drew-style tiptoe down her steps and over to her neighbor's porch.

Mrs. Whitehead slowly stepped backward to get closer to Rose before she whispered, "Can you hear them?"

Rose closed her eyes and listened a moment, catching a male voice though she couldn't understand what he was saying. Then, a female shouted, much louder, angrier. "You lied to me again!"

Mrs. Whitehead's stare pierced through Rose's closed eyelids, and when she opened them to see if her mind was playing tricks, the woman was in her face, shaking her head, wringing her hands. "I don't know what to do. These arguments are getting worse every day." She kept her voice low as she leaned in close.

"Should we be listening to this?" Rose followed her neighbor's lead, keeping her tone to a whisper. She'd suffered enough pain from being the center of gossip while going to school and didn't want to even appear to be someone who might spread it. Some wounds took time to heal.

The elderly woman ushered her into the house and pointed out a seat on her davenport before plopping down next to Rose. "I don't want to overhear, but when it gets loud, I worry. Should I do something?"

"You say this has been going on for a while?" So it wasn't a gossip thing, it was a worried thing.

"About two weeks. Oh, dear."

Rose needed more information, not to share, but to understand if there was anything to be done. There definitely might be a problem, but should the neighbors get involved? "How well do you know them?"

Mrs. Whitehead smoothed out her apron before tucking a rogue gray curl behind her ear. "The Prescotts have lived there about a year. They haven't been married all that long. At first, we were very friendly. Evelyn would come by to chat sometimes and bring over a treat so we could have tea. But then she mentioned she wanted to get a job. They've only got the one car, and he takes that to work. So she found something downtown that she could walk to. Said she was clerking at Woolworth's."

The picture grew clearer. This Evelyn was married to a chauvinist who was trying to keep his wife tied up at home. Just the idea made Rose's blood pressure jump. Ooh, would she love to get her hands on that man. "So he won't let her work? He keeps her trapped in their house?"

"Oh, no, no, nothing like that. Roger is very good to Evelyn. She even told me that several times back when she came to visit. Might be this has to do with her wanting to get her own car."

Not a chauvinist? "What makes you say that?"

"Well, I know she's wanted one for some time. And he mentioned that her birthday was coming up not that long ago. I've got a feeling he wants to give her one as a gift, and she thinks because he doesn't want to go car shopping, he's broken his word. I'm guessing, of course. But it makes sense. The problem is, if she keeps throwing these tantrums, there's going to be hurt feelings before he gives her the surprise."

"Oh. Couldn't he have just told her that for her birthday he was taking her out so she could pick out what she wanted?" That's what Rose would prefer.

"I guess, but what if she wants something out of their budget? I know he'd hate to tell her no." Mrs. Whitehead wadded her apron in her hands and then smoothed it out again. "What should I do? I don't want to spoil the surprise, but maybe I could drop a hint?"

Rose shook her head. "No, that would make Roger upset with you. And Evelyn might even agree with him because you spoiled everything." She took a moment to consider what Mom would do. The answer flashed quicker than expected. "You could pray."

"Oh, dear me, you are right. Why didn't I think about that? Probably because I've missed so much by not gathering with our congregation. I'm out of the habit. Of course. I just can't get out by myself anymore, so the pastor or his wife try to stop by sometimes. The company is lovely. But being away from church is so hard. I miss it so, and now I can see that I'm forgetting to do things I would have done automatically. Thank you, Dr. Crackinbush."

"Just call me Rose. We're neighbors. You know, I haven't looked for a church home since I moved here. Would you allow me to take you?"

Mrs. Whitehead's eyes glistened. "I would so appreciate that, but I'm not sure you can get me down those steps and to your car."

"Don't you worry about that. I'm a whole lot stronger than I look." Rose patted the woman's hand. "Would you like me to stay and pray with you? I'm not one for praying out loud, but I'm good at listening while you do."

Now a tear skittered down Mrs. Whitehead's cheek. "Please." She took hold of Rose's hands and started.

At first it was like greeting someone she loved. Then she moved on to Evelyn and Roger, mentioning the rift, the surprise, and asking for things to work out and for the couple to forgive each other. Just when Rose figured she'd covered that well, Mrs. Whitehead went into a litany of her family and friends—Rose wasn't sure who they all were—and added in healing requests for herself. She wrapped it up by praying for Rose, thanking God that He'd sent her such a kind neighbor.

The woman might not have thought that if she'd had any idea what had run through Rose's mind before she called out from her porch. That piece of shame made her cheeks heat while she silently asked for forgiveness.

The amen came, and Rose added hers before withdrawing her hands from Mrs. Whitehead's. That gave her a moment to glance at her wristwatch. "I need to head back. I've an appointment this evening and have to get ready."

"Appointment, you say? Is that what you young folks are calling dates now days?" Mrs. Whitehead winked.

"Oh, no, nothing like that." Rose's cheeks warmed. "I'm meeting a colleague for dinner to talk about business."

"Is this colleague a handsome young professional? I think I saw him a couple days ago stopping by your house." Those eyes that had been glistening with unshed tears now glinted with mirth.

Rose cleared her throat. "Yes, that was him." So it was a good thing she hadn't invited Brett inside with Mrs. Whitehead watching. "We've been working on a project and will hopefully finish it up this week. I ought to be going."

At the door, she paused. "I'll keep Evelyn and Roger in prayer too. By the way, when should I pick you up for church?"

"The late service starts at 10:45. I think that might be best, so we've got time to judge how this goes. What if you come by around ten?"

Rose couldn't imagine it taking that long to get the woman in her car, but better safe than sorry. "Then I will see you at ten tomorrow morning. Have a nice evening, Mrs. Whitehead."

"You too."

Rose waved from the bottom of the steps before crossing the yard to her own porch. Not exactly what she'd envisioned happening when she called out her greeting, but maybe this was a good thing.

No maybe about it. She had put off finding a church for too long. It was time.

Tomorrow, she would set aside her excuses and do what her mother had been pushing her to do. Could be this would give her a brownie point or two.

Though heaven knew that there weren't enough brownie points to get her in good with her stepfather. That was already a lost cause.

What *was* it about that lady chiropractor that continued to rob Brett of sleep? He would have sworn he was tired enough that just plopping into his Lazy Boy would have sent him off to Slumberland. Nope. Here he twisted and turned in his bed, having given up the usually comfortable chair, with Rosie's voice and flashing eyes darting from his subconscious every time he closed his lids.

He was almost to the point of shouting "uncle" to whatever devious device kept him awake, but the idea of giving in was feeding his stubborn nature. It's what had gotten him through his healing after the tornado and sustained him through med school and his internship. Brett punched his pillow once more. He'd set his alarm anyway, so he might as well keep trying.

That is until the phone rang.

"Brett here."

"Hey, kiddo. Wanted to give you a call." Alma. Hadn't he talked with her in person last night?

"What's the matter?"

"Hey! Can't I simply phone my favorite little brother?"

Brett snorted. "You say the same thing to Bart."

"Yeah, but I mean it right now. Are you busy?"

Something was determined that he would not get a nap. He ran his fingers through his hair, pushing back on the instinct to rip it out. "No, I'm not."

"You sound like I interrupted something."

"Nah, nothing. Just a Saturday afternoon examination of the inside of my eyelids. What's up?"

"You were sleeping? I'm sorry."

"I wasn't sleeping." Yet. Brett tried hard to keep his voice even, but he was sure there was no fooling his sister.

"You're positive?"

"Alma. What gives?"

She hemmed and hawed until he was ready to hang up on her, but then she sighed. "I liked your friend Rose and was hoping there was something going on with you two."

Oh, good grief. "She's a colleague. Sort of."

"She didn't look like a colleague when you were dancing. Besides, she definitely can hold her own, with all that give and take we had at the table last night. I think you need to—"

"You planning to manage my love life?" Now Brett sat on the edge of his bed. "I'm incapable of handling things myself?"

"Currently you are the only one of us not in a relationship, and it won't be long before you're the only single member of the Shoffner kids."

"Big deal. Wouldn't it be better for me to find someone compatible rather than rush into something to keep from remaining a bachelor? A station in life that is well-respected, by the way." He'd have adjusted his tie Rodney Dangerfield-style if he were wearing one.

It was Alma's turn to snort, derision unmasked. "Only among other bachelors. For your information, Buster, I read a bit of research that married men, on the whole, live longer. So there. I'm just looking out for you."

"Where did you get your statistics? I don't recall reading them in the Journal of the American Medical Association."

The soft cough gave him an idea where she'd dug up her research. "Uh...*Cosmopolitan*?"

"Seriously? Well, if it's in *Cosmo*, it has to be the truth."

"Stop making fun or you won't remain my favorite little brother. All I'm saying is that now that you've got your practice up and running, you should take some time to think about starting a relationship. Since you and Rose have hit it off so well, she'd be a great candidate."

A noise filtered through the line, and Brett suddenly realized there were three of them on this call. "Hey, Mom, do you agree with Alma?"

His sister sputtered. "How did you—"

"Let it go, dear. He's your brother. I'm just surprised it took him this long to figure it out. And yes, my darling Brett, I heartily agree with your very smart sister. I didn't get to speak with Rose last evening, but from what I've learned, she is remarkable."

Brett blew out his breath knowing it was going to take more than he could explain for them to understand. "She is. Remarkable and intelligent and witty and passionate about chiropractic. If Doctor Eilert ever got wind I was dating a chiropractor, let alone a feminist, he'd disown me."

"That's the problem? Really? I figured it was more like she clashed with your old-fashioned girl delusion." He'd been doing better with Alma. Once Mom got tag-teamed into the ring, he was going down for the count.

"Delusion? What's so wrong with wanting a woman with aspirations like my mother?" Let her deny that she'd chosen home and family. Mom should be the poster child for United Homemakers of America. If there was such an organization. But then, if there wasn't, there ought to be.

"I didn't have the option to choose. They expected women to stay home in my day. I would have loved to have gotten out once you all left the nest, but my skill set leaves me with few options. This young woman made it through chiropractic school, and that is no easy feat. And I'll let you in on a little secret. I've been to a chiropractor, and it helped immensely."

"Mom, you what?" He was up now, pacing. "You could've been hurt. Your back ruined beyond compare. The things Oskar has told me about that. I know Rose is wonderful. Maybe if she were less confrontational, and maybe if she'd consider being a housewife instead of a chiropractor. But no matter how much I enjoy being with her, there is no future."

"I'm sorry, Brett."

"Me too, little brother."

Brett ran his hand over his face, knowing he'd just spewed out the reasons he needed to keep his distance from the lovely Dr. Crackinbush. "Yeah, me too."

They must have heard something in his voice because they wrapped up the call. "We'll go now, sweetheart. But don't close the door too fast. It might surprise you where things could lead. You take care and call soon."

"And you can call me too, kiddo. I only want what's best for you."

It was like having two mothers. "Love you both. And I promise to call. Bye." Brett returned the handset to the cradle and flopped back on his bed.

Maybe he needed that conversation to show him how he'd been lying to himself. Asking Rosie out, even with the pretext of going over their interviews and making it Dutch treat, was still hoping for a date with her.

There was something compelling about Rosie that went beyond how easy she was on his eyes. As much as he hated to admit it, even her sass that challenged him was appealing. He'd never want a relationship with a woman who was milquetoast and let him walk all over her.

No, he wanted someone who, like Alma said, gave as good as she took. Plus, Rosie had a sense of humor. At least when she didn't feel insulted. And she hadn't acted offended around him in a while, Okay, they'd only known each other almost a week, so a while was relative.

Still, Rosie Crackinbush was getting to him like no woman ever had. He wasn't sure even now if that were good or bad, but he knew beyond a shadow of doubt, it was dangerous.

He stood and stretched, carefully working a kink out of his back. A nap today was a lost cause, but he still had time before he needed to get ready to meet Rosie. Wandering into the living room, he turned on the TV, finally landing on an old *Three Stooges* episode. If he couldn't sleep, then laughter was the next best medicine.

Apparently it was just what the doctor ordered, since while he was helping Moe knock Larry and Curly into submission, a clanging jarred him back into his life. The alarm in his bedroom that he'd forgotten to turn off. Good thing.

The shower did a better job than his alarm clock of waking him. After a moment of vacillating on how casual to go, Brett settled on his brown and navy striped short-sleeved pullover with the placket and collar, jeans, and his white belt. If that didn't say relaxed, he didn't know what did.

He double checked the time on his 1972 Prestige as he buckled the leather band around his wrist—a gift from Mom and his siblings for his birthday last month. He'd make it, just. Which niggled at him. Didn't his dad say if he wasn't fifteen minutes early, he was late? Though he had a feeling Rosie's family motto was a little different. Maybe she wouldn't hold it against him.

Ten minutes later, he pulled into Krieg's parking lot and shut off the ignition. That's when he noticed his hands trembled. Thankfully he wasn't a surgeon. Was he really in that bad of shape? He needed to get over himself. It was one simple business dinner. With a woman who had no interest in him, he pointed out to his edge-of-panicked self. In fact, she didn't even think he was funny. If anything, that was a deal-breaker. He needed to keep that forefront in his thoughts.

So why was this making him so crazed?

You really have to ask?

Brett shook off the question without naming whose voice popped in his head. He didn't need more to mess with his mind. Instead he plastered a grin on his face. There. Just one meal and some strategic planning. That's all. No. Big. Deal.

And if he muttered that all the way to the entrance, maybe he'd believe it.

He pulled open the door to find Rosie waiting on the other side. Looking cool as a cucumber in her blue sundress flecked with tiny daisies. "Thought we weren't going to dress up, though you look very nice."

"Thank you for that left-handed compliment, doctor. And no, I didn't dress up. This is one of my most comfortable outfits." She glanced down and swished her skirt as she finished speaking.

"Well, it looks lovely on you. Is that less left-handed?" He really hadn't meant to sound that way. It just surprised him that she'd wear a dress after requesting more casual attire.

"Yes, and thank you. Actually, you look nice too. I like how that shirt brings out the color in your eyes." Then her cheeks took on a warm glow, and he had the feeling she hadn't planned to express that, or at least not in that way. She glanced away and then turned back, her expression schooled. "I sort of expected you to be waiting for me. Didn't you say your family insists on being fifteen minutes early or they're late?"

That's what she remembered? "I did say that. However, you didn't seem to appreciate that quirk, so I made myself wait. Just about caused me to check in with Mom to make sure I belonged to the Shoffner clan. Not sure what I'd do if she told me I was adopted. But I think I can handle five minutes early without going into a spasm."

Rose chuckled. Maybe he and his humor were growing on her. Only to his mind, that was plain silly. He could do better.

The hostess came to their lame conversation's rescue, grabbing menus and guiding them to a small table where they sat in silence choosing their dinners.

Maybe the conversation hadn't been rescued. Could be it was dying a slow death, heaving out its final gasps. Whatever was happening, the surrounding silence remained until the server returned with glasses of water and her order pad.

"These will be separate checks, please." Rosie's voice fairly squeaked.

Shirley, the waitress, turned an eye on Brett, and he squirmed beneath its laser stare. This wasn't on him. He might have tossed out the idea to soften the invitation, but he preferred to be the one to pay. Or maybe ol' Shirl was just wondering about his shiner. No matter. All he could do was shrug and allow Rosie the courtesy of ordering first.

"I'll have a cheeseburger, medium, with pickles on the side." She smiled and handed back the menu.

Now it was his turn, and with all the weird vibes since they arrived, he couldn't remember anything. So he did the only sane thing he could think of. "I'll have what she's having." Whew! He also handed back his menu.

"What can I bring you to drink?"

Great, another question? Hopefully, Rosie would choose something he liked.

"I'll have a Coke."

"Make that two." Double whew. It felt like he'd just finished a round of dodging Joe Frazier.

Rose slid her napkin onto her lap before fixing him with her gold-flecked green eyes. "So, how has your afternoon been?"

If only he could tell her. Everything he did, even down to the patients he saw, had a cord of connection to her. Somehow she'd wormed her way into all the varying facets of his life. And that was something he was not about to admit. "Fine. Met a friend for lunch, talked with my mom. You?"

She seemed to wince. "Brett, I've got to say it one more time. I'm very sorry about your eye. It just looks so painful, and I'll bet you got questions today, probably from patients."

Now that made him smile, especially when he remembered how Mrs. Tomlinson had done her best to ferret out the story. "There were a few interesting probes, but I kept your reputation intact."

"I'm not sure how to take that. Maybe I'll say thank you and we can move on."

Great, he'd said the wrong thing again. Should he ask for a rule book so he could better prepare and not end up with a terminal case of foot-in-mouth disease?

Chapter 8

Ever since she realized there was an attraction, Rose's ability to hold a conversation with Brett had disintegrated into nothing more than hovering her toe above the water and pulling it back for fear of getting scalded. Brett wasn't out to hurt her, she was sure of that. Well, pretty sure. He had a kindness about him despite his misled chauvinist habits.

So why wasn't she able to hold a simple conversation with him?

"Earth to Rosie." He grinned and tapped her hand.

"Oh, sorry. Guess my mind was elsewhere. It's been a long day and I sort of feel...I don't know. Hazy? No. Just things aren't clear at the moment, and I need to pull myself back into my routine. It'll get better when I do."

"What's got you so mixed up?" Those blue eyes filled with concern nearly undid her.

Rose should have seen that question coming. She toyed with the edge of her napkin in her lap. There was no way to honestly answer. How did she say "You are the source of my discombobulation?" How would he take that? Would he suspect she'd started to have some feelings for him?

Had she?

No. That wouldn't happen. Not only was it not in her life plan, but it made no sense. They were too different and had only known each other six days. Six measly days.

God created the world in six days.

That didn't help.

"There's just a lot happening on so many fronts. Looks like my neighbor is in need of some help, and I've got equipment that ought to be sent from my grandfather's storage unit to my house for set up—I have to get that settled and soon so I don't keep paying to house it—and of course, Teri and Bart's wedding coming up. You know, as the best man and maid of honor, we're supposed to do some planning."

"We are? Like what?"

"Bart never told you about what they'd decided?" Rose had really hoped Bart would have talked to Brett so she didn't have to be the one to explain it all.

But Brett merely shook his head. "He went off to his room. I crashed on the couch and got up before he did. There wasn't a lot of conversation."

She knew men didn't converse the same way women did, but for cryin' out loud, they were twins. Wouldn't it have been normal for them to have some sort of discussion before going to sleep? She and Teri had talked until their eyes drooped and their words trailed off.

Rose inhaled and held it a moment, pulling everything together in her brain. "They've decided they want us to handle the rehearsal dinner. It is all set to happen in Kokomo. They found a location here that specializes in weddings. The Weather Girls Wedding Shoppe and Venue. It's over on the west side. They figured it might help if things were closer for us, and this place is pretty great. Anyway—" Rose grabbed another breath, swiped a sweaty palm across her napkin, and plunged in, "they want us to plan with the Weather Girls to make it a surprise for Teri and Bart."

"Make it a surprise? Like they won't know that the dinner comes after the rehearsal? It does, doesn't it?"

She nodded but waited for him to finish his thoughts.

"How are we supposed to surprise them when they've set it all up?"

Rose swallowed and rubbed her hand again. "We're to pick the menu, get everyone's choice, and come up with after-dinner entertainment before we whisk them off for their bachelor and bachelorette parties. We have to plan as well. They were imagining this as a precursor to the separate wingdings, as Teri put it, something that they'd share."

"Oh."

That's all he had to say? He always had plenty of words, and now he shut down when she needed him? Great. Just simply spectacular. "Food wise, the Weather Girls can help with those decisions. It's mainly the entertainment afterward, before the bachelor and bachelorette parties, that will take the work. Do you have any ideas?"

"W-e-l-l." He drew each phoneme out so long the word might as well have had twelve syllables. "Do you?"

"I'm not sure. We can keep it simple, offer two choices on the menu, maybe have dinner and dancing?" That's as far as she'd gotten, but she knew Teri hoped for more.

"They'll have that the next night." Brett drummed his fingers on the table before capturing her gaze, all full of hope. "Do you sing?"

"I sang in the choir at church growing up. I sound great in the shower. But I don't know about singing before an audience." She winced and hoped he'd take her word for it. There was no way she wanted to audition for him.

Brett rubbed his fingers at his hairline. "Okay, I'm going out on a limb here. But we have to contact the wedding party anyway, to get their dinner order, right?"

Again, Rose nodded.

"What if we ask them to put together a two-minute skit? Let's make it funny. They can do it with a partner or solo. Could be the Weather Girls will have a place to set up a makeshift stage. It won't be the same as the toasts the next night. Maybe pretend to sing a song, mouth it. I don't know. What do you think?"

He stared at her so earnestly that it grew apparent he really liked this suggestion, or at least the nexus of it.

"I think... Yes, something along those lines might work. Let's figure out the rest of this survey stuff and then we can begin honing your idea. It's definitely better than anything I've come up with." She offered him a smile, and he grinned back. And he did it because she smiled at him, not because he was trying to pull one out of her. That undid something inside, like a flower blooming only in her heart. They were still far from a doable idea for the dinner entertainment. Still, perhaps with a lot of luck, they might pull this off.

Dinner arrived and conversation slowed. Afterward, while sharing a slice of sugar cream pie, they each sipped coffee and finally got to why they were supposed to be meeting.

Brett laid the paperwork out on the table. "Here are the names left to call. If they respond like the first ones, it's a cinch. Do you want me to hang onto the notes from the finished meetings and start a tally sheet? Maybe I could make a graph. Or would you prefer to do that?"

Rose had to laugh. She'd intimidated him to the point he was timid about stepping up to do anything for fear she'd take it the wrong way. "It's fine. Since I'm taking the notes, I'll put the tally sheet and a graph together. Should I call you when I'm done so you can see it before we turn it in?"

"I trust you. You are one competent woman, and you'll have it all..." He wiggled his fingers. "I don't know, color coded and alphabetized with a legend. I'd just throw it all together and hope for the best."

Is that how he saw her? Over-the-top detail oriented? Okay, maybe she was a little. Or even a lot. But was that a bad thing? Now she felt guilty about that intimidating thought.

"I can't imagine you'd do it up too haphazard. Not with your efficiency skills. But color coded makes it pretty." She winked, plenty aware that he wasn't one to say mean things. At least not intentionally. Maybe now he wouldn't feel so timid either.

"Efficiency skills? I like that. I might use it with Belinda and Pam the next time they complain." He chuckled and somehow the atmosphere felt lighter.

Rose tucked the paperwork into her purse and glanced up to see Brett signaling the waitress for the bill. Guess they were done. A little part of her cringed at the stab of sadness that reality brought.

Clasping the receipt, he held her chair and then walked her to the cash register, keeping his hand at the small of her back. Rose hated that she enjoyed that bit of civility so much. Of course, she could stand on her own and needed no one to guide her out. But his touch radiated warmth and something else. Gentle excitement? Whatever it was, it was wonderful, and she craved it. How had an enlightened woman like herself fallen into such a primal trap? And enjoyed it?

He allowed her to go first. She paid her half then stepped to the side feeling strange. The worst was when he removed his hand to take out his wallet, leaving an empty coolness where his touch had been. He was all smiles with the hostess too, and that stirred something in Rose's belly that her intuition could name but the rest of her refused to believe. Jealousy.

"Would you take a walk with me before we go our separate ways?"

Despite the slowly descending temperature that must still be in the mid-eighties, Rose agreed with a small nod. She hated the idea of saying goodbye to him more than strolling through a blanket of humidity, a notion she chose not to examine now. Or ever.

"We could go together and check out a park. Berkley Park isn't far. I'd bring you back for your car."

The idea of letting him drive tempted a lot more than she wanted to admit even to herself, but it made better sense for Rose to follow him there. "I'll take my car. You lead the way." She leaned against him, for just a moment, hoping that would convey it was simply logic and not independence making the choice. Logic. She had to hang on to that.

Brett turned and slowly tucked a curl behind her ear. When he spoke, it was soft and full of smiles. "Okay. In case you lose me, take Jefferson to Berkley and head north. It will be on your left."

His touch, small as it was, electrified her nerves. She nodded, not trusting anything that might come out of her mouth.

Still with his hand at her back, he walked her to her car. She could have handed him her keys to unlock it for her, but that was just silly. He would have done it though. She was well aware of that. Instead, he watched while she turned the key and then he opened her door for her to slide in. He was a gentleman through and through. What would Betty Friedan think? Would Gloria Steinem call her a traitor? Right now, with Brett leaning in her open window, his face so near and dear, Rose didn't care.

She followed her impulse and brushed his cheek with a kiss.

His eyes widened before his grin complied.

It surprised them both.

But Rose's hands covered her face before she saw more. "I'm sorry. Maybe I should go."

"Rosie, look at me." He gently tugged her fingers away. "Rosie, I'm not. Do you really want to go home?"

Impulse took over again. "No."

"Then don't. Follow me. I promise to remain on my best behavior."

She nodded and started her ignition so she wouldn't get lost in those eyes of his. With the lights of the parking lot, they were a dark denim blue and they twinkled, almost danced. Oh, how they made it hard to just think.

He moved away, walking backwards a few steps before tossing her a wink and heading for his car.

Now that his lack of proximity allowed her room to use her brain, all she did was berate her impulsivity. Apparently the problem wasn't whether he'd be on his best behavior, but would she? Rose leaned her head against her steering wheel. What had she been thinking? Well, that answer stared back in bright neon letters. She didn't think. Heat that had nothing to do with the outdoor temperature crawled up her cheeks.

What did he imagine had been going through her mind? Did she really want to know?

Most of all, why, oh, why had she kissed him? She pulled from the lot, following his taillights.

Granted, it was just a tiny peck on the cheek. Nothing romantic in the least. Gratitude for his kindness. That had to be all it was. Had to be.

But would it give him ideas for something that could never happen?

Wait a minute. Why could it never happen?

Oh, her heart was gaining a mind of its own, and it was time to explain the facts again and set the record straight. Because a romance of any kind either led to her dreams being crushed or heartbreak. *Do you get that heart? We're talking real, painful, soul-crushing heartbreak.* How could she have both in her life—her career and a... What was she thinking Brett could be? Friend? Boyfriend? Husb—

Don't even imagine it!

She needed to take Barney Fife's admonition and nip this, nip it in the bud.

But you started it.

Fine, so she would finish it. Now. Tonight. Before it all rode away with her like a runaway train with no escape.

Right.

She'd make sure Brett knew there was no way under the sun that things could progress with them. Zero, zilch, nada.

Was she willing to be just friends?

The thought of never having him in her life made her chest ache, and she rubbed the spot as they braked at the traffic light. Friends would be acceptable. She would agree to that. They could end up as good friends. Special friends. Through thick and thin.

What happens when he finally meets that old-fashioned girl and settles down? Think she'll appreciate her husband having a woman best friend?

Will you be able to handle the loss of your friendship when she takes that special place in his life?

Stupid heart. Now her chest really hurt, and she did an internal scan of her body to rule out the probability of a heart attack. No, not a heart attack. Something that drastic was ill-advised considering Brett was a doctor and would end up treating her and they'd become even closer.

That left only one other possibility. Heartbreak. Her traitorous heart was broken. Possibly permanently damaged.

Rose braked into the parking spot next to Brett at Berkley Park. There were things to get straight with that man, and nothing would be right until she did.

Brett locked his car door and rounded his trunk to aid Rosie from her vehicle. The drive over, and that sudden peck on his cheek, had left him wondering. Would she really want to take a chance with little ol' Doctor Brett Shoffner, MD?

If Rosie thought it was worth the exploration, maybe he did too. There was no getting around the fact that he was attracted to her, but he also wasn't stupid. Usually. Would she be willing to investigate possible compromises? Would he?

However, that was a long way off. They'd need to take this slow and do their due diligence to make sure there were no misunderstandings, since they were coming from such opposing mindsets.

Somehow, that thought had overtones of his lawyer brother.

Brett glanced at her again, his smile peeking while he held her door.

She climbed out and locked up.

Then he guided her hand to the crook of his arm. Less intimate than holding hands, but there was something endearing about being connected this way.

Rosie peeked up at him, then back at her feet. Those feet clothed in shoes designed to make her appear taller. Even with them, she barely came to his shoulder.

"I didn't think about your footwear. How are you holding up?"

"Fine. Don't worry about it. I wear them all the time unless I'm working on someone. Then I have a platform built around the table. If I tried to manipulate anyone, especially a larger man, I'd be off balance in my wedges. But after I deliver my last patient of the day to Mildred, I am out of my flats and into my preferred shoes."

"Who's Mildred?"

"Oh, she's Doc's wife. She oversees the office and business end of things." She kicked a larger pebble from the sidewalk.

They continued along the path until a park bench appeared and they ambled toward that. It'd be easier to watch her face while they were seated.

"What made you choose chiropractic?"

Rosie clasped her hands in her lap before fixing him with a stare.

"What?" Wasn't he clear?

"Just checking to see if you really want to know and aren't making fun of me."

A thousand responses bombarded him, but the look in her eyes ruled out all but one. "I really want to know, Rosie."

"Okay. My grandfather was one. My father's father. My dad died when I was seven, and Grampa became my world. Even after Mom and Howard got married, he was there for me. Howard... Well, now isn't the time for that. Let's just say I loved my grandfather, and he inspired me. I'd dreamed of learning to become a chiropractor, but Howard refused to pay for the Palmer School of Chiropractic. He had other plans for me—nursing. According to him, doctors were men and chiropractic was not a recognized form of medical practice. Grampa paid for my tuition at Ball State, but he died my senior year and left the majority of his estate to me. He'd set aside a chunk for Palmer's tuition and left me all his equipment besides the estate. My brother didn't mind. He understood, though Howard wasn't all that keen. It thwarted his plans. Wally, my brother, had his education paid for by my stepfather because he went into pediatrics. He was a male, so it was fine for him to be a doctor. He didn't need everything that I did. Not that Grampa forgot him, but his inheritance was a lot smaller than mine."

Brett's fingers inched their way closer to Rosie's. "So that's the stuff you've been paying to store? Your grandfather's equipment?"

She nodded. "He set it up to come out of the estate, but the sooner I have it delivered, the quicker I can use that money for other needs. Once the survey is done, I'll contact the storage place and make arrangements. I have to get the name of a reputable company that calibrates X-ray machines to ensure it's properly set up."

"You do your own X-rays?" Brett had never known a doctor to do that.

"It's so much easier than sending patients to the hospital where they won't accept my request for one, let alone allow me to see the results. I've had training and know how to read them."

Brett's fingers had met their goal and slowly encased her small hand in his, a weight lifting when she didn't pull away. "You amaze me. Your fire and passion are persuasive."

"So you don't think I ought to be burned at the stake?"

"Where would you get that? Of course, I don't." He scooted closer to her, protective mode kicking in.

She stared at her hand in his, still not withdrawing it. Was she thinking of pulling back?

"I've learned a lot from you."

"You have?" Now her gaze held his, her green eyes round and wide, the gold flecks glinting in the park lights.

"Definitely." He began making small circles underneath on her palm with his thumb while she released a small sound, not quite a whimper. "Should we talk about something else? I hate to make you uncomfortable."

"Then maybe you shouldn't do that?"

"Do what?"

"That thing you're doing to my hand."

"You don't like it?"

She sighed, though it sounded more contented than exasperated. "I never said that. But it doesn't necessarily make me comfortable."

"Is that a bad thing?"

She closed her eyes and tipped her head back just the tiniest bit. "Oh, no. Definitely not. But comfortable isn't what I'm feeling. Not by a long shot."

He chuckled. "Then I'll keep going. Should we talk about the rehearsal dinner?"

"Don't expect me to, um, make sense." The final word breathed out softer than a whisper.

"Okay, I'm thinking maybe we do little skits. I haven't heard how large the wedding party is supposed to be—"

"It's us, and then two bridesmaids and two groomsmen."

"Okay, then. Each couple creates a skit. Do the other people know each other?" An idea churned in his brain.

"Well, Alma and her husband do. Of course. The other two have yet to be asked since they couldn't make the party."

"I see. With Alma and Ed, that should be easy. I'm thinking if each of the couples did a skit, we'd give Teri and Bart a glimpse of life after the wedding through mouthing the words to songs, or something along those lines." Several duet choices were coming to mind. This could be good.

"I'd have to get up in front of people and sing?" Her hand stiffened but at least it remained with his.

"Pretend. Unless you wanted to—"

"No! Um, no, I don't think so."

"So you'll lip sync with me?" Now he had trouble breathing while waiting on her answer. That seemed a long time coming. In his head, mouthing turned into code for something else. Did it seem like that for her too?

"I guess. I won't be up there alone, right?" She relaxed.

He squeezed her hand and watched a smile begin to form on her lips. Sort of like a sunrise in how it brightened her face and made her eyes twinkle. "Never. I promise."

"Okay. Maybe we can talk about it after we finish up the survey." She paused. "I probably need to head for home. I promised my neighbor I'd take her to church in the morning."

"Ah, right. I understand. It was an early start for us today too." Though at this point, he could stay up all night if Rosie sat beside him like this.

"Yeah, it was." Those gorgeous eyes captivated him again, and he hated for all this to end. However, he stood, breaking the spell and pulling her up with him. Releasing her hand was not something he was ready to do though, just yet. "I'll walk you back."

This time their fingers wove together and as genteel as it had felt to amble with her fingers in the crook of his arm, it didn't come close to the euphoria of the clasp between them. All he could do was pray the stroll to the vehicles would never end.

Again, there was no chatting as they retraced their steps. Instead, she leaned her head against his shoulder, and his chest filled to near bursting. Could anything be better?

And then they were in the parking lot.

Her sigh caught his ear. This time it had no contentment tones. "Here we are."

"Yeah, here we are." Not exactly brilliant prose, but what else was there to say? *Can we do this again? Would you let me take you on a real date?* None of those thoughts made it to his vocal chords.

She fumbled in her purse, finally pulling her keys free and unlocking her car.

He opened her door and barricaded her in the triangular gap. It was almost as if he had her trapped, not that he was hunting her or anything. No, she'd appeared on his horizon out of the blue. And thank God she did.

Rosie raised her gaze to meet his, her bottom lip caught between her teeth. "This was nice." He could get lost in her gaze and never want to be found.

"It was. Rosie... " Brett's heart had taken over as he studied her glistening eyes, her mildly flush cheeks, her mouth that tempted him more than he'd ever been tempted. He knew to go slow, not rush. He realized moving too fast would make things weird between them. His head yelled all this and more thoughts his heart didn't listen to. Before he could stop himself, he leaned down and brushed a kiss, not on her cheek, like she'd done with him, but on those amazing lips, so soft but firm, warm, and inviting.

She responded, her hands rising to trace a trail up his chest, slide up to his shoulders, and then around his neck, drawing him in.

No longer did his forearms rest on her door and car. Instead, they engulfed her, bringing her closer still. She tasted of sweetness with a little coffee flavor, and he imagined enjoying that on a regular basis. An SOS from his brain told him to hold back, to not overwhelm her, but she overwhelmed him. He'd never kissed, nor been kissed, by a woman so perfectly, so completely. As if they were created to do just that. Dreams of Rosie replaced his old-fashioned girl ones as his fingers wove into her blonde hair, softer than bunny fur. Sweeter smelling than a garden. There was no other place to be than in her arms.

A throat cleared behind Brett. Rosie jumped back.

"Sorry, sir, but you might want to take that somewhere else." The patrolman who'd parked his cruiser at the rear of Rosie's car tipped his hat and didn't try to hide his grin before climbing back into his vehicle.

When had the guy even pulled up? How long had he been standing there? Should he try to start again?

"I ought to leave." Rosie's hand moved to pat his chest but stopped just short of connecting. She spun on her heel and climbed into her driver's seat. "Thanks again, Brett." Her fingers briefly brushed over her lips.

He stepped out of the way while she pulled her door securely closed and rolled down her window.

"Goodnight." She wouldn't meet his gaze but focused on starting her ignition.

"Rosie. I, I'll wait for your call." It was the best he could come up with. She obviously didn't want to talk about what just happened, at least not now. Had he made a mistake?

Now you ask?

"Okay." She backed from the space and headed out. Of the parking lot, for sure. Out of his life? Maybe. It wasn't something he could figure out at the moment.

Brett jammed his hands in his pockets and strode for his car. This was not how he'd seen the evening going. If anything, he'd probably have stopped the whole thing if his brain hadn't taken a station break at such a critical juncture.

All right. He knew what he was doing, that he shouldn't, and that he went ahead anyway.

Now, what did he do?

Nothing. Rosie was in charge of calling him once she had everything ready. He hadn't given her his address yet, but she'd said she'd call on Tuesday evening to bring him up to speed. So between now and then, there wasn't anything he could do.

Not one blessed thing.

Except pray. And go to church tomorrow just in case the pastor had a word for him in his sermon.

It could happen.

Chapter 9
Sunday, August 27, 1972

Rose woke, tracing her smile with her fingers as filaments of her dream continued to dance in her head. The stars, the warmth, the tender touch.

The kiss.

Her eyes popped open, and the silly grin disintegrated into a mass of holy-smoke-what-did-I-do, all wiggly like some gooey, melted Jell-O salad in the summer sun. Rose groaned. It wasn't just a dream. A deliciously— No! Bad dream! Bad Choice! Bad Rose! She pulled her pillow over her head and groaned some more.

Oh, heavenly days, what did she do now? How in the world did she face Brett again? And she had to. On Wednesday.

What had she been thinking?

She tossed her pillow to the side and sat on the edge of her bed. Her brain had not been engaged. That was certain. If it had, she'd have remembered how important it was to avoid entanglements. Nothing romantic, no extra self-inflicted challenges to thwart her from reaching her goal, especially since it was so close. So. Very. Close. Rose could almost reach out and touch her objective, her lifelong dream. It was that tangible now.

So was that kiss.

Had she messed things up? She dropped her head to her hands, searching her thoughts for a way to rewind last evening. A do-over. That's what she needed. Howard and his golf buddies would call it a mulligan.

No, Howard would tell her she'd come to her senses and had found someone sensible to build a life with.

That alone should have been enough to discover a way to wipe the last twelve hours out of existence. If only.

A shower was what she needed. She did her best thinking as the spray peppered her clean, and besides, it was time to get ready for church. Mrs. Whitehead expected her at... Rose glanced at the clock. Nine thirty-seven? To top it all off, she'd overslept.

Rose jumped from her mattress and yanked open dresser drawers before attacking her closet, tossing all her needed clothing on the bed. Then she raced for the bathroom, took the fastest shower in history, and donned her clothes. Fighting the fear of what the clock face revealed, she checked her alarm. Seven minutes left. No time even for hot curlers. She settled for a ponytail and added mascara and lip gloss for good measure. No one would recognize her there. Probably. She hoped. Maybe she should pray. Fast, because now she had two minutes to get to Mrs. Whitehead's. Ack!

A race down her stairs, a grab for her purse, and a moment to lock up left her with forty-five seconds to cross her yard and knock. She skidded to a halt and raised her fist as her neighbor pushed open the screen door.

"There you are, Rose. Right on time."

If only the woman knew. "Are you ready? I parked in the driveway last night thinking it might be easier on you."

"I'm all set. I ought to take my cane, just in case. Getting to the car once we're off the porch steps shouldn't be so bad, but taking those stairs is my biggest concern." The woman chewed at the corner of her lip, revealing she was more worried than she said.

"Like I told you, I'm pretty strong. Let me get on the side opposite your cane. You set the pace and just lean on me. I'll keep you steady."

Mrs. Whitehead nodded, though she still didn't look sold on the idea. However, she maneuvered to the top of the steps before she paused and stared.

"You can do it. I'm right here." Rose had her arm around the woman's back and gave her waist a gentle squeeze. "On three we'll take the first step. One, two—"

"Maybe I ought to stay home."

Rose shook her head. She couldn't let the poor soul stop when she was so close to victory. "You can do it. I'm right here. But how about we pray about it?"

Mrs. Whitehead agreed and gripped Rose's far hand while mumbling out a "Help me, Jesus" prayer. That should do it. But just in case, Rose added her own *Please, God!*

After they both said amen, Rose tried again. "One, two, three."

The fearful woman stepped down a tread with Rose and stopped. "We did it. We really did it. Okay, again."

Rose counted and they went down another level. Five more attempts put them at the bottom of the porch steps.

A tear trickled down Mrs. Whitehead's peachy soft cheek. "I haven't been here in over a year. I can't believe it."

"But you did it. And if you can do it once, you can do it again. I'm happy to take you to church or to the store, run errands with you. You don't have to stay shut up in your home."

Mrs. Whitehead pulled Rose into a hug with a chuckle. "Let's just start with the service today and see how that goes."

After getting her neighbor into the passenger seat, Rose started her car. "I forgot to ask where we're going."

"Oh, I should have told you. Wabash Community Church. It's on the west side of town, off Superior Avenue."

On the drive over, Mrs. Whitehead talked of the wonderful people who attended the church. The pastor and his wife. The new music director, who was a professional musician. The fabulous cooks who made dinners on Wednesday nights.

How there were people of all ages, all backgrounds who attended. At least that's how it was a year ago.

It was obvious that Rose's neighbor had only good thoughts for all the members, but if they were so great, why hadn't they tried to help in the past year? Had no one missed Mrs. Whitehead? Well, she did say that the pastor and a few others had come by to visit with her. However, didn't anyone consider helping the woman get to church?

She must have grown too quiet because Mrs. Whitehead touched Rose's arm. "Are you okay?"

"Yes." Rose paused, then plunged in. "I just can't figure out why no one tried to help you get there after all this time."

"Oh, they did. I didn't do it because it scared me too much. Somehow, with you being a doctor and all, I decided to give it a try."

Oh. "I see." Sort of. If her neighbor knew what kind of a doctor she was, would she still have been as brave about taking a chance? Had Rose been deceptive in not sharing her specialty? True, it had never come up in conversation, though there were times Rose could've explained. Had she really wanted to, that is. Why hadn't she wanted to?

She needed to answer those questions. However, that was a self-reflective discussion for another time. They pulled into the parking lot and found the closest empty space. "Think you can walk this far?"

"Definitely." The smile on Mrs. Whitehead's face beamed away any trace of fear.

There were no steps into the narthex, which made life much easier. Rose helped the woman from her car and walked beside her into the church foyer.

"Amelia Whitehead! It is so good to see you!" A middle-aged lady in a cream-colored dress rushed over to give Rose's neighbor a hug.

"Gloria, this is my new friend, Dr. Rose Crackinbush. Rose, may I introduce our pastor's wife, Gloria Mussing."

Mrs. Mussing held out her hand, and Rose shook it while they both said, "Nice to meet you," and then laughed.

"I'm so glad you got one of my favorite people to come back. We've missed her around here." Gloria Mussing's praise was warm and genuine. Made it hard to have judgy thoughts about her.

"I'm happy to do it. Besides, being sort of new in town, I needed to find a church home. Mrs. Whitehead assured me this was the place."

"It's good to be back, Gloria, but I think I ought to go sit down now." One glance at Mrs. Whitehead's paling face showed she'd used up a chunk of her energy.

"Then I won't keep you. Welcome to both of you." Mrs. Mussing patted their shoulders and moved to the side.

Rose allowed Mrs. Whitehead to grip her arm and lead to the pew she wanted. About a third of the way from the front.

"Oh, shoot. We didn't get bulletins."

"No problem. Let me grab a couple." Rose was back up the aisle before her neighbor could object.

Which was why she was there as the glass doors opened, causing her to glance over.

Out of curiosity.

As Brett Shoffner stepped into the large narthex.

Rose's breath caught as she spun away and raced back to the pew, sliding in, and passing Mrs. Whitehead a bulletin while she opened her own and held it smack dab in front of her face. *Please, please, please don't see me!*

How could he be here? Had she mentioned where she was taking Mrs. Whitehead? Yes and no. She'd said church. There had to be at least a half dozen churches in the area. And she hadn't known which one they'd be attending until she was in the car this morning. So there was no way she told him. Was it a lucky guess? Was he stalking her?

How did he know? Why was he—

"Good morning, ladies. Glad to see you again, Dr. Crackinbush." Brett. He'd found her.

Rose lowered the bulletin and summoned a smile in hopes Mrs. Whitehead wouldn't catch on to the problem.

"Good morning, Dr. Shoffner. May I introduce my friend and neighbor, Mrs. Amelia Whitehead. Mrs. Whitehead, this is Dr. Brett Shoffner." Rose's face started to hurt from the fake smile, and her heart rate must be through the roof.

"It's lovely to meet you, Mrs. Whitehead." He shook hands with the woman. "I didn't know this was where you attended, doctor."

"It's my first time. I hadn't found a church home so far, and Mrs. Whitehead invited me."

Then the words she'd been too afraid to imagine popped from her kind-hearted neighbor's mouth. "Dr. Shoffner, why don't you join us? There's plenty of room." She glanced at Rose as she scooted farther in.

What else could she do?

"Sure." *Please don't join us.*

"Thank you. Don't mind if I do." His gaze never left Rose's, while a smile teased his lips.

Rose slid closer to Mrs. Whitehead, giving him the end seat. At least if he started whispering to her, her neighbor shouldn't be able to hear. Maybe. *Please, God, don't let her overhear anything.*

But Brett didn't whisper. He spoke nothing other than small talk that he directed to both women. However, once the sermon started, she noticed him inching his fingers her way. He did that last night too. Worked them slowly over to cover her hand and eventually wove his digits with hers. Such an innocent, sweet move. She'd fallen for it beneath the romance of the moonlight. But today, in church no less, she wasn't about to get caught in that trap. She knew where it led, and she was not about to kiss Brett Shoffner ever again.

Rose moved her fingers out of his reach.

He withdrew his hand. In fact, it seemed he withdrew himself, though he continued to sit next to her throughout the rest of the service. But she could feel it in the surrounding atmosphere.

She'd hurt him.

Great. She didn't want to do that. She just wanted to set her boundaries. They could be friendly colleagues. But romance was not going to be on the agenda. Not now. Not ever. If that hurt his feelings, well, better to learn that before things got more complicated.

Oops. Her mind was so filled with that problem that she couldn't remember a word the pastor said.

"Romans 8:28 tells us 'And we know that all things work together for good to them that love God, to them who are called according to his purpose.' People tend to focus in on that first section of the promise—all things working together for good—but turn a blind eye on the rest. But the Apostle Paul is quite clear. We have a part in this. We need to discover the purpose God has intended for us, the one He calls us to. There are overarching corporate purposes, as in we are called to give God glory. Then there are group purposes, as when our church comes together to help the needy. But that's not what Paul is referring to here. Sometimes our experiences will seem random but over time will work together to point us toward and prepare us for the true purpose God has for each of His children. Those events, the struggles we go through, both good and bad, can be used to give Him glory as we reach out to one another in His love. Sometimes it is to comfort with the comfort we've been given. Mourn with those who mourn, rejoice with those who rejoice. There are times our skill set makes us the right person at the right time. The calling comes first. We know God equips the called. And those things we go through can equip us if we will put our trust in Him. Do you know the purpose for which God has called you?"

Pastor Mussing didn't pull any punches. Now Rose wished she'd listened from the beginning.

She knew her to-do list—do her best with her patients, finish up the survey, call to get Grampa's equipment delivered, ask Doc about who calibrates his X-ray machine. She could check that off in her sleep.

But her purpose?

Rose was pretty sure about that. At least about being called to be a chiropractor. She'd wanted to be one her whole life. To help others find healing without putting poisons inside them. To help encourage bodies to heal from the inside out. To be dedicated to the cause.

But did any of that give God glory? Was this really her sole purpose in life? She sneaked a glance at Brett.

Had God called her to only be a chiropractor?

Rosie's walls were back up.

The thought made Brett plain sad. She'd chosen to not take a chance just when he'd convinced himself possibilities were there if they both tried.

It had seemed like a divine appointment to spot her in a pew at his church, like maybe God was in on it and rooted for him. Though if he'd taken a moment to understand instead of thinking her hiding behind her bulletin was so cute, he might have gotten the message a bit sooner. Now he and his thick head were stuck in the pew next to her.

Brett had toyed with asking the women to lunch, but why risk the no? Uh-huh, that'd be a negatory, good buddy. He'd shake their hands and they could part ways. He had a life of his own long before he realized there was Dr. Rose A. Crackinbush, DC in the world. Though to be honest, his ignorance wasn't exactly the bliss that knowing her was. When things went well, that was.

Okay, that notion made him smile. When he'd had information look up her phone number, he'd discovered her middle initial. Brett had meant to find out what the A stood for, but now it was probably a moot point. The less personal they got with each other, the easier it would be to go their separate ways after the survey.

Oops, and the wedding festivities. Oh, brother. All he wanted to do was groan. But not here. Definitely not in church where he was already missing Pastor Mussing's sermon for lack of focus.

The organ kicked in and people around him stood. Looked like he'd almost missed the last hymn too. He held in a sigh, stood with the congregation, and sang to the end.

Time to put on his polite face. "Thank you, ladies, for allowing me to sit with you today. Enjoy your week." Then, as an afterthought, he added, "Rose, you'll call me?" Did she notice he'd kept his word? No Rosie when in public.

She nodded while Mrs. Whitehead glanced back and forth between them. Hopefully Rosie would set her straight. They were nothing more than friendly associates. Period.

Friendly associates. That didn't sound so bad.

Eh. Not exciting either.

Brett wasn't good company, so he made a run through Frisch's Drive-In and left with a to-go bag for home. He probably ought to see Mom, but after that phone call, she'd be fishing for more details, and he didn't have any he wanted to share.

The malaise lasted the rest of the evening, despite putting on his favorite comedy records. Flip Wilson's *The Devil Made Me Buy This Dress* and *The Button-Down Mind of Bob Newhart* always cheered him up but fell flat this time. Finally, after channel surfing for anything funny on TV, he gave up, locked up, and went to bed. The extra sleep should give him a better attitude when he woke, anyway.

One would think.

However, though he should've been fully rested, Brett was the poster child for "Not a Morning Person" come Monday. A fat lot of good going to bed early did when all that happened was a remake of Bobby Lewis's "Tossing and Turning." Now he questioned if his staff would be safe around his growl-ly attitude.

"Hey, boss, want to talk about it?"

"What?" He glanced up from the open JAMA on his desk that should have been giving him a clue for one of his patients, except that he'd read the same *Journal of the American Medical Association's* article five times and retained nothing. "About what?"

Then he got a closer look at Belinda's poor-thing expression. "Nope. Don't want to talk about it."

"You do know you might feel better just getting it off your chest?"

"Probably not." He searched for his place in the article, gave up, and closed the magazine. "Fine. I thought I'd met someone, but she apparently isn't interested. Now let me grumble and bellyache for a day until it's out of my system, and then I'll return to normal."

"Oh, boss. I'm sorry."

"See? That's the reason I didn't want to tell you. All that pity stuff. I'll get over it." Eventually. Hopefully.

Belinda moved in from the doorway, giving him a quick hug.

"Aren't you afraid I'll snap your head off if you come too close?"

"You? Never. You're a pussycat."

"I don't want to be a pussycat. I want to be an enraged lion."

"If I call you king of the jungle instead of boss, will that help?" Belinda followed up with a wink.

"Maybe."

"She shot you down, huh?" She wasn't letting go it seemed.

"Let's just say I got the message."

Now she was making herself comfortable against his desk, pinning him in his chair. "What does that mean?"

"It means I got her message. She's not interested."

"Did she actually say that? Maybe you misread a signal."

He shook his head. "I don't think so."

Belinda pushed away with a sigh. "Okay. I can see I'm not getting through to you. Apparently, you're under the impression you've mastered interpreting female signals. Just saying that sometimes women get confused too. Maybe she's not telling you no. It could be she's trying to figure it out herself and might end up deciding in your favor. If you take yourself out of the picture though, then she's out of luck and so are you. Unless she tells you so with real words, you still have a chance." She started for the door before she turned back. "Of course, I'm merely another female. What would I know?" Belinda tossed him a second wink and headed to the front.

Yeah, what did she know? Probably a lot more than he did.

Hey, blockhead, women are more than a jigsaw puzzle to be figured out and thrown back into a box when you're done. And now Alma was back in his brain.

He wasn't the top of his class like Rosie, though he worked hard and learned and was becoming a respected physician—at least he imagined he was—so he had some mental acuity to problem solve. So why were women so difficult to understand? And why did that mystique attract so much? Augh! Brett wanted to hit something. However, he got the message from Belinda along with the subliminal one from his sister. Be patient. Don't assume. What he needed... Yeah, he knew what he needed. A busy waiting room to get his mind off this mess.

For a Monday, they were having a slow spell. No scheduled appointments right after lunch and no walk-ins for an hour. It was not conducive to keeping his head on straight, and that was a fact.

Maybe everyone was on vacation.

Brett had no sooner considered that when he heard the front office bell. Moments later, Belinda called him to handle a patient. From that moment on until they closed up, it was nonstop. *Thank You, Lord.*

After the previous night of not sleeping, Brett was happy to grab a bite and fall into bed early again, full of hope that he'd not wrangle with the what-ifs surrounding Rosie's decision.

This time, he slept. And dreamed. Of Rosie, of course, while Belinda's words echoed through his brain. Did he still have a chance? Or was wishful thinking finding an audience while the rest of him blindly dozed?

He had no answers when he woke. Just the certainty that Rosie must now make the first move. So he wouldn't take himself out of the picture. Yet. For now, he'd work on being patient. Besides, they still had obligations to fulfill, and there was no reason to make life more uncomfortable than it already was while trying to get things accomplished.

However, once the survey and wedding were out of the way, if she hadn't given him a reason to stay in the game, he was done. Someone had to protect his heart, and it looked like the only one to do it was Dr. Brett Shoffner.

Boy, he hoped this was no game.

His Tuesdays in his office were lighter as a general rule, and today was no different. Just enough patients to keep the day rolling, lessen interpersonal thinking time, and get him home at a decent hour. No hospital rounds to prolong his day. His mood had improved each minute closer to Rosie's call. She had to reach out this evening so he could give her his address.

It still felt weird to have her come pick him up. Maybe she'd let him drive? No, whatever part of his mind conjured up that piece of brilliance had been living under a mental rock. That would not happen. How he responded to all this could be the make-or-break moment for them, so he'd better suck it up.

Brett was simply going to have to accept that he'd be the passenger while a woman drove him around. Shades of Mom and his freshman year of high school. He managed that, barely, until the time he got his learner's permit, no matter that his mother was an excellent driver. It had irked him to no end. His Mommy had to drive him like he was some kid. Okay, he was a kid back then, but at the time he'd considered himself more adult than child. Rosie probably was a great driver too. She expected excellence of herself. He'd figured that out already.

At six on the dot, his phone rang, and he knew it was her. Even before he picked up. Something about the ring, though it was the same as any other clang, brought him assurance that this was Rosie. His stomach did a sudden flip, and his hand hesitated over the handset. *Seriously? Get a grip, man!* He raised the receiver after the second ding-a-ling, hands shaking. "Hello?"

"Brett? It's Rose. Just wanted to touch base with you about tomorrow. How about I pick you up at 8:45? That will give us fifteen minutes to arrive at the first vet's house. Actually, it shouldn't take that long, but I want to be prepared, and I know how you are about being early and all." She was rambling, her words pouring out quickly. Like she was nervous too. Somehow it helped him relax.

"That works. Got something to write with?"

She paused and confirmed, so he recited his address. "I'll see you then tomorrow at 8:45."

"Guess you will." His turn to pause. Before he could over-think it, he added. "Rosie, are we okay?"

She grew quiet again, and he wanted to take back the question. "I don't know, Brett." At least she didn't feign ignorance. "I'm feeling confused and need to sort things out. Thank you for giving me space to do that."

So Belinda was right. He shook his head. Why was he not surprised? "I'll give you all the space you want. But could we talk abou—"

"Better go now. Thanks for understanding."

"See you tomorrow." Her click came through, like she'd waited just long enough to make sure he was done and hung up. No high school shilly-shallying about it. Good. He'd actually expected that. They were both adults. But nothing reminded a guy of his awkward teen years more than being attracted to a beautiful woman and hoping the attraction was mutual.

Now he prayed he wouldn't break out in acne in his sleep and that his voice didn't start cracking all over again by morning.

Chapter 10
Wednesday, August 30, 1972

The apartment was one of many cookie cutter buildings set in an elongated half oval. Was this the right place? Rose checked her notes again. Yup, this was it.

As she shifted her car into park, the front door opened, and Brett stepped out to wave. Good, he was ready. She didn't have to wait, though if he'd been sitting on his stoop watching for her, she wouldn't have been surprised. Yet, despite the fact that putting off being in a confined space with him might seem a smart idea, the anticipation had been worse. Far worse.

He hurried down the three steps and walkway to her car, opened the passenger door, and climbed in wearing tweed dress slacks and a chocolate brown oxford shirt rolled at the sleeves, revealing his forearms, and making his eyes all the more azure. When had she turned into a sucker for forearms? Rose averted her gaze.

She'd half expected him to come around to her side and insist on driving, but she somehow knew better. He might not be comfortable with her in the driver's seat, but he wouldn't protest. He was too well-mannered for that sort of response. And kind. And thoughtful of others.

She accepted his metaphorical olive branch.

"Hey, how's your day going?" His grin wasn't as big as usual. Despite his words, she couldn't get away from the knowledge she'd hurt him.

I never should have let it get this far.

Still, as much as she dreaded being with him, she did so because of her own reactions. Her heart picked up beats and outshouted her brain. She didn't want to grow excited about being with him. She didn't like enjoying his company or laughing at his corny jokes that were becoming funnier the longer she knew him. At least cerebrally she disapproved. Her emotions were another story. They demanded she turn the car over to him and let him drive her wherever he chose. Stupid emotions.

She glanced his way.

He'd cocked an eyebrow, and she realized she'd been too much in her head to respond. Oh, no. What was his question?

Ah, right. "Fine. Good. I'm good." Sure she was.

Now his smile gleamed in his eyes, as if he knew how she felt. "Me too." He followed up with a wink.

Great. It was like he understood her thoughts as clearly as she did, maybe more. Not helping.

"Um, our first stop is over by Bellaire." *Just focus on the task at hand.*

"Let's go." He settled into the passenger side as if it were his most comfortable chair. Wasn't he itching to be in the driver's seat? Why wasn't he? How long before he reached over and yanked the steering wheel from her hands?

Rose put her gearshift into drive and eased from the curb. She would never figure this out, especially when her brain had to scramble to simply maintain her semi-lucid adult facade.

Brett kept up small talk, telling cute stories of his work week. He never crossed the line into diagnoses, just the medical silliness that occurred, and he gave everyone a goofy name. There was something about the cadence of his speech that lulled her to possibilities. It had nothing to do with what he said, just the rhythm of his words. He wasn't all excited or morose, merely even-keeled. Soothing. Secure. Steadfast.

No, she couldn't let herself fall that way. There was no coming back if she fell in—oh! *Think something logical, something... Anything. Brain start working again.*

Ten days. It had only been ten days. Not even two weeks. No one fell in love that fast. So it was impossible that the cause was that four-letter L word. Probably just her female instincts betraying her sound judgment.

It got quiet.

"I figured for sure you'd laugh at that. Even Belinda thought it was funny."

Oops. "Sorry. My mind is going in a thousand different directions. I apologize for not paying attention." She peeked his way a brief second. If he only knew that it was the sound of his voice wrapping around her like warm caramel that kept her from understanding what he said. It might even make him laugh.

He was back to the sadder smile. "That's okay. What's on your mind?" She'd hurt him again. But he'd never say it.

She peeked again as a ball rolled out in the street. Rose braked hard and checked for a little one racing after. *Keep your eyes on the road, girl.* She blew out a breath.

Brett had stiff-armed the dash but sat back, meeting her gaze. It must have taken enormous willpower for him to not say anything.

Rose resumed driving and framed her answer to his question. Anything to get their minds off what just happened. "I'm taking Friday off. I've got a moving company bringing my grandfather's equipment to my house and need that all set up. Then Saturday afternoon, Doc's guy who calibrates his X-ray machine is coming over to adjust mine. Thinking of all that is overwhelming and exciting. But to do it, I've had to move a few patients around, and I'm hoping it works for everyone. Doc says I should start scheduling days at my place and slowly transfer over. I don't want to take business from him, yet this was the plan all along. So it has me conflicted that my dream is so close, but will it end up hurting the person who has helped me reach it?" Rose had turned into the queen of rambling. She glanced over. "Sorry. You asked." The good news was she hadn't needed to include how his presence messed with her mind.

"Wow, that is a lot. I get it, sort of. When I took over for Dr. Eilert, I'd figured we'd work together for a while before he retired. Then, about the time I finished my residency with him, he said he was done, and the practice was mine. I'm purchasing it from him, of course, but he was out of there. I couldn't help but wonder if I'd messed up something, but he stays in contact. We meet for lunch, usually once a week. So I guess it's not me, but I can't figure it out."

This was something she hadn't realized. Maybe because she'd taken so little time to learn about him.

Rose pulled into a trailer park and stopped in front of a mobile home. "We're here." She was out of the car before he could get to her door. That was okay. She'd never have asked him to do it, but the thought that he put out the effort didn't exactly rankle. In fact, she rather appreciated it. Hopefully no one of the Phyllis Schlafly ilk would make anything out of it.

They walked to the front door, Brett's hand at the small of her back making goosebumps go all the way to her toes. Boy howdy, their day was underway.

Every stop went pretty much the same, with each vet showing interest in learning more about the VFW.

By 11:30, they'd finished the last visit. Now what did she do? Drive him straight home? Offer to grab a bite?

"Rosie, I know you said you'd prepare our findings. Would you let me show my thanks by buying lunch? We could do Fenn's this time. Have you ever been there?"

She allowed the idea and all its implications roll around in her mind a moment. "Okay. Just this once. Because you are saying thank you." It was perfectly innocent. What could happen? Nope, she didn't want to answer that question. "I've never been to Fenn's, though Doc has mentioned it. You'll have to tell me what you recommend."

His smile grew again. Good. She hated the guilt when it dimmed. "I suggest a grilled ham and cheese with a lemonade. They make the best."

"Sounds great."

The rest of the drive, he told her about Fenn's menu. Even after that, she still planned to go with his suggestion. But if he was to the point of reciting sandwich possibilities, they were running low on topics of conversation. That was sort of a concern. Not that she wanted to share her life story or anything, or at least any more than she already had. Still, if they couldn't talk, the awkwardness would be overwhelming.

He gave her directions to the soda fountain shop and made it to her door to help her out this time. As he walked her across the street to the tiny store front, he again had his hand at the base of her back, making her lower half tingle as if it had electrical currents running through it.

Rose reached for the door, wanting to do something, anything. The tingles were driving her mad.

She gave it a yank.

Ouch! Her hand went to her nose. Was there blood? It was as if the hinges had no resistance and plowed the steel edge into her face. How did she get so clumsy?

"Here, let me see."

Rose tried to pull away, but he held her still, lowering her hand.

"I'm a doctor, remember?" Brett flashed her a wink, which only heightened the embarrassing heat flooding her cheeks. "It's not broken, but it's sure to be sore and probably bruised. Just in time for my black eye to be fading."

"I don't play favorites. I'm as hard on myself as I am on you." It was the first thing that came to her mind.

And it made him laugh. "I'll give you that. How about we move out of the doorway, and I'll get our lunches ordered. They should be able to get us some ice for your nose too. At least it isn't bleeding."

Rose nodded carefully and allowed him to lead her to an ice cream parlor table and chairs, farther back in the shop. She picked the side facing away from the front so she was less likely to be noticed by other customers who entered. Patrons who were smart enough not to bang themselves in the schnozzola with the door.

Brett returned quickly with a clean bar rag wrapped around chunks of ice. "Here. You know the drill." He winked again, and she realized he was trying to restore her dignity and sense of humor. He was doing a decent job.

"I guess I need to be easier on us both."

"I think you're right. Let's make a pact. No more assault and battery on either of us." He stuck out his hand.

She shook it. That was one agreement she'd be happy to keep.

The kid behind the laminated counter called, and Brett retrieved their drinks and sandwiches. That should keep her busy and out of trouble. Only she felt every chew as it jarred her nose.

"Hurts, doesn't it? I'm sorry." He captured her hand with his.

"You've nothing to apologize for. I did it to myself. But yeah, my nose isn't too happy with all the mastication. It feels every vibration."

Brett gave her fingers a little squeeze then released them. "That's why I'm sorry. You're hurt, no matter who's at fault, and I hate to see you in pain."

"Are you this empathetic with all your patients, doctor?" She tried to add a smile but could only manage so much stretch to her upper lip.

"Yeah, I sort of am. I don't like to see anyone hurting. However, if I know that pain is part of the healing process, as in recovery from a procedure, I accept it as necessary. Once a person has encountered real, honest-to-goodness physical suffering, I can't fathom them not having some form of empathy for others." He shrugged and took another bite of his sandwich.

"Tell me about your pain." She spoke the words without thinking, but then decided that was what she needed to say.

"I, um. You mentioned before that you remembered the Palm Sunday tornado. Right?"

Rose nodded and waited.

"I remember it too. It destroyed our house and put me in the hospital. Changed the trajectory of my future. I'll tell you about it one day, but not now. Not here." He glanced around at the others in the shop.

"Okay." Whether she agreed or not, that was his decision. But she understood. There were too many ears in the place, and it was obviously a private story he didn't readily share.

They finished up their meals with only sprinkles of small talk.

Brett paid their bill and escorted her out. "Would you like me to drive? Not trying to take over, just inquiring in case you don't feel up to it."

"I'd still have to get home from your place." Rose shook her head gingerly. "No, I can handle it. But thank you for asking." His question hadn't threatened her. Rather, she grew empowered. Respected. Honored, sort of. He cared enough to ask and was willing to abide by her decision. She'd never known a man who would do that, except for her grandfather. Maybe Doc too.

Still, he walked her to her side of the car and held her door while she climbed in. Knowing he respected her made it easier to accept his manners without looking for ulterior motives. No reading between the lines but taking them—and him—at face value.

Perhaps that was the key.

After dropping him off at his apartment, Rose drove for home to get ready for work. But that thought wouldn't leave her. Should she simply accept Brett for who he was and not for everything he symbolized? Was it even possible to do that?

Could be it was time to find out.

"You were right." Brett nearly snorted as Belinda whipped her head around and stared.

"Really? About what? Oh, I need to mark this on the calendar and set up an annual memorial holiday. To have a male acknowledge my being right about something is huge. Gotta find my transfer notes where I keep all the yearly repeats for the next year's planner." Belinda paused, tipped her head, and gave him her laser stare. "We ought to take the day off." All that and with a straight face too, until the last second when she cracked up.

"Oh, c'mon now. I've said that before. I'm positive."

She pinched her lips closed while she shook her head.

"Well, I thought it. That should count for something."

Belinda was back to laughing. "I'm sure it does, at least in your mind. So what was I right about?"

"Rosie. I followed your advice and am giving her time to decide. She has some trust issues, understandable ones, and I represent things that have caused her pain. Getting her to view me as different and not lumping me in with others is my challenge."

"That is very fair-minded of you, boss." She popped him on his arm and handed him Mrs. Brown's folder. "Room two."

He nodded, scanned the latest blood work results, and headed in to see his patient.

Good thing he'd had lunch with Rosie, because there wasn't a down moment from that point on until they closed the office for the day.

The rest of his week went the same, topped off with quiet evenings at home trying not to conjure the petite chiropractor who'd adjusted his way of viewing medicine, at least a little. He didn't completely write off the chiropractic method anymore. Not if Rosie was the result of their training. She was too smart, too intuitive, and too professional for him not to respect her. If other chiropractors were like her, then he needed to rethink his stance. However, since she was the only one he'd ever met and he'd never seen her in action, he would remain cautious. At least before recommending a chiropractor to his patients. And he still probably wouldn't, especially while Oskar was in the picture. How would he explain it?

Spending time with Rosie when they were both open, no barriers, made him crave more. The look, the laugh, the touch when conversation just naturally flowed. It was like they'd found a bridge to reach each other.

Funny how her doing the driving hadn't bothered him. At least not much. He was sure that would have started an itch he'd never fully scratch, but turned out it wasn't a problem. And asking her if she'd mind if he paid or drove her home was simple and straightforward. He was one for two on that. If all it took was to consider her opinion, then that wasn't so hard. Mutual respect, he agreed with. He just needed to remember to view things from her standpoint as well as his instead of charging ahead, making all the decisions. She had a brain, an astute one too, and so had opinions of her own. Talking it out, agreeing to disagree when necessary, that all made sense.

Did she understand that's what he was trying to do?

Boy, he hoped so.

By Saturday, Brett was going through Rosie withdrawal and couldn't wait for Sunday for his fix. Strange way to describe it, but with how he was feeling, Almost climbing the walls to be with her. He'd diagnose it as a full-blown addiction to Rose Crackinbush.

But he wouldn't get to see her until tomorrow at church. Hopefully. And in the meantime, he still had his lunch with Oskar. Who would undoubtedly start in again on his kick about women in medicine. For the first time, Brett was not looking forward to seeing his mentor.

He nearly picked up his phone to cancel the weekly date. But that might hurt the old man's feelings. He owed Doc Eilert more than he'd be able to repay in ten lifetimes, so even if it meant sitting through a lecture on women in the workforce, it shouldn't be a big deal. Brett might be the only connection the guy had to the outside world. Hmm. Did Oskar ever get out to do things other than their lunch? Wait. He must have some connections with the VFW, because he'd told Brett about the bequeath program, and he'd learned about Rosie applying. Wonder who all he knew at the post besides Frank Brown?

There was another call he wanted to make, too. To Rosie. To see if he could pick her and her neighbor up for church. Logic seemed to work with her, and it simply made sense for the three of them to go together. Would she agree? The more he thought about it, the more he wanted to just hear her voice. He reached for the phone five times before he had the guts to follow through with dialing.

In the end, it rang seven times before he hung up. He took that as his answer and left to meet Oskar.

Same place as always. Same order, too. Seriously, few lunches were as satisfying as a breaded tenderloin sandwich.

Fortunately, the conversation wasn't the same. Oskar had stepped off his soapbox. Instead, he seemed down in the dumps.

"So what's going on with you?" Brett dropped the question as casually as possible and took a big bite of his sandwich the moment the words left his mouth, just to keep things easy.

"Not a lot. I'm moving to Florida."

Brett choked. He grabbed his Coke and hoped the liquid would push the bread and meat where it needed to go, then steadied his breathing. "Florida?"

"Didn't see that coming, did ya?"

"No, sir, I didn't. What brought this on?" Brett couldn't imagine.

"These old bones aren't looking forward to another Hoosier winter. I've got a sister living down there. She's been after me..." Oskar let his voice fade away as he stared at his plate.

"I'm sure the winters are better down there. Why not just split your time?"

"No. The change will do me good. I've already put my house on the market. It's what I need to do." Oskar waved his hand as if wiping the words away. "We need a different subject. I hear they plan to announce the medical team who'll be part of the new program at the VFW. Should decide in a couple of weeks."

Brett lowered his sandwich without taking a bite. Not exactly what he wanted to discuss. It would only lead to comments about Rosie. "I hadn't heard."

"Have you been back over there? They need to see you actively helping so you'll stay foremost in their thoughts."

"I'm planning to go on Monday. I completed the survey, so I can drop it off then." All that first person made it sound like he'd done it alone, though any clarification would only cause difficulty.

"Good. Maybe you should stay and talk with some of the guys. Let them tell you their stories."

"I'll do that. Not a problem. Just take a longer lunch. Belinda is great about working around schedule anomalies."

Oskar smiled at that. "She sure is. The girl is a jewel." His fondness for her was evident though a sadness lingered after his remark.

It was time for another subject change. "So what are your plans for the rest of the weekend?"

"Nothing much. Probably get a jump on the packing. Hoping the house sells quickly, clear that all out of the way before I leave."

The last thing Brett wanted to do was make his friend feel melancholy again, and he sure didn't want to encourage this rush to Florida. It was selfish, he knew, but there was something secure in knowing the guy who'd saved his life and shown him a new purpose when his entire future had been ripped from him was only a phone call away. It'd been a while since Brett had discussed a case with Oskar, but it could still happen. Maybe that's what he ought to do. Bring up cases and ask for opinions from his mentor so he'd feel needed, valued. Was that at the root of the problem?

Things grew quiet while they finished their lunch. When the waiter brought the bill, Brett was faster.

"Hey!"

"It's time I took a turn. I owe you a lot more than a meal." Brett squeezed the old man's shoulder before heading to the cash register.

Once outside, they shook hands. Oskar held the grasp a moment longer and cleared his throat. "I, um, tell Belinda I don't hold a grudge."

Brett opened his mouth, but Oskar cut him off before he could ask. "Don't. It's private. Just deliver the message."

"I will, sir." Brett stood on the sidewalk watching as his friend shuffled to his Caddy and climbed in. What in the world had he meant? It was obvious he didn't want Brett to know, and that understanding needed to be honored. But those good intentions couldn't entirely push away the curiosity warring for victory. Should he ask Belinda to explain?

No. That would be sneaky and dishonest. After all that Oskar had done for him, no, Brett wouldn't do that.

Instead, he'd do as requested. Deliver the message without questions.

Now he just needed to decide whether to call her once he got home or wait until Monday. Holding off might lessen his resolve to not investigate. Calling today was the better choice.

So before he lost his control over the curiosity still running rampant, he dialed Belinda as soon as he walked in his apartment.

She picked up on the second ring with her cheery hello.

"Hey, Belinda, it's Brett. I just had lunch with Dr. Eilert, and he gave me a message for you."

There was a pause before she came back with considerably less cheer. "Okay."

"Um, he said to tell you that he doesn't hold a grudge." He chewed his lip to keep all the questions from tumbling out.

"Oh." That tiny little word suggested a world of possible interpretations. She followed it with a sigh. "Thanks for letting me know." She paused again, and Brett was sure she was about to say goodbye. But she didn't. "Did he explain?"

"No. He said no questions. Just asked me to deliver the message."

"Okay then. Thank you. I appreciate that. Anything else, boss?" The nickname had lost its fun.

"That's it. I won't keep you. See you Monday?"

"Yep, see ya. Bye." The only part of the exchange that sounded anywhere normal, aside from her greeting.

He rang off and decided to go see his mom. If he stayed around his place with no one to talk to, he'd probably call Belinda back and beg her to tell him what in the world that was all about.

Again in his car, he headed for Russiaville and a woman who knew how to say the right thing when he needed it.

Cars filled Mom's driveway when he arrived, forcing him to park on the street a few houses down. Had he forgotten her birthday? No, that wasn't until next month. Did he miss a phone call from her inviting him to some event? She wouldn't throw a party and leave him off the guest list. Would she?

The front door flew open before he'd even locked his car. "Brett, sweetie, I didn't expect you."

"I can see that. What's going on?"

Mom met him halfway and gave him a hug followed by a kiss on his cheek. "Well, if you must know, I'm having a little get-together."

"And you forgot to invite me?" Gee whiz, could he sound more pathetic? "Sorry, of course you don't have to include me."

She threaded her arm around his. "You are welcome to come in, but I don't think you'd be all that comfortable. It's a Sarah Coventry party."

Who was Sarah Coventry? "What does that mean? Like Tupperware?"

Mom giggled. "Well, sort of, only with jewelry instead of plastic dishes. We're trying on necklaces and earrings and such. Don't say anything, but Teri is here looking for gifts for the bridal party."

"Okay, I get it." He hugged her this time. "Go back to your brood and have fun."

"Brood? Now you're calling us chickens? Are you accusing me of flapping my wings and laying eggs?"

Brett kissed her forehead. "If the cluck fits."

She swatted him. "I think I could still bend you over my knee, so you better skedaddle before I try it in front of all my chicken friends."

"Bye then." He chuckled all the way to his car. Only, once inside, a loneliness he'd been ignoring for some time came crashing back with a vengeance.

Brett didn't want a relationship just to stop feeling alone. If that were the case, anyone he got along with would do. No, he wanted a connection with someone he could share with, listen to, laugh together with. A woman to hold who'd understand him, who'd allow him to cherish her for as long as they lived.

That sounded dangerously matrimonial. And it didn't scare him. Wow.

The kicker was that someone now had a face.

Chapter 11
Monday, September 4, 1972

"I 'll be back after lunch, Doc." Rose jerked open the bottom desk drawer to retrieve her purse, then closed it with her foot.

"No rush. Hopefully now they'll start figuring out who they'll invite to serve on the VFW's medical team." Doc gave her shoulder a fatherly squeeze. "You can tell me the latest when you get back."

Rose tossed him a thumbs up and headed to her car, balancing a plate of cookies she'd baked last evening. So maybe it looked like a bribe, but who was going to argue with an oatmeal raisin treat?

Setting them on the roof of her Fairlane, she dug her keys out and got the door open. Rose was on her way.

She'd agreed to meet Brett out front in order to deliver the paperwork together. For some reason, the lawyer, Mr. Brown, chose the VFW and not his office for them to drop off the findings. Apparently, he wanted the process to be completed with member input.

Brett waited by his car as she parked and walked over to open her door.

"Forget something?" His grin told her he had information she didn't.

However, she had no time for his games. "Not that I know of. Let me give you thi—" The seat next to her was empty.

"You mean this?" Somehow her plate of cookies materialized in his hand.

Oh, wow. How had that managed to stay on top of her car? "Yes." *Don't show your embarrassment. Stay cool.* She allowed him to hang onto the treats rather than taking his outstretched palm. It was important to keep her wits about her, and he was already messing with her mind. Even if he were only trying to help her from the vehicle, his mere touch could make her thoughts go in all sorts of ways, none of them helpful in this situation.

He didn't react, just held her aluminum covered offering while she extracted herself.

"Thanks for the assistance. I'll take them now." All that work and she nearly lost them on the drive over. After that, allowing the vets to believe Brett had brought them? Not going to happen.

He gave them back, though he did cock an eyebrow.

She wasn't fooling him. At least, though, she could carry the plate with both of her hands, keeping them occupied and out of trouble. Of course, that meant he had to open the door for her, but it was a small price to pay.

"May I peek at the graph and tally sheet before we turn them in?" Man, he had great manners.

"Sure." She stopped at a table in the lobby, set the treats down, and pulled the documents from her purse before handing them to Brett. "I clipped all our notes along with."

He perused her work. In fact, he took so long she almost snapped at him. But when he met her stare, he sported that big grin that twinkled in his eyes. "This is amazing, thorough, and well done. I'm impressed, Rosie, and I knew you'd do a good job. This, though, is beyond what I imagined."

His praise warmed her, not like the humid summer days they'd just gone through, but as if lowering herself into a relaxing bath. It swirled around her, the perfect temperature, making all the knots of anticipation release their hold on her insides. Places she'd not realized had been tensed now succumbed to a satisfying limpness. In fact, she needed to sit before her knees gave out.

"Are you all right, Rosie?"

She sank onto a nearby chair and tucked a curl behind her ear. "I guess I didn't see how much pressure I'd put on myself about this. It means a lot, but logic tells me life will go on even if I'm not included in this venture. But your compliment made me realize..."

"Hey, I get that. My practice is going okay, but this is important to me too. And I think what you put together should help us both. I'm glad we were partners."

Rose raised her gaze to his. "Me too." She meant it. Despite how his presence had shaken her well-ordered world, she knew she spoke the truth.

"Ready?" He held out his hand.

"Ready." She accepted help up but didn't hang on. Just that momentary touch caused a disruption in her psyche. That was more than enough. Remembering the cookies, she grabbed them, and they headed for the stairs to a room Mr. Brown had said he used as his on-site office.

The door was ajar, so Brett knocked on the jamb.

"Come in."

As Brett pushed the door wider, Rose caught sight of the lawyer coming out from behind an old desk on the far side of the room. Looked like he was in the middle of a working lunch.

"Dr. Crackinbush, Dr. Shoffner. Thank you for bringing your findings here. Makes it easier to share with the members who are on the bequest committee." He shook their hands, and Brett turned over the spreadsheet and notes. "This appears quite thorough. Great job. How many do you think will join now that you've contacted them?"

"They all seemed interested and appreciated the contact." Rose found herself needing to speak up so as not to become background to the men's conversation.

Brett glanced her way. "That's true. I wouldn't be surprised if every one of them joined, though a few had some situations that might make it a challenge. However, there was nothing that showed the VFW in a negative light. Right, Dr. Crackinbush?"

Rose nodded, knowing Brett was aware of her need to be heard. "Is there anything else?"

"We have another group working on a different project. Once they finish, our committee will go over everything we've learned and make a decision. That's about all I can share for now." Mr. Brown dropped the survey onto the desk, a definite cue that he'd dismissed them.

"Oh, one more thing. I've brought cookies for the vets. Where may I leave them?" Rose was not going to drop them off with this man.

"Hmm. How about on that table in the lobby? Anyone coming in will have an opportunity that way." Maybe he wasn't the chauvinist she'd imagined.

"I'll do that. Thank you, Mr. Brown." She turned for the door, only to have Brett's hand at her back again. Now she needed to walk as if nothing was amiss, keep the cookies from dropping, and maintain a semblance of dignity. Only all that.

The way things were going, she'd probably take a header down the staircase.

Fortunately, her feet remembered how to put one in front of the other and she made it to the stairs. Even better, the stairwell was narrow enough that they couldn't walk side-by-side. Brett went before her. Just when her brain questioned ladies first, she realized he did it in case she fell. He was too thoughtful for her own good.

As she set the now-uncovered plate on the table, Brett stood alongside, his hands shoved in his pockets.

"What would you say to lunch? We both need to eat, and there's a great Chinese restaurant not that far. The China Clipper."

Did she dare? "You'll go Dutch treat with me?"

"If that's what you want. We can walk. It's just a few blocks."

That was better than getting in the car with him, plus taking both cars and finding two parking spots downtown could be tricky. "Okay. Let's go."

Now that the survey project was done, what would they talk about? Of course, there were still their duties with the wedding project where they had to come up with the entertainment. "Have you decided on an idea for the rehearsal dinner show?"

He chuckled at her description. "Yes. In fact, I planned to share my ideas at lunch. China Clipper is just a bit down Mulberry Street. It'll be easier to explain when we're seated."

It was that complicated? Great. Did she want to hear this? He wasn't going to make her sing in front of people, was he? He told her they could lip-sync. Didn't he? She was sure he had.

They politely chatted about the weather—agreeing it might be a tad cooler now that September had arrived—while her stomach knotted.

Brett had another funny story about his practice. "You should have heard Mrs. Calabash fishing for information on my black eye."

"Mrs. Calabash? As in Jimmy Durante's Mrs. Calabash? You know where she is?"

Brett stopped walking and stared at her before busting into a laugh. "That was good, Rosie. Great timing too." He put his hand over his heart, took a Durante-type stance and did his best imitation. "Goodnight, Mrs. Calabash, wherever you are."

Rose snorted. "Okay, not half bad. But you don't have the schnoz to do it justice."

"Fine. But it's better than just naming her Mrs. X. That's too mysterious."

"Good call. Did you ever explain to Mrs. Calabash?"

"Nope, and she even pumped Belinda without success. The restaurant is on the next corn—"

A screech and boom split the air.

Rose found herself pinned to a brick wall, Brett's arm holding her still, while the backend of an old Ford pickup crashed onto the front end of a newer-looking sedan.

Brett released her. "They need help!"

She joined his race to the vehicles. The elderly gentleman in the truck said he was okay, waved them on, so they ran to the car.

It was a woman. She appeared stunned and had a bump growing on her forehead. Brett yanked at her door, but it wouldn't budge. However, her window was down, and he was able to reach her that way, though he couldn't get her out of the car.

It was a two-door, so Rose ran to the passenger side and got that one open, sliding in next to the driver. "She's going into shock."

"I know. Can you scoot her out your side?"

"Baby. My baby." The woman continued to mumble, turning her head and fixing her glassy stare on Rose.

Rose leaned over the backseat to see a padded basket on the floor. No noise came from it. Her heart froze as she reached behind the seat to pull a blanket away.

Two little eyes blinked, and one tiny fist found a mouth. A baby. Less than a month old.

"Brett, there's an infant on your side in the back. Can you reach her? Or do you want to come take the mom while I climb behind the seat?"

He raced to her side. "Switch places with me. I'll get the woman out, then you grab the baby."

Rose nodded and moved, giving Brett room. His neck muscles bulged as he tugged, but he got the mother free. She'd lost consciousness by now, but sirens grew closer.

The tiny one began to cry. Did the sirens scare him? Or her?

Brett scooped the woman into his arms and carried her away from the crash.

Rose shoved the bench seatback forward and brought out the carrier, holding it close to her, hoping to soothe the poor little thing. By the time she'd joined Brett, an ambulance pulled up.

Brett waved the attendants over. "We're doctors. The woman lost consciousness after we got to her. She has a contusion on the forehead, but her pulse is steady." He had them bring out a stretcher.

Once they'd loaded the woman into the ambulance with the baby placed alongside, they realized no one knew who the young mother was.

Brett and Rose returned to her car. He found her registration, and she retrieved the woman's purse. They gave both to the attendants who said to head for St Joe's hospital if they wanted to meet there.

Brett nodded and stepped away.

Rose's arms felt empty, leaving an emotion she struggled not to name. Now was not the time. She blinked to clear her eyes, took a deep breath and exhaled. They'd need to go back for one of their cars. Lunch today was definitely out.

The crowd that had formed cleared as a policeman spoke with the elderly man still in his truck.

Rose glanced around for Brett, spotting him as he leaned against that brick wall, his back to her.

She touched his shoulder.

He nearly jumped from his skin.

"Brett, what's wrong? Are you hurt?"

"Just gimme a minute." He wouldn't meet her gaze.

"Talk to me. Do you need to sit?"

"If I do, you won't be able to get me up."

She had to think. "Can you walk?"

"Slowly."

"Lean on me then."

"You're not st...tall enough."

"I'm tall enough and strong enough. C'mon. It's better that I'm not so tall. That would put pressure on your anterior longitudinal ligament. Try me." She lifted his arm around her shoulder.

He groaned softly but didn't fight her, though he might on the re-mainder of her plan.

"I'm taking you back to my place."

"No, just my car."

"You can't drive. At least you can rest at my house."

Silence.

Rose pursed her lips. Something was definitely wrong. His breath was ragged, and he wasn't arguing with her. Dr. Brett was in a lot of pain.

"C'mon. Let's keep moving."

He grunted but obeyed.

It was much slower going, but eventually they arrived in front of her home. The next challenge would be her porch steps. It was as if they mocked her. This was something she hadn't considered when setting up her office, but her future patients might welcome a ramp to the entrance. She would right about now.

Brett used her banister to pull himself up, one tread at a time.

Rose followed close behind. She hurt just watching him.

Slowly, she let out her breath as they reached the porch deck. "A few more steps to the wall. Hang in there while I unlock the door."

Her fingers didn't want to cooperate with the keys, and she dropped them like a butterfingered goof. This was why they tell doctors not to work on people they love. Love? The whole ring fell again. Finally she got the aggravating piece of metal into the slot and turned. Success.

"Hope you're better at helping me than opening that door." Brett's teasing didn't even faze her. She knew false humor covered pain, and with Brett that only made sense.

"C'mon, step over the threshold and you'll be in my office."

She steadied him as he lowered into a chair and then he glanced up to capture her studious gaze with a worried one of his own.

"So, Dr. Crackinbush. What now?"

This was all wrong. True, Brett was well aware he wasn't able to drive. He also knew that he couldn't sit on the sidewalk next to where the accident happened. He probably should've had the ambulance attendants take him in with the woman.

But that young mother was in a worse condition. Brett had gone through his back betraying him before, although it caused agonizing pain with each occurrence. Maybe even more so this time.

However, now that he was in Rosie's house, he had no inkling of his next step. Should she walk over to the VFW and get her car to drive him to the ER? That seemed the only sensible idea.

"Suppose you tell me what's going on with your back." Rosie stood over him with a glass of water.

Brett had to admit he was dry from mouth-breathing to get here. Hungrily downing the fluid, he realized he hadn't bothered to thank her. He wiped his forearm across his lips. "I should have said thank you. Sorry."

"You're in pain. I don't expect good manners. But returning to the topic at hand, what's going on with your back?" She took the glass from him and placed it on a cabinet.

"Remember I told you about the tornado? I planned to go to officer candidate school out of ROTC when that happened. I would've been the fourth generation of Shoffners to be career military. Bart wasn't interested, but I was and had planned for it my whole life." He paused while the events of that April day played through his mind. It had been nice outside, enough that his parents had invited family and friends over for a barbecue after church. Dad had been there, so proud of Brett's career choice.

"You said it changed your life."

"It did. We'd had a gathering. Fortunately, by the time the sky started to appear green, most were headed for home. Our house had no basement. It was a newer model, so those still there tried to take cover in the center of the structure. Dad and I were working to get everyone else safe when we took a direct hit. It knocked me unconscious. My dad... When I woke in the hospital, I heard the whispers. The staff doctors didn't think I'd even walk again. But Dr. Eilert stuck with me. I was in traction longer than I like to remember. And then I had close to six months of physical therapy. Dr. Eilert saved me. And when they told me I wasn't fit for military service, he gave me a new goal, a future I poured myself into." He glanced up at her.

Rosie's eyes gleamed with tears ready to drop, but she kept a professional tone to her voice. "When was the last time you looked at X-rays of your back?"

That's when he realized he'd never seen his own X-ray. Why? Of all the X-rays he'd checked, why hadn't he seen his own?

For the same reason his patients hadn't ever seen theirs. He was the gatekeeper with experience. They wouldn't know what they were looking at. Of course, he could explain, but no one asked. They trusted him.

Like he'd trusted Oskar.

"I've never seen my X-rays."

"Do you want to?"

He knew in that moment if anything came out of his mouth, it would be wrong. But apparently, his eyes telegraphed his thoughts.

"They calibrated my machine last weekend. I've taken and correctly read hundreds of scans. I know you don't trust chiropractors, but I promise I can do this. It's only an X-ray. Will you take a chance on me at least that much?"

Everything inside him shouted no—using Oskar's voice. Everything, that is, except his heart. That was a soft but steady beat of acceptance. Brett nodded.

The touch of her hand on his told his brave heart this was right. "Okay, let me get things set up. You rest here, and I'll come back for you. Do you want more water?"

He nodded again, still not trusting his voice.

She refilled his glass and then left the room where he could hear drawers squeak open and closed. When she finally returned, she had her lead apron on. "Think you've rested enough that I can help you up?"

"Let's give it a try." It was better to do something instead of sitting and waiting. Now he was plain anxious to see his films.

Rosie brought over a walker to use to pull himself up. Once standing, he set the aluminum structure to the side. He'd take one step at a time and hold himself rigidly erect. As long as he didn't need to hurry, this would work.

She led him to another room, definitely set up for taking X-rays, and had him stand next to a wall. A pocket for putting in an X-ray film cassette was attached behind him. "Normally I'd have you take off your clothes and put on a gown, but I don't want to make things worse before we see what we're dealing with. Do you have any metal on you?"

"I'm wearing a necklace under my shirt. Oh, and my belt and the zipper on my trousers." *Yeah. Oh.*

Though her cheeks heightened in color, Rosie unbuttoned his polo and found the chain that led to the cross he always wore. "Put the cross in your mouth. That will hold it up out of the way. The pain is in the lumbar region, correct?"

"Yes, it shoots down through the lumbar."

"Can you manage your belt and pants? I'll get a sheet to wrap around your waist."

Brett loosened everything but wrapped and tied the corners of the cloth together on his right hip before letting his trousers drop and sticking the gold cross in his mouth. She'd returned to the machine, keeping her back to him. He'd never been so glad that Mom always said to wear clean underwear. Of course, he'd not expected to model his boxers today, so his mom was batting a thousand. Again.

Then he closed his eyes, listening for her directions on when to hold and release his breath, when to turn, where to place his arms. Her voice soothed in ways he couldn't explain despite the far from sexy position she had him in. Took all he had not to think about what he looked like in this moment and to keep from worrying how he'd reach the pants puddled at his ankles. Every *Three Stooges* episode where at least one stooge ended up in his undies paraded through his brain. Sure, Brett wanted laughs, but dropping his trousers to get them had never been a consideration. Now he knew why. This was excruciating.

"That's it. Let me help you into this chair, and I'll go develop them." First she raised his pants to where he could reach them—filling him with horror and gratitude—and then guided him to a seat by the wall. They were professionals, but it was still difficult having her dress him, even partially. He couldn't force himself to make eye contact to be sure, but he was certain she was as embarrassed as he was. He redid his pants and laid the sheet on the chair arm.

The wait seemed to take forever. He needed to check those films. Finally he heard her call out. "It's a good thing they only used traction on you and not surgery. Come see."

Rosie had left the walker near his chair, so he swung it around and employed it to hoist himself up. But he refused to use it to walk. That he would do on his own. There'd been too much fuss over him. Besides, he had to see what she was talking about.

Rosie stared at his films. "What was your diagnosis?"

"Spondylolisthesis. Grade two, almost grade three."

"Umm, I don't think so. I don't know how to tell you this, but you don't have a spondylolisthesis. Take a look. You do have subluxations, which are the misalignment of the joints—"

"I know what they are." No need to treat him like he had no training.

"Then you also know that that's what's been causing the pain and spasms you are experiencing. A chiropractor could have fixed this without a lot of physical therapy."

Brett switched his view to her. "You don't know that."

"Yeah, I do. I've seen bunches of cases. The traction you had moved your vertebrae back into position, but an adjustment would have done it quicker. Look, you were unconscious. Getting you to the hospital was the smart thing. But until medical doctors agree to consult with chiropractors, needless choices are going to be made. I don't know why they ruled out surgery when they diagnosed spondylolisthesis, but thank God they did. That would have been catastrophic and permanent."

"So they came to the right decision. Medical doctors aren't stupid." He was tired of tiptoeing around her feelings, and the pain in his back didn't afford him much in the way of patience.

"I never said they were. However, just as I'm obviously untrained in matters not improved by chiropractic, they are failing to see even more possibilities and potential help because they won't consider it. And it's the patients who pay the price."

He ran his hand through his hair. "Maybe."

"One more thing. I can help you. This can be fixed. If you'll trust me."

All he could do was stare.

She wanted to work her snap, crackle, and pop voodoo on him? Fear had an odor that shouted hospital clean. Her X-ray room and viewing space smelled antiseptic.

Just like when he woke up in St. Joe's.

And learned his future, and more, was gone.

If he let her adjust him, would he be able to continue working as a doctor? Would he end up confined to a wheelchair? Life... God gave him a second chance. How could he throw that away?

"I realize I'm asking a lot for you to trust me. I don't know how else to prove I can help you. But I can. And there's something more I don't know if you're processing yet. You could have gone into the military. The adjustments would have trained your vertebrae and ligaments to stay in place. You'd have a military career now. What I don't understand is that whoever diagnosed you obviously saw the films because they treated your injury with traction, though I think that long in traction and physical therapy was a bit of overkill for your true diagnosis. And babying your back all these years didn't help it grow stronger."

His diagnosis was a lie. They lied. More to the point, Oskar lied. The man he trusted had told him his military career was over before it began. Anger that Brett had never experienced welled from his core. "They told me that my lumbar region was permanently compromised and that lifting or reaching in the wrong way could cause me to be in traction or even worse, paralyzed. I've carefully worked out ever since to keep my muscles strong to support my damaged lumbar. But you're saying correction is possible?"

Rosie nodded. "I can help alleviate your pain now and with a few more visits, your back will be good as new."

Brett suddenly realized he was more angry than fearful. Maybe he should think about this. But to be pain-free after all these years? "Yes."

"You're sure?"

Was he? "Yes. Let's do it."

"Okay then." Rosie led him to the adjoining room that had more the look of one of his exam rooms. Only there was a platform that surrounded the examination table. She kicked off her wedges next to a desk and slipped into more practical footwear. "Can you get there yourself?"

"With that step all around, it shouldn't be a problem. How do you want me?" His nerves started to dance, but something about Rosie's professionalism kept them under control.

"Hold it." She stepped on something on the floor behind the table and it started to tilt.

"What in the world?" He'd never seen anything like that. The head came up and the foot rested at his feet.

"This is newer technology. I had the table retro-fitted Saturday, about the same time as the guy calibrated my X-ray machine. They were both working on things, and all I could see was I'd be ready for patients. And now, here you are."

Yeah, here I am. Still he stepped up to the table and gripped the sides with his hands as she lowered the top back into place. It ought to be a ride at the county fair.

"Now that your prone, let's get started. Here, I've got a bolster." She slipped it beneath him. Then her hands gently traced his spine until at the spot, stretching him over the bolster. "I'm going to use my massager on you to help relax the muscles." Again she was gentle, moving the vibrations in and around the affected area.

His back released tension, and he melted more onto the table.

"Ready to go for another ride?"

"What?"

"Hold on." She stepped again behind the table but this time he could see there was a button on the floor. The tabletop's head, and his, rose making him vertical. Once it stopped, she came around to him. "I want to get you on your side and figured it would be easier on you to do it this way. Turn to your left and hold the table again." Rosie made sure he stood correctly before going back to her button. "Here we go." The table took him from vertical to horizontal. "Now I'm going to use my pretzel technique on you.

Before he could mount an objection, she pulled his left knee toward her and pressed his right shoulder toward the table, adding, "Take a deep breath and let it out."

As he exhaled she pressed. *Pop!*

Relief flooded him. Blessed, blessed relief! How had he never considered chiropractic help before?

"Take another breath and let it out." Rosie tried it again, with a slightly different maneuver. Not as much reaction as at first, but still a definite difference. "I'm not going to do more at the moment. Let's see how this goes. Hold on while I raise the table for you."

Brett obeyed and soon stood on the floor facing her. "I can't remember feeling this good. Rosie, I apologize for doubting you."

He'd never seen anyone beam as Rosie was doing at this moment. "That's the nicest thing you've ever said to me, Dr. Shoffner."

"Then I doubly apologize, Dr. Crackinbush. When do I need to come back to see you?"

"After work tomorrow? You're my first patient to be seen at this location."

Somehow, that made him proud. "You name the time, I'll be here. Should I come every day?" That wouldn't be such a bad thing, would it?

"No. I want to see you sooner than later after this first adjustment, but once a week after that is plenty. Then we can taper off." She changed her shoes.

"You really are short."

Rose turned on him, and he raised his hands in surrender. "I didn't say it was a bad thing. I kind of like it. Besides, you are very strong."

"You've got that right, Mister. Sorry. Doctor." She winked. "Let's walk over and get our cars. Are you up for that?"

"Absolutely. I'm even breathing easier. This is amazing. *You* are amazing, Rosie." He turned her toward him. "Thank you."

"I was glad to help. But Brett, there's one thing that's been gnawing at me."

"What's that?"

"You knew everything they'd told you, about not lifting anything heavy, not reaching at wrong angles. And yet you crawled into that car, picked up the woman and carried her out, holding her until the ambulance came. You were aware of what they said it had the potential to do, and you still did it." She stared up at him as if seeing him for the first time.

Then he said aloud what he'd told himself back when he climbed into the wreck after the woman. "What else was I to do?"

Chapter 12
Saturday, September 9, 1972

After her alarm startled her awake, Rose lounged under the sheet. Normally she'd have been preparing to see patients at Doc's, but they mutually decided it was time to offer treatment at her own place on Fridays and Saturdays. She'd had a few who she'd called to redirect to her new office for yesterday, but no one booked with her today. That meant she was free to do as she pleased, though there was an internal neon sign warning she ought to stay close to home. Just in case.

She stretched and yawned before throwing back the sheet and padding to her bathroom. Being presentable, just in case, was also a great idea.

After a shower and getting dressed, Rose treaded downstairs. Her office and therapy room were in perfect order, waiting for a patient. Memories of Brett sitting on the exam table, feeling better than in forever, made her smile. She'd won him over to a fuller picture. It was exactly as she'd known it would be. Once a person experienced relief, the next thing that happened is wondering why they waited so long.

He truly saw her. Not only that, he respected her.

This was not what she was used to. Especially in her family. She had to stop bemoaning this and move on.

Brett understood though. She had an ally. Finally. Oh, sure, there was Doc, but this was something else. Something more. If only they were allowed to work together. The American Medical Association stated that they would kick any MD out of the AMA just for sharing patient data with a chiropractor. They had zero tolerance for collaborating chiropractors and MDs. Which was why he chose his words with care when he told stories about his practice. She wouldn't want that to happen to Brett.

What if he shared information with his wife?

That thought froze her where she stood. Getting married wasn't her destiny. She'd accepted that when she chose chiropractic. It would never work since she'd dedicated herself to this career.

Yet, those few minutes of soothing the baby last Monday still made her ache a little. Or a lot. For just that moment, Rose cradled her arms, remembering how the infant's body heat seeped through to mingle with her own, and how handing her over—she was sure the little one was a girl—had left a coolness that leached to her core.

What if she and Brett did build something permanent? What if they married? Since he now understood the value of her work, she couldn't imagine him telling her she had to quit. He would never do that. She was positive. But how would he feel about children? Was there really a way?

Her mind began sorting ideas into a mental graph until she stumbled on a possibility. What if she and Brett married? And they lived in this house—he only had a small apartment anyway. He'd keep his practice and she hers. Then if she did get pregnant, she'd take some maternity leave, like the big corporations did. Doc would see her patients for however long she needed. Of course he would. Besides, it wouldn't be forever. As healthy as she was, she'd probably work almost to the day. Maybe. And then, once she had their little boy or girl on a schedule, and had a couple weeks of recovery, she'd take her practice back. The baby would be with her at home. Or if she were able to help Mrs. Whitehead get her strength back, maybe her neighbor would babysit. Yes. It might work.

No. What was she doing? Those were simply fanciful dreams. She didn't even know if Brett would be interested. Especially with all that talk about an old-fashioned girl his brother and sister tossed at him at the engagement party. No, she wasn't the one for Dr. Shoffner.

Still, she couldn't escape the knowledge that she was. Interested, that is. In him.

Rose glanced at the clock. Her morning without any appointments was slipping away. She needed a task, or she'd lose her mind. What else could she do, besides daydream, until her office hours finished at noon?

Bake. Great idea. It would be better to do it while the weather was cooler in the day anyway. And she could make something for Mrs. Whitehead and for the vets. Now she had a sensible plan.

She pulled out her favorite kitchen tool, *The Woman's Home Companion Cookbook*. Thoughts of her mother's face when she asked for it a couple Christmases ago flitted by. She'd specifically asked for one just like Mom's and oh, the cheers. As if Rose had changed her mind and was going to bring peace to the family. Nope. Instead, all it meant was she enjoyed baking as a hobby and appreciated good recipes. Mom finally accepted that, sort of.

After flipping through the cookie section, she settled on brownies. Everyone liked those, right? And this was a great recipe.

An hour and a half later, she'd arranged the gooey, chocolaty bars on two of her older plates that she didn't mind much not being returned—though she did put masking tape on the bottom of each where she'd printed her name—and covered them with aluminum foil. The clock read 11:57. Technically, she was still open for business. A little longer couldn't hurt. So she paced.

First stop, go see Mrs. Whitehead.

And avoid Miss Kitty.

Then to the VFW.

Rose held out those last three minutes before turning the sign in her window, locking up, and taking her treats next door.

Her neighbor appeared surprised to see her. "Come in, please, Dr. Crackinbush."

"I just wanted to check on you and bring you these." She handed off the plate. "We're still on for church tomorrow morning, right?"

"Of course. But what is this?" Mrs. Whitehead pealed back a corner of the foil. "Oh, my, they look wonderful and smell delicious. Will you stay and have one with me? I have coffee."

"Yes, thank you." Rose glanced about, but apparently Miss Kitty was occupied elsewhere.

"Go ahead and have a seat. I'll be right back." Mrs. Whitehead set the plate on her coffee table and headed for the kitchen, returning in a moment with two plates, napkins, and two mugs. "I couldn't remember how you liked yours. Oh!"

Rose hopped up to grab the wobbly tray before it slid from the woman's hands. "I've got it. You should have let me bring it in. It's okay. Black is fine." Though she preferred a little cream, she'd gotten used to black in college. However, that was trivial next to seeing the difficulty the woman had bringing in her cups and plates. "Have you thought any more about letting me help you? I'm not soliciting business. I wouldn't charge you. But I'd like to see if I can make things better for you."

"I have. And yes, I want you to check. I couldn't get out to my doctor when I started having problems. And when I finally called, hoping he'd do a house call, he was no longer working. I don't even know who the new man is. So I let it go and told myself it's just old age."

"Then let's start with an X-ray so we can check that off our list. Think you might be up to it after we finish here?" The sooner she started helping her neighbor, the faster the woman would become more mobile and less fearful.

"Yes. Let's." Mrs. Whitehead drained her mug and popped in the last bit of brownie. "That was a special treat. Thank you." She wiped her mouth and stood. "I'm ready." A woman on a mission. A body had to respect that.

Taking it slow and easy, Rose helped her neighbor to her house. Of course, after having assisted Brett to her porch, she should have thought about the walker, but it was too little too late at this point.

This time she had Mrs. Whitehead lay on the bed for the scan. It was safer, and she was less likely to wear out so fast. Afterward, she guided her patient into the dressing room to change before viewing the films.

The X-rays revealed three areas showing a loss of disc height, two thoracic and one in the lumbar region. No wonder the poor woman had trouble. Rose returned to give Mrs. Whitehead the news.

"You have herniated discs. Three to be exact. I'm basing this on what I saw. Loss of disc height indicates long term trauma and damage to the discs and misaligned joints." Rose lightly touched the woman's spine to indicate where the problems were. "Which can aggravate the discs. I believe this is your source of pain and declined mobility." She took her neighbor's hand. "Mrs. Whitehead... Amelia, I can help you, but this will take time. I also have some exercises you'll want to do to help promote your healing. Start small and build. You'll feel better after treatment, but don't overdo it. Let's go nice and easy, and soon you'll be back to your old self."

Mrs. Whitehead swiped her cheek, catching a tear. "You really think so?"

"I know so. But remember, the exercises are important. Increase your repetitions slowly day by day. I'll write up a schedule for you. Are you ready for your first adjustment?"

"Yes." The woman stood a tad straighter, her chin tipped a teeny bit higher.

"Good. Let's do it."

Afterward, her reaction was similar to Brett's. There'd been relief she hadn't experienced in a long while. Which was wonderful, because sometimes it took more than one visit before the patient found full relief.

However, Rose reminded her to not overdo, or she might wipe out all the improvement they'd made. She also went over the exercises before walking Mrs. Whitehead back to her home.

On the way, she thought of something. "How are your neighbors on the other side? Did they get things worked out?"

"Oh, my, yes. But they almost didn't. However, now Evelyn has a car and has been trying to make it up to Roger for all the tantrums she threw."

Rose shook her head. "Misunderstandings will mess up relationships faster than anything."

After reaching her neighbor's door, Rose declined to go inside again. "I have more brownies to deliver. But I'll be over to get you tomorrow for church."

Mrs. Whitehead pulled Rose into a sudden hug. "You are a gift, young lady. Thank you for caring about this old woman."

That made Rose tear up. "You are the gift, Mrs. Whitehead. It means so much that you trust me. I promise to honor that."

"I know you will. Now scoot. No one should have to wait for those delicious treats." The woman's smile spoke straight to Rose's heart.

Even without any paying patients today, it was shaping up to be a wonderful Saturday. Rose fairly skipped up her steps into her home, grabbed the plate designated for the vets, and smiled her way outside again.

The short walk gave her mind time to wander. Would she see Brett tomorrow at church? He'd said he felt even better after his second adjustment than the first. That thrilled her to no end. And if she missed him there, he had an appointment for next Wednesday morning.

If she could stand to wait that long to see him. Her head tried to talk some sense into her, but thoughts of Brett filled her heart. She was willing to attempt a relationship, despite the internal warning.

Rose practically flew across the street toward the VFW building. That lightness in her step stemmed from the realization that her dreams were coming true. Even ones that she'd written off as a needed sacrifice for her calling. Okay, maybe she was jumping the gun a little, imagining a life with Brett.

Wait. That's what she was doing?

Yes. It's exactly what she was doing.

And it didn't scare her.

Or maybe it did a tiny bit now that she focused on it.

She passed a familiar car about then, parked in the VFW lot. Brett was here. Yes! Another lovely gift for this Saturday. Donna Fargo had nothing on Rose Crackinbush. "Happiest Girl in the Whole USA?" That warbler wasn't even in the running next to this chiropractor.

Rose pulled the door open to loud voices. Yelling. Shouting. Anger. Part of her wanted to turn and run, but the other part ruled her feet that continued to enter the lobby, searching for the source.

"You *ought* to be thinking about it. And you'd better do something about it."

She stood quietly in the room where three men huddled. An older gentlemen—though he was sounding like anything but—ranted at Mr. Brown while Brett stood silently by, his cheeks a mottled red. "My friend, Dr. Shoffner, isn't looking for a partner. Not with a chiropractor. And you do not want one on your medical team here. They're quacks and will kill off your members."

Oh! The plate slipped from her hands, crashing onto the floor.

Brett turned. "Rose?"

She couldn't meet his eyes, focusing instead on the bits of brownie and broken ceramic mixed together in a pile at her feet.

"You're the one, aren't you?" The older man shoved past Brett and stepped on the mess to point his finger at her nose. "You think you can pass yourself off as a doctor because you've got a pretty face and talk a good game? Well, let me tell you, Missy. No bribe will change the fact that you are *not* a physician. You don't belong here. Get out." He pointed at the door.

Rose heard a gasp, then realized it came out of her mouth. She stared from Mr. Brown, who peered at his shoes, to Brett, who remained silent, his hands shoved in his pockets. Breath locked in her chest, burning.

No one had ever betrayed her this much. Not even Howard.

Rose fled out the door, shoulders straight, tears in a strangle hold to stay back until... Until she could make it home.

And never see Brett again.

"Oskar, she didn't do anything wrong." Brett had to find her. He'd been too stunned to say a word while his mentor ranted, especially when Rose herself walked in.

Dr. Eilert grabbed Brett's arm as he moved toward the door. "Don't you go chasing after her. You can't have people thinking you agree with her witchcraft. You'll get kicked out of the AMA."

That made him pause for a split-second. But no, he needed to go after her. Brett shook off Oskar's grip and hustled outside.

She was halfway to her house.

He trotted to catch up. "Rose!"

She spun around. "Don't you dare follow me. Stay away."

"Rose, let me explain."

"Explain what? That you let him attack my character? My integrity? My profession? And you did nothing to say anything different, even when he wagged his finger in my face. I should have bitten it off."

Brett froze. "You wouldn't do that. You couldn't harm someone."

"But you can. Without saying a single word." She turned and raced toward her house.

"Rose! Stop, please. You walked in on the middle. That's not everything."

Again she spun on him. "Oh? Were you going to stand up for me?"

He paused. Because that hadn't been his plan. Standing up for her would have pushed Oskar over the edge. He might have done that already by following after her. Brett sighed.

"Just as I thought. Coming to see me was some big, dark secret. As long as no one found out, it was all hunky dory, but when it comes to something in public, that's another story." She made a beeline for her steps and stumbled.

He ran like he hadn't in years. The irony of why he could flitted through his brain at that moment. But he caught up to her on her porch and turned her to face him. "Are you alright?"

"What do you care?" She shrugged him away, but he recaptured her arms.

"Rosie, I've never avoided you in public. That's where we've been most of the time."

"Only because you were forced."

"Not true. If I had my druthers, we'd be seeing more of each other privately." Then he heard his words.

"That's what this is?" She tried to twist away.

"No, that didn't come out right. Rosie, I want to spend more time with you where we can be alone. I'm tired of sharing you. I'd prefer to have just some you and me time." He drew her closer, let his finger trace her arm. "I've been thinking of that all week. Even Belinda noticed." He lowered his voice to a whisper. "I'm falling hard for you, Rosie." Her lips were inches away, and that was too far. Brett leaned in, his eyelids slowly shuttering closed, the warmth of her breath leading him nearer.

Ow! He held his cheek. "You slapped me?"

"Tell me this, doctor. Would you have told them that I adjusted your back? Had you planned to mention that you're feeling better due to my quackery?"

"Rosie, you heard Osk—"

"I did. What I didn't hear was you."

"It wasn't the right moment. There are things I haven't told you."

She faced her door and stood still a moment before turning back. "I realize we have to work together for Teri and Bart. Mail me the information I need. Then, after the rehearsal dinner, forget my name. I never want to see you again."

Before he could react, Rosie was gone, in the house, the door slamming closed.

Should he lean on her doorbell until she answered?

She'd probably call the cops and he'd make the headlines in the Kokomo Tribune.

Crazy Doctor Caught Trying to Break into Chiropractor's House.

Brett turned and spotted Mrs. Whitehead watching from her porch. Rather than saying anything, he simply waved.

Her face gained color and she went back inside. Great.

He stepped down the stairs to the sidewalk. Less than a week ago, he'd struggled to walk up them. Now, because of Rosie's talent, he could jog up and down them without trouble.

Then he thought of something else. He had an appointment with her next Wednesday. Would she refuse him as her patient?

He'd paid for his appointments, had insisted on it. She wouldn't risk his back going out, would she?

At this point, he deserved it—his back going out and her turning hers on him.

He returned to the VFW where Oskar sat while Mr. Brown swept up the mess left on the floor. The lawyer glanced up and nodded toward the older man.

Brett took the cue and sat next to Oskar. "Are you alright?"

Oskar turned as if he had no clue where he was or who Brett was, flashing a sweet smile. "Oh, I think so, but I don't remember where my car is."

Driving at this point wasn't a safe idea. "I'm not sure where you parked, but I'm happy to offer you a ride."

"Thank you, young man. Do you know where I live?"

Brett's heart seized. "Yes, Dr. Eilert, I do."

"Oh, good." But he continued to sit.

"Would you like help up?"

"Yes. Please."

Brett aided his mentor, who was as docile as a lamb. He'd get Oskar to his home, but then he and Belinda were going to have a conversation.

As they walked out, Brett worried that if Oskar spotted his own car in the lot, he'd attempt to drive it. But he didn't, and within a few minutes, Brett pulled up in front of Oskar's home. Now the worry about leaving him alone rose. If the man couldn't recognize Brett, there was a lot he wasn't remembering. Who knew how bad his dementia had progressed, especially when no one had informed Brett of the diagnosis to begin with. There was no danger of him driving off in his car right now. But still.

"Sir, may I use your telephone before I leave?"

"Of course, young man. Say, you do look familiar. Have we met?"

This was crushing Brett. He was angry and scared enough to hold it together, but he knew what was going to happen when he was alone. Oskar was the only father figure he had left. Even if he still wanted to have it out about the deceptive diagnosis, it was obvious now wasn't the time. He'd hoped to broach the subject over lunch, but they never got to the restaurant. Oskar had wanted to meet at the VFW first. And now this.

"Yes, sir, we've met. My name is Brett. Let me help you into the house."

"No need, Brett. You just follow me in, and you can... can... What was it you wanted to do?"

"Use your phone."

Oskar nodded. "Ah, that's it. Well, come on in." He climbed from the car as if he had no problem. The docile lamb was melting away, but hopefully the argumentative bulldog wouldn't return.

Once inside, Oskar pointed to the kitchen. "The phone is in there. You can leave your nickel on the counter." He laughed at his own joke. There was a glimpse of the kind man Brett knew.

He needed to make two calls. But he'd handle the second from his apartment if things worked out. He dialed the number by memory, and soon Belinda picked up. Brett turned his back and kept his voice low. "Belinda, I'm at Dr. Eilert's. I've got some questions for you, but right now, are you available to come here?"

"What's wrong?" She sounded worried, which was better than what he expected.

"He doesn't know me. I'm concerned about leaving him by himself."

"On my way." She hung up, so he did too.

"What do you mean you're afraid to leave him by himself? Who are you talking about? Not me. You can't be referring to me." Oskar stood behind him.

"You seem a little confused, and it has me concerned."

"So the big and mighty Dr. Shoffner who pushed me out of my practice is now worried about my sanity? How dare you. Get out of my house."

"Oskar—"

"Don't Oskar me. You're a snake in the grass, and after all I've done for you." He picked up a metal trivet from the table and brandished it.

"What did I do, Oskar? Tell me. I'm trying to figure out who did what and now that you are accusing me, I am at a loss." Brett stepped backward toward the front door, keeping his eyes on Oskar and what was in his hand.

"You stole my practice."

"No, I didn't. You invited me to do my residency with you and stay on and work together. Then you decided I needed to buy you out right away. I only did what you said."

"Liar!"

"Oskar. How did I steal your practice?"

"You... you... ah..." The weapon lowered, dropped, and the old man sunk to the floor.

Brett collapsed beside him, holding Oskar while he sobbed.

There was nothing he could say. This pillar of the community had been a giant to Brett. Strong, knowledgeable, doing his best for his patients. Well, Brett knew that somewhere the hero had fallen off the pedestal. He'd kept Brett from back surgery, but he'd let him live a lie, keeping him from the military. However, with the state of mind Oskar was in, there was no getting at the truth.

They sat that way even after Oskar quieted. Brett only noticed when Belinda called him from the front door. It stood open with the screen door blocking the entrance. The lines of light on the floor from the sun beaming through the window blinds told him they hadn't sat there that long, though it may as well have been a hundred years. He motioned her in, fearful his voice would trigger something for Oskar.

Belinda joined them on the hardwood floor.

Oskar raised his head. Spotting her, he wrapped her in an embrace and began crying again.

"How long?"

She glanced over at Brett. "How long have I known?"

"Yeah."

"Since before you finished your residency. He made a mistake with a patient. I was called in to give a statement to the lawyer. He was terrified you'd find out and leave, so he convinced them to stop the suit if he retired from medicine. That's why he did everything so quickly. And why he wants to move to Florida with his sister. She's said she'll take care of him."

"Oh."

She sniffed. "He can stay with me until his family makes other arrangements." All three of them were crying.

"Are you sure?"

"Yes. Can you do without me for a few days in case this takes longer?"

Doing without Belinda might destroy his practice. "Don't worry about it. I'll talk with Pam and work out something. Just make sure you do come back though. We need you to survive." He squeezed her shoulder.

"You've got that right, boss. Gather up some clothes and check for meds he might need. I'll stay with him until you've packed his stuff." She turned her attention back to Oskar.

Took a few minutes, but Brett found all Belinda had requested. Then he walked the two of them to her car and helped Oskar settle inside. "I'll be praying."

"I know you will. I also figure you'll have more questions. Hang on to them until we can talk, okay?"

"Yeah. Sure. Thanks, Belinda." It seemed so little to say.

But once she drove off, he closed up Oskar's house and realized the second call really should be an in-person visit. So he headed to his mom's.

This time there weren't cars all over. He found her out back on her porch enjoying the early evening.

"Mom, we need to talk."

Chapter 13
Monday, October 9, 1972

The days and weeks blended into each other. Somewhere around the middle of September, Rose's desire to hibernate and live in her bed fizzled. Doc had refused to let Rose do that, though he hadn't pried. Just reminded her she had patients who counted on her. So she went through the motions as the calendar changed.

Rose finally realized October was more than a week old before she noticed it had arrived. And the only reason she did then was because Teri had called yesterday.

"Have you made your appointment for your fitting with the Weather Girls?"

"Not yet. I will."

"Don't wait for the last minute. The wedding is in three weeks." Teri squealed. "Can you believe it? I'll be a married woman in twenty-one days! It's going to be the longest five hundred twelve hours of my life." Next thing the girl would be counting minutes.

"Your day will get here, and yes, I promise to call them." Rose meant it too.

Only there was no way to phone on a Sunday, so that task was on her to-do list for today. Sundays had enough drama trying to make sure she didn't see Brett. Or at least not more than his profile across the sanctuary so she had a fighting chance to escort Mrs. Whitehead out before he spotted them.

Over the past couple of months, she'd managed to transition with most of her patients. She only went to Doc's on Mondays and Tuesdays, hoping to add more to the roster of who she saw and seeing the ones who needed to stick with those specific days. Of course, that meant she had to schedule enough space between visits in order to handle the bookkeeping and payment part since hiring an assistant wasn't in the budget. Yet.

There was another reason niggling at her that she might have jumped the gun on starting her own practice. When she didn't have a patient at her office, she was alone at home with her thoughts. Um, no, that really wasn't a good thing.

She'd ended up between a rock and a hard place with Brett's continued therapy. As a doctor, she couldn't risk her patient's health. However, there was no way under the sun she'd keep treating him. So she'd sent him a letter stating that Doc was willing to see him on Wednesday mornings but that Brett would need to call to make the appointment. Doc wasn't about to do anything that smacked of soliciting business.

That relieved her conscience to an extent. When she thought about how he'd betrayed her, that took care of the rest.

Fortunately, Doc didn't discuss his patients with her, so she had no worries concerning knowledge of Brett's progress. Most of the time.

Brett sent her a letter, as well explaining his plans for the rehearsal dinner show. He'd tried to be charming and funny but didn't say anything specific about their blow-up. Rose didn't know if that was a good or bad thing, but at least she wouldn't have to sing. Thank you, Lord! Only mouth the words to Marvin Gaye and Kim Weston's "It Takes Two."

Part of her was sure he'd sent her a coded message with that choice. Maybe he had, and maybe he hadn't. However, after everything that had happened, if he wouldn't stand up for her, she wasn't going to be the only one trying. Period. She needed to know the man she gave her heart to also had her back. It was fortunate she learned this lesson before she got more involved. Yeah, she kept telling herself that. It only proved she'd been right all along. Her calling left no room for romance. No romance, no heartbreak.

Now she just had to figure out how to heal what was already broken. The Palmer School of Chiropractic had no classes on that.

Brett had requested the third couple's addresses, and she'd mailed them without anything else on the page. Hopefully that made her point clear. If it weren't for Teri and Bart, she'd have nothing to do with Brett Shoffner. Ever again. The idea of dumping the whole thing, asking Teri to find another maid-of-honor, and getting out of this mess actually crossed her mind. It would give her battered heart a rest.

It wasn't just seeing Brett, or even having to interact with him. But at a wedding? It was nearly killing her. Then she'd think about Teri and what a great friend she'd been through the years—listening to Rose's whining about her stepfather, all the plans to become a chiropractor, standing up for Rose when classmates were cruel, inviting her over to get her out of the house and away from the pressures of life with Howard.

Teri had heard it all and still stood by her. Why hurt her because her fiancé's brother was a jerk?

All these thoughts and more knew better than to show their faces when work kept them at bay. However, in the wee hours, especially in her dreams, they haunted her. Take last night. She'd awakened herself sitting up in bed, calling for Brett to warn him not to hurt his back. It was like her subconscious betrayed her. Rose cried into her pillow for an hour afterward. Made her wary of sleeping, but as a medical professional, she realized the importance of a good seven to eight hours. She'd be no use to her patients without rest. So she prayed for dreamless sleep and occasionally got it.

Just not always.

Now today she'd be at Doc's, trying to hide her yawns and praying for clarity of mind. *Please, please, please.*

After a shower and getting dressed, Rose headed for her door only to be stopped by a phone call. Frustrated, she raced back and swiped up the receiver. "Yes?" Her breathlessness evident even to her own ears.

"What's the matter?" Teri.

"I was on my way out."

"Good, I needed to catch you before you left." Teri sounded too bouncy.

Rose hadn't mentioned the problem with Brett to her but assumed she'd probably heard from his family. Surely he told his brother how she was mean and spiteful and deliberately misunderstood him. "If I was gone, I wouldn't have answered."

Teri giggled. "Someone got up on the wrong side of the bed today. I booked appointments for try-ons. Can you get there Wednesday morning by ten?" At least she remembered Rose's work schedule.

"Yes. I really was going to call them."

"I know. But this way I made sure everyone has an appointment. Besides, could be we'll have some time before you go to your office. I still haven't seen your new place. If we finish early, would you show me around?"

Rose sighed. Normally that would be a wonderful idea. But right now, she just wanted to be left alone. She was turning into a regular recluse. However, that was not the way to treat her best friend. "Sure. Sounds great."

"Don't overdo your excitement there."

"Sorry. I didn't sleep well, and I really need to be out the door. Let's talk Wednesday, okay? Love you."

"Love you too. See you then. Bye!" Teri's chipper closing rang in the space where Rose should have echoed *bye* until finally the line disconnected.

Rose was not a good friend. Teri deserved better.

After replacing the handset, she locked up and headed for her car, ending up only two minutes late getting to Doc's. He didn't say anything, but the glance he gave let her know he was worried about her.

Fortunately, her patient arrived before Doc could try to draw her out. That's how he put it. He showed interest but let the other person supply the details. Well, her details didn't want to be shared. So she threw herself into her work and took a walk outside in what was left of Mildred's garden during her lunch break in order to not be an easy target for Doc's drawing-out strategy.

Her avoidance counter-offensive worked well enough that she tried it again the next day. Tuesday.

At least Rose had slept better last night. Hard not to as tired as she'd been. And no dreams that she could remember. But she only had to get through today and then she'd be back home until next Monday with her thoughts and problems and no one encouraging her to let it all hang out.

"Rose, we haven't had a chance to talk this week."

Uh-oh. Doc figured it out and had followed her. Him and his sleuthy feet. She never heard him come outside.

"I'm just not in a talking mood, Doc."

"That's fine. May I walk with you?"

What could she say? "Sure."

It took a good three minutes before Doc broke the silence again. "You've seemed down for some time, Rose, and I have to admit, I'm worried. I thought it was temporary, but did I push you out on your own too fast?"

That was the last thing she'd expected him to say. She'd been so wrapped up in her own problems, she hadn't given a thought to how Doc might interpret it all. Poor guy. "Oh, no, I'm seeing patients. Maybe not quite as many as I had here, but it is picking up a little more each week. Besides, we knew it would take time."

He clasped his hands behind his back and his gaze tracked his steps. "That's good, good. Um, are you feeling all right? Today is your scheduled appointment before you leave. Should I check you for... anything?" He shrugged.

She shook her head. "It's private, Doc. I really don't want to talk about it."

"I'll respect that. Only know you can discuss anything with me. I won't judge, and I promise not to try to fix. I'm just a sounding board who is on your side."

"Thanks, Doc. I appreciate that." She wanted to leave it there. Funny how, despite her doubts about men, this man had proved very dependable and cherished by her. Which was probably why her mouth had other ideas. "Have you ever felt betrayed by someone you trusted?"

"Yes. That is painful. It's happened on occasion. The times that hurt the most were when it happened with those I was closest to." He didn't ask any follow-up questions, for which she was grateful.

However, her mouth continued to work from a different playbook. "I had someone I trusted, who I believed respected me, yet stood by and said nothing when his colleague attacked my character and integrity."

"I'm sorry. That really must have hurt deeply."

Rose noted he never asked for details nor if she got the other person's side of the story. He was simply there for her.

"I'd started to imagine my future in a different light. Maybe even consider a relationship. And more. Then he stood there. Mute. Not one word. How could he do that, Doc? How could he make me feel as if we had something special worth working toward and then allow someone to trash me like that?" The dam she'd erected to hold it back burst. Where did the tears come from after all this time?

Doc put his arm around her and let her cry without trying to answer her questions. The man was wise.

When she'd pulled herself together and stepped back, he squeezed her shoulder. "I can't tell you why. Only he can. If you want to know, you'll have to ask him. Decide which you want more. Answers or him out of your life for good. You're the only one able to answer that."

She ran her fingers under her eyes and nodded. "You're right. Thanks."

"I'll go back in so you can think." He patted her shoulder this time and left. Not only was Doc a great boss and mentor, he'd also accepted her like a daughter, treated her that way too. Had Howard ever done that? Had he wanted to?

It was too much to think about now. She'd have plenty of time at the end of her workday when life got quiet.

After a busy afternoon of back-to-back patients, she finally made it home, pulling into her driveway and resting her head against her steering wheel. She was almost too weary to leave her car.

Someone tapped at her passenger window. Mrs. Whitehead. She even walked down her porch steps to greet Rose at her car.

That was why Rose became a chiropractor—to see lives healed. Just the encouragement she needed right now.

Rose climbed out. "Wow, Mrs. Whitehead, that's a big difference."

"Yes, it is. I even took a walk to the corner and back today. It was enough to wear me out so much I took a nap too, but oh, it feels so good! I thought I'd see if you wanted to come over for dinner tonight so I could say thank you." The woman appeared hopeful, almost animated.

Rose's mind flashed a glimpse of her almost-empty refrigerator. She needed to get a grocery routine. This was getting embarrassing. "Sure, I'd like that. What time? What should I bring?"

"Just yourself. Dinner is almost ready now, so come anytime." The woman's smile nearly dazzled with joy.

"Give me a few minutes to clean up, and I'll be right there."

That was an answer to prayer, both the great dinner and Mrs. White-head's results. If Rose had needed a sign to prove she'd found her purpose, this was it. It was the pick-me-up she'd needed, as well as the reminder of the importance of her calling.

Rose had all of her patients listed on a pad on her nightstand where she could pray for them before bed each night. Other than the scratched-out name of Brett Shoffner, she faithfully lifted each one.

That evening, as she climbed into bed with a satisfied tummy and a revived mission, she reviewed her day—the talk with Doc and the delicious meal fixed by a walking miracle. Rose studied that list more carefully. Praying for Brett didn't mean she had to open her heart to him again. She didn't have to like him or speak with him. It was his health and healing she prayed about. That was fine. So she added his name back over where she'd tried to remove it.

Then, as she spoke his name in her prayers, she also realized she had to stop holding the grudge against him. Forgiving him didn't require trusting him. Instead, she gave it over to God and refused to let bitterness strangle her life.

That night, her dreams were sweet. She could call them up when she woke, but there was nothing painful to remember. Maybe she'd rounded a corner.

Still, she hadn't decided whether to ask Brett for the answers or continue her life never knowing. With the tranquility that flowed around her this morning, she didn't want to do anything to dispel the almost holy atmosphere. So with a breath, Rose knelt by her bed one more time, lifting that decision to God too. She would abide by His answer. If He wanted her to say something, He'd arrange the right moment. If she were to let it all go, there'd be no chance for questions, and that was fine too.

Even more peace flooded in, if that were possible. And a few tears leaked out, but they were from joy, not sorrow. Rose was ready for whatever came.

Today she needed to meet with Teri to try on her dress for the wedding. And she'd get to see what Teri would wear. Her beautiful friend deserved an equally beautiful day. Rose added that to her prayer list and headed for the shower, looking forward to a fun time. This felt as if it might be a good day. And she welcomed it.

CRACKLIN' ROSIE

Friday, October 27, 1972

"Remind Dr. Fisher that he's taking my emergency patients through the weekend." Brett ran his hand through his hair, positive he was forgetting something. "Oh, and make sure it's set with the exchange."

"Got it, boss." Belinda came around the corner. "How are you doing?"

He knew what she meant. Though he hadn't mentioned his feelings for Rosie, he had confided what Oskar had done at the VFW. Belinda realized he'd see Rose again at the dinner tonight.

"It's all good. I've been psyching myself up for it. Not a problem." And if he told himself that enough times, it should become true.

"You might tell her Oskar is gone. Even if you don't share his diagnosis. I know you didn't make it, but ethics dictate you can't tell her. You're aware of that, right?"

Oh, yeah. "Yes, of course. But he spoke with a lot of vets before I met up with him that day. He had a group there that he was good friends with who might be swayed enough to keep her off the medical team. The lawyer, Frank Brown, called to say they should finally have a decision next

233

week. Apparently the other group's project ran into a snag, and they just finished yesterday." That was one big thing that nagged at him. Would Oskar's rant persuade the vets on the committee against Rosie, even though most of them figured out the man was dealing with dementia?

And there were more nagging issues.

It took a while for that talk with Mom to settle into something where he could understand her side—not agree. He'd never agree. But if Rosie would give him five minutes, that was one thing he could share with her.

Five stinkin' minutes.

The evening would shove them together for longer than that. As the best man and the maid-of-honor, they would have to sit next to each other, interact, perform a skit, and pose for photos.

It was a lot.

He wasn't sure if he could do it if Rosie remained angry.

"Get going. You'll be late if you don't get a move on."

"Right. Boss." Brett cracked up at Belinda's expression when he called her that.

"Glad you understand. But let me be the one to call you boss, so nobody gets confused. We can keep the truth of it our little secret." Belinda winked.

"I doubt we've muddled the truth about who runs this place for anyone. Especially after your having been gone for a week taking care of Oskar until his sister came for him. I have no idea how we survived."

"Now you're talking baloney. And you'll be late. Get going."

"Yes, ma'am." Brett tossed her a salute and left through the back for his car. He had enough time for a shower and to change clothes. In fact, he probably could have worked tomorrow's regular half schedule, but he had only one twin brother and would take the day for the special occasion.

An hour later, he headed for Ferguson House. Bart had told him there was parking in the back if he entered from the alley. As he climbed from his car, he noted that the lights in the outer building were on. Looked to be an old, refurbished carriage house. Peeking inside, he spotted his brother and sister in an animated conversation with their mother. He still wasn't quite ready to talk with her yet. Just because he could see her side didn't mean he was over the betrayal.

Another glance, and he saw Rosie and Teri talking with a third woman he hadn't met. Taking a minute before going in, he studied Rosie. Was she an equal party in her conversation? Did her smile reach her eyes? Did her attention wander while someone else spoke?

Was she looking for him?

This not being able to explain was killing him.

If he told her, who would know? Technically, Oskar hadn't been his patient. And she most likely wouldn't let the information go elsewhere. What was the harm?

The harm was breaking with the AMA. They could cause his privileges at the hospitals to be revoked, leaving him to send patients to other doctors in order to get prescriptions for tests that could only be conducted in a hospital facility. Worst case scenario, he might end up putting his whole practice in jeopardy. Not just his, but Pam and Belinda's livelihoods too. And they needed the money. Work was not a hobby with them. They had no other income to survive.

Either he had ethics, or he didn't. Was he a man of integrity only when it was convenient or even when it was hard?

Yet keeping silent didn't feel all that ethical.

Enough. Get this over with. Brett opened the door and forced a smile on his face.

Mom caught sight of him first, and the worry lines between her brows clenched his stomach. He hated that she'd peer at him, trying to assess his reaction.

"Hey all. Happy wedding eve, Bart. Just so you know, the family has appointed me the official keep-the-groom-happy-healthy-and-here person. So, no shenanigans."

He held out his hand and his twin shook it, pulling him into a guy hug.

"You've got an easy job, little bro, because I don't have cold feet." Bart glanced over at Teri, who was laughing at something the other woman had said.

Rose raised her eyes at that moment, meeting Brett's gaze. He tried to give her a no-big-deal smile to put her at ease, but who was he kidding? Neither of them would be that way all weekend.

They'd set a small platform up at the front with a couple of microphones. A blonde he hadn't met walked up and spoke to the group. "Hello. My name is Stormy. My sisters and I want to welcome you all to

Teri and Bart's rehearsal dinner. This is actually where we'll be hosting the wedding and the reception. However, there'll be a few changes tomorrow. This stage will be gone, and a more traditional podium and arch in its place. Also, we'll roll out the tables after you leave tonight, and set up the chairs. We're pretty fast at the transformations but decided for this evening we'd keep it like this. The aisle is still the center, and we've made sure to have a clear path through the tables." She paused and exchanged a nod with Teri before continuing. "Looks as if everyone is here. How about you all take your seats, and we'll show each of you what to do."

The practice was on. He and Rosie didn't have to be together until it was time to exit. She barely let her fingers touch his bicep and never even squinted at him.

"You look lovely tonight."

"Thanks." She still refused to glance his way.

They made it to the back of the room and waited for the other couples to join them.

He tried again. "How have you been?"

"Fine. I'm fine." At least she peeked at him for a moment as she finished her words. "You?"

"It's been a little crazy."

"Umm." That was all she could say? He'd given her the perfect opening.

"I learned something though."

"That's good." She wasn't taking the bait.

"I found out who started the lie and why."

237

"What lie? Oh, about your back?" This time, she made eye contact. "Who?"

"My mother."

Now Rosie didn't look away. "Why would she do that? She knew the military was your dream."

Brett took a breath and kept his voice low enough that Bart and Teri couldn't hear. "My father died in that tornado. I was only hurt. She was afraid if I went overseas, she'd lose me too. His death had just happened, and she was worried about me besides grieving. So she asked Dr. Eilert to tell me I'd never be able to serve. He felt so guilty that he mentored me into medicine and even sold me his practice when he retired." That's all he'd say on that part.

"Brett, I'm sorry. That must have been a blow."

He nodded.

"So how did you go about forgiving someone close to you who betrayed you?"

He knew what she really asked. In fact, the irony wasn't lost on him. "I'm still working on it. She's my mother. I love her. I understand her motives, especially when I think about what all she was going through. I guess putting myself into her shoes, so to speak, helps. I also know she feels bad about it now and probably wouldn't have done it if Dad hadn't just died. Yet she crushed my dreams, so I'm still dealing with it. But I'm choosing to forgive because the alternatives offer no healing."

Rosie studied her shoes. "That sounds like a healthy attitude."

Stormy called for another run through, so everyone returned to their starting spots. This time, when they exited, Rosie's hand tucked in at his elbow a little more securely.

Afterward, dinner was served. They'd seated him at the same table as Rosie but not next to her. When the teen waiters and waitresses brought out the dessert—apple pie a la mode—Brett nodded to her, and they mounted the stage.

"Good evening, folks. We thought it might be fun to have some entertainment before the bridal parties go to their separate functions." He tossed a wink to his brother. "So, Teri and Bart, we've got a little program to musically depict your romance."

With a nod to Stormy, who'd agreed to play the records, the show began. The music to "It Takes Two" started, and he and Rosie mouthed it to each other with great flourish and finished to laughter and applause. Next came Alma and Ed with their song "Hey Paula," only when the singers sang *Paula* or *Paul*, Ed and Alma sang *Teri* and *Bart*. Again, the audience, especially the about-to-be newlyweds, enjoyed it.

Finally the last couple in the bridal party, Cindy and John, sang "I Got You, Babe." Cindy even had Cher's habit of brushing her hair from her shoulders down to a tee. It might have been the best duo, though when Brett thought about Rosie up there on the stage with him, he wished it had been for real.

The party broke up with lots of see-you-tomorrows.

Brett finally grabbed another moment to speak with Rosie. "So, what all do you have planned?"

"We're going to do some fun things at my house."

"Oh." He shoved his hands in his pockets, trying to work up the words he wanted to say.

"Brett, I'm really sorry about what your mother did. And I'm working on forgiving you. I appreciate that you told me. Sort of helps, like I can tell you understand how I feel. We'll be able to get through this weekend better than I figured. But I don't think anything more will come of this. I'm not sure I can trust you. I apologize if you hoped for more." Just for an instant, he thought she was going to pat his arm but then changed her mind. "I'll see you tomorrow."

Then she left.

Sucking all the hope out of the room.

Chapter 14
Saturday, October 28, 1972

"Hey, sleepyheads. Get up! It's my wedding day!" Teri's voice broke through stronger than any alarm clock.

Rose rubbed her eyes. It was morning already? She tried to stretch, but something heavy lay on her feet. Oh, Cindy. Teri's other bridesmaid.

Now she remembered. Rose crashed on her own sofa giving the bride-to-be her bed for a good night's rest. She and Cindy tried to share the couch, each taking an end. Not the most comfortable way to sleep, but Rose had been so tired that she dozed off anyway. The crick in her back was payment for her bright idea.

"Cindy, Rose, get up!"

Someone annoyingly woke up on the right side of the bed. Rose's bed, to add insult to injury. Oh, who was she kidding? She'd do the same thing all over again for Teri. Too bad there wasn't time for a nap in today's schedule.

"I'm up. Let me put some coffee in me." Rose shuffled for the kitchen. "When do we have to be at the beauty shop?"

"In an hour. Did you two stay up talking while I slept?" Teri fell in step behind her, clearly not understanding the lack of bravado this morning.

So Rose stopped and gave her friend her full attention. "No, not really. The couch wasn't designed for two sleepers, despite our short statures. But it was more important that you get a good night's sleep. It's your big day."

Teri pulled her into a hug and spun around. "It is my big day. I never really imagined it would come."

Rose gently broke free and started the percolator. "If you let me grab my coffee, I'll get ready. Appears you already are. If Cindy wants first dibs, she'd better hustle."

"Deal. I'll handle it. Cindy!" Teri floated back to the living room like a happy balloon.

Rose had portioned the first floor off, so her office and patient rooms took over what had been the original living room and dining room. The current living room was simply a small den off the kitchen. The new floorplan didn't allow for a lot of personal space downstairs, but Rose had a complete upstairs for that. In fact, she was toying with the idea of turning everything downstairs but the kitchen into business area. Maybe eventually she'd even move the kitchen upstairs and divide the house with her practice on the ground floor and her private life on the second.

They made it to their hair appointments at Wright's with not a moment to spare. There were enough stylists that they saw all three of them at the same time.

Normally Rose didn't go to the shop, instead saving money by going to Catalina Beauty College. The hairdressers-in-training there were good, but the woman working on her today, Julie, was amazing. Rose let herself relax and enjoy the splurge while Julie's expert fingers massaged her scalp during the shampoo.

She closed her eyes.

Immediately, Teri's happy conversation found Rose's ears. "At first I thought he was arrogant, and I didn't want to talk with him. But then he brought me a small box of cookies that his mother baked for him. I wondered why, and he told me he remembered hearing that snickerdoodles were my favorite."

"Aw."

"I couldn't believe he knew that. So when he asked me out, I said yes."

"Where did you go?"

"He took me to dinner and a movie. But he waited to pick it out with me instead of deciding for me. It felt like he cared for my opinion. I think that's what started my falling in love with him. He's so kind. What I thought was arrogance was really only knowing his craft. He's a lawyer in the building where I work, and I'd hear him talking with his colleague in the elevator. Nothing specific regarding clients, just general law topic stuff. He's amazing."

"Good thing you are marrying him. I don't think he could ask for a better fan club."

"Ha! I'm definitely the president. But more important than that, I can trust him with my heart."

Teri's words were a fist to Rose's chest. She'd thought she could trust Brett with her heart, but now... Last night, once they started talking, the same old feelings nearly overwhelmed her. She came that close to asking him if they could try again, and she was pretty sure he almost made the same request.

I'm not sure I can trust you.

She'd really said that to him.

The problem was, she'd have to take a chance to find out if it were possible. Should she risk it? The pain of his betrayal pricked her again.

Julie wrapped the towel around Rose's hair and raised the back of her chair. "Let's move to my station."

Rose watched as Julie combed her hair out and put it on rollers before she went under the dryer. Now with the warm air swirling about her head, staying awake was a challenge, and she didn't want to think about Brett. It was too hard. She tried focusing on the McCall's magazine Julie handed her, but no amount of flipping through the pages found anything that caught her attention.

Maybe it was because she kept going over her conversation with Brett last night. How horrible for him. It must have been so awful to learn his mother lied to keep him from the military, knowing that was what he'd trained for his whole life. Could Rose forgive her mom if that had happened to her?

Well, it sort of did, almost. She didn't exactly hold a grudge against Mom for marrying Howard. It was no secret she'd been lonely. And raising two teens without her husband must have seemed a difficult road.

But why Howard?

He made her happy.

True. Most of the time.

She wasn't happy when Rose and Howard squabbled. Then Mom tried to placate everyone. How did she not see how Rose felt, how it hurt that her mother practically severed all ties with Dad's side of the family?

Wasn't it time for Mom to take her side for once?

Oh. That popped out of nowhere. Or from some place deeply repressed. Rose felt warm, and not from the dryer. At least, not all of it.

Was she jealous of Howard when it came to her mother's attention?

Maybe. A little. Okay, perhaps some of the difficulty was of her own making. To be honest, she hadn't gone out of her way to build a rapport with the man. Having been a daddy's girl, that was asking too much of Rose.

However, it was time to act like an adult. She'd offer the olive branch. Howard's choices were on him, but she could definitely make better ones than she'd been making.

The timer dinged, and Julie raised the dryer hood, checking for doneness. "You're dry. Let's move you on over to my station again."

Rose followed and tucked her thoughts away.

"So you're the maid of honor. How long have you been friends?"

It was hard to think of a time when Teri and Rose hadn't been. "Forever, I guess. We met when we were four and just stayed connected even through family moves and going to college. She's the best friend anyone could have."

"Sounds like you're a good one too."

That made Rose think. How much of a friend had she really been to Teri? It was Rose's life that had all the drama, and Teri had stuck by her through it all, always taking her side. Teri hadn't experienced the turmoil of losing a parent, or a second marriage, or the upheaval of a stepparent. Still, she'd had her own ups and downs, times when she cried and needed Rose to listen. But more often than not, it was Rose asking for comfort and Teri calling to celebrate. And even then, Teri was the better cheerleader. She remembered every victory and proclaimed each one a moment of honor.

That's it. Rose had moped around long enough. This was Teri's big day. No more feeling sorry for herself. Even if she never got to experience the joy of finding true love, her best friend had. Rose would be the most amazing cheerleader Teri had ever seen. She might learn to do a handstand or a flip. Oh, what about the splits?

Don't get carried away.

Okay, no physical gymnastics, but in every other way possible, Rose was going to make this day shine for Teri. Or die trying.

Julie spun her around.

The image peering from the mirror seemed a lot happier than the one who walked into the shop. That was a good sign. Plus, Julie had done a great job, pulling the sides into a barrette with tiny silk flowers and banana curls hanging down her back. "Thank you. You understood what Teri and I tried to express."

"Not a problem. I get it. Hope your friend has a wonderful wedding."

Rose pulled out a tip and handed it to the stylist. "She will. Guaranteed."

The next stop was the Stone Hut for Mexican food and to meet up with Alma and her mother. It was the only opportunity to grab a bite before the wedding, though Rose had her doubts about Teri eating anything. Still, Alma had suggested the restaurant, claiming she had taco cravings.

Because of the baby, Alma hadn't stayed last evening with the rest of the girls. She said she had to go home to her own bed with her own pillows or she wouldn't sleep. She was less than a month from her due date.

It also helped because there was less time for Alma to ask Rose difficult questions about Brett.

After the women gave the waiter their orders, the conversation tended to split a little with those seated next to each other talking in small groups.

Rose hadn't meant to eavesdrop. She'd been so introspective after her thoughts under the dryer that she remained quiet, letting the world spin around her. But then she overheard it among the other snippets of conversation. "...had to have Dr. Eilert's sister come get him and take him to Florida." That was Brett's mother's voice.

Rose turned just as Alma answered. "I didn't realize he even had dementia, let alone that it was so advanced. That has to be a nightmare for Brett."

"I know. He's always looked up to Oskar. Called him his mentor. Brett said something about wanting to go visit Oskar but was afraid he wouldn't recognize him. I guess that happened once already."

Rose excused herself and went to the ladies' room.

She shouldn't have been listening and needed to get away from the conversation before she got herself in trouble.

The door had just closed behind her when it opened again. Teri entered. "Are you okay? You had a funny look on your face."

Rose stared into the mirror and adjusted a curl. "You need to focus on you today. Not me. This is what you've been waiting for." The puzzle pieces were dropping into place, and she needed a private moment to think this out. *I love you, Teri, but go away.*

"I'm not leaving until you tell me what's going on."

Don't do it. Don't do it.

Rose faced Teri. "I owe Brett a big apology, but I don't know if I can ethically give it." Now she'd done it.

"What could ethically keep you from apologizing?"

"We had an argument a while back. I thought he'd done something hurtful. However, I just learned by accident that he had no real choice. If he'd tried to explain, he'd have broken an AMA regulation. A stupid one, but there are better ways to change it than getting yourself kicked out of the American Medical Association."

It still didn't make clear why Brett stayed silent when the doctor began his verbal attack. Maybe it shocked him? Or could it be he was trying not to add fuel to the rant for fear of causing the old man to have more trouble?

Who knew?

Teri wrapped her arms around Rose. "You can't tell me, right? I get it. Medical rules and lawyer rules are similar. Bart can't give me details on cases either. But he can let me know that there's a problem and to start praying. Want me to do that?"

Rose's heart picked up its pace. "Yes. Please. I have a couple theories based on what I overheard. And if either one is close, then I've badly maligned Brett. I can't just tell him I learned something from his mom and sister. Besides, even if I did, he wouldn't be able to deny or approve my statements. He couldn't comment. Period."

"So you're stuck. There's only one way to get unstuck. You got that, right? God's going to have to arrange it. I'll keep praying. You let me know what happens."

Rose nodded and they returned to the table. She was now more determined to make this day perfect for Teri and to mend things with Brett.

Brett glanced at his watch again. "It's two minutes after the last time I told you. Just settle down. Remember, you're the one who said you weren't going to have cold feet."

"I don't have cold feet." Bart stopped pacing long enough to drop into a chair. "I just want to get the hullabaloo over with and have my wife to myself."

That made Brett chuckle.

Just the twins were in the upstairs room of the main house now, since John and Ed had gone down to act as ushers.

"Tell you what. Maybe you can advise me with a hypothetical problem." Hopefully, Bart could help him with this mess, and it would get the poor guy's mind off counting the seconds until the wedding.

"I'll have to charge you. Hypothetically." Perfect. It grabbed Bart's attention.

"I can handle that. Suppose a certain medical doctor had knowledge about a person who was not his patient. At the time of the incident, the information was merely theory, an educated guess, because there hadn't been an examination and the hypothetical diagnosis resulted from observation without confirmation."

Bart nodded. "I'm with you so far."

Brett's hands grew sweaty. He rubbed them inside the pockets of his tux trousers. "This person who was not the patient had an episode in front of a chiropractor who did not know all the details and hadn't had time to make their own diagnosis. If the medical doctor explains what was witnessed to the chiropractor, will he still get kicked out of the AMA?"

"Wow, bro, when you get hypothetical, you really get hypothetical. Look, I figured who all the players are. Mom told me last night what happened with Dr. Eilert. Besides, it makes sense, especially since Rose is a chiropractor. Personally, I think you can trust her with the information. Professionally, I cannot promise that you aren't breaking some AMA code of conduct, or that if it should somehow accidentally leak out, you wouldn't be in hot water. Of course, if you married the woman, she can't testify against you if you try to fight back with a lawsuit. Just an idea. I seem to have matrimony on the brain." Bart popped up. "What time did you say it was?"

"Augh!" Brett punched his brother's arm. "Cool it, bro. It's going to happen."

A knock sounded. "It's Stormy. Everyone decent?"

"Yes, come in." Brett answered for his brother since he'd suddenly taken on a deer-in-the-headlights appearance.

Stormy peeked around the door. "If you two are ready, you may go downstairs and into place." She stared at Bart and cocked her head. "He's alright, isn't he?"

Brett laughed. "He's never been alright, but he'll make it. Fortunately Teri loves him, mess and all."

"I so get that." Stormy was still chuckling as she led them down the back stairway and out to the carriage house.

They'd transformed the inside. Brett wasn't one for fashion or interior design, but he could tell whether he liked something or not. This autumn-themed color combination looked nice. With all the guys in dark blue tuxes—and from what he'd been told the girls would be in navy dresses—it contrasted well with the yellows, oranges, rusts, and golds of the arrangements.

As soon as the men all got into position up front, music started, and the back doors opened again.

Cindy was the first down the aisle. Brett tried to see behind her to where Rosie would be waiting her turn. Instead, his sister came next. She looked cute despite her insistence that she was too pregnant to be in the wedding party. A brief glance Ed's way confirmed he agreed with Brett, even more so.

When he resumed watching the bridesmaids, Rosie stood in the doorway, just starting her walk down the aisle. She stole his breath. How had he not seen she was this beautiful? Oh, he'd always thought she was pretty. However, today she'd left pretty in the dust. Stunning was more like it because she wiped out anything and anyone else in the room. As if everything in the world fell away and she was all he saw. Wow.

Could she tell what he was thinking? Maybe. He spotted a tiny smile zeroed in on him. It *was* for him, wasn't it? Otherwise, he'd fall apart.

The rest of the ceremony was a blur. All he could think about was that she smiled at him. Did it mean something? Like she forgave him? Still, she'd said she was working on that, but anything more was out of the question. Did he just hear his heart snap in two?

The recessional music began, and he escorted Rosie on his arm. He was the luckiest guy there, that was for sure. As far as he was concerned.

Stormy had informed everyone that the bridal party photos would be under the giant sycamore. Her sister Windy would take them while the carriage house underwent another transformation to accommodate tables, guests, and a dance floor.

Brett led Rosie out where they all congregated, waiting until Windy set their positions. They started with the bride and groom along with the wedding party. Then Teri alone with her attendants. When they hollered for the groomsmen, Brett had to be called twice, since his attention was all on Rosie.

They tried different mixes—family, just the guys, just the girls, and then each of the attendants as couples, starting with Cindy and John. Then Alma and Ed posed, adding some cute shots focusing on the forthcoming baby.

"Alma, don't worry, it's perfect. You're going to love having these photos." Even with Windy's assurance, Alma still had a strange expression. Brett wasn't so sure that's what was on her mind, but something definitely was. He'd check afterward.

Then it was Brett and Rosie's turn.

Just before Windy posed them, he opened his mouth to speak. It was now. He had to get the words out.

Only they both spoke at the same time.

"Can we talk after this?"

The look on Rosie's face made him crack up. She joined him, and the bit of tension he'd been harboring slipped away. Without thinking, he leaned in and brushed a kiss on her forehead.

Someone gasped behind Windy. He glanced up to see Teri bouncing and tugging Bart's arm. Something sure had her excited.

Windy finished the photos and none too soon. Brett couldn't wait to dance with Rosie in his arms. First though, there was the matter of dinner. And the toasts. And other festive traditions.

At least at today's meal he was next to Rosie. "So, Dr. Crackinbush, we meet again." He held her chair before taking his seat. "Come here often?"

Rosie chewed at her lip before grinning. He'd missed her smile, and the tiny one as she came down the aisle only whet his appetite.

"I heard a new joke. What did the bare foot say?" Rosie scanned the rest of their table mates, but her gaze came back to him.

Brett shrugged, glanced around to see if anyone else knew. They didn't. "I don't know. What did the bare foot say?"

Rosie looked like she was about to bust. "Sock it to me." Then she snorted.

Man, he'd missed this. He'd missed her. She wasn't just tolerating him for her friend's sake. They were having fun with corny jokes. And afterward they'd go for that private talk and maybe get things straightened out.

But what if she'd decided not to see him anymore? That this was it.

No, that couldn't happen. Not when—

"Brett, would you take a walk with me, please? Me and Ed?" Alma, seated on his other side, had that same strange look on her face. Now he had an inkling why.

"Sure." He scooted from the attendants' table and helped Ed assist Alma out of her chair. Slowly they worked their way around the tables, Brett on one side of her, Ed on the other.

When they reached the back where the doors were, Stormy was there. "Is everything okay?"

All at once Alma took hold of Stormy's hand and leaned forward.

Stormy's eyes got big as Brett's hunch was confirmed. "Oh, I get it. Do you want a private place, or are you going straight to the hospital?" Stormy already had the door open for them.

Brett spoke for the trio. "A private place first. We need an idea of how far along she is."

"I've been having mild contractions since lunch. But they are now stronger and less than five minutes apart. So how about we head for the hospital? Stormy, would you please tell Bart and Teri to keep the party going?" Alma straightened. "Let's get moving guys while I'm in between."

"Stormy, tell Rose... " Brett shook his head. He had no idea what to say and no time to think. "Gotta go. Ed, you'll to have to drive so I can time everything. Sorry, man." Brett figured his brother-in-law would rather be taking care of his wife.

"Gotcha." Ed pulled out his keys. "Glad I parked out back."

Once at the car, Alma climbed into the rear seat behind Ed and leaned against the side window. Brett took the other side and set her feet on his lap. He'd never considered he might end up delivering his own niece or nephew.

Hopefully Alma was okay with it because his gut told him her obstetrician in Lafayette was not going to make it in time. "You know, Belinda can call your doctor. I just need to find a phone at the hospital to let her know."

"Think he'll make it?"

"Hmm, I doubt it. But he might try. It could happen. I mean, this is your first. Suppose you fill me in on what your doctor has said at your visits so I'm better prepared. I thought you still had a few weeks left." Brett turned on professional mode, hoping that his big sister wouldn't see him as her little brother right now.

"You sure you can deliver this baby?" That was Ed. Brett hadn't counted on doubts from him.

"Yes, I'm positive. I've delivered dozens of babies."

"But never a relative before." Ed sounded worried.

"True, but I think it still happens the same way."

"Oh, Ed. Stop it. Brett is a great doctor." Alma turned to him. "You are a great doctor, right?"

"I don't like to brag—"

She grabbed his hand and squeezed until he was sure something would pop out of place. "Say it. Say you are a great doctor. I need to hear it, you idiot."

"I'm a great doctor whose hand is about to break."

Alma let go. "Sorry."

"It's fine. I just want to make sure I can catch your baby. I only know how to do it with two hands."

Ed snorted and Alma giggled. "Fine. I won't break your hand then."

"A little tip. If you were having a contraction while you were doing that, you really could break something, so when you hold Ed's hand in the delivery room, only grasp one of his fingers. You'll both thank me later. Also, when we get to the hospital, the on-call doctor will eventually take over. I'll still be there but just preparing you."

Brett noted the expression on her face and placed his palm on her belly. It was tightening. He checked his watch and confirmed how long the contraction lasted. Over sixty seconds. It had only been about three minutes since that one at the door. "Ed, stay safe but go a little faster."

At least if he had to deliver the baby on the side of the road, he was a medical professional and not a scared father with no background to help.

However, Brett was still cautious. This was his new niece or nephew.

Ed pulled into St. Joe's and drove up to the emergency door.

"I'll stay with her, Ed. Go park. I'll let them know to bring you back." Brett climbed out and then helped Alma.

An eagle-eyed attendant came rushing with a wheelchair. "Are you Dad?"

"No, I'm her doctor. She's in full labor. You need to get the delivery room ready, stat." Brett decided that later, when he told this story, he'd have the attendant salute while Brett assisted his sister into the wheelchair.

Ed must have found a space fast because he ran up just as they entered the glass sliding doors.

"Then you are the dad?" The orderly was dying to pin that title on someone.

"Yes. What information do you need?" Ed was puffing from his run. Poor guy.

"Get the info while you prep her for delivery. I'll take Dad and we'll find some scrubs." From tux to hospital greens, a big difference. Brett shook his head. "Follow me, Ed, or do you want me to help you get used to your new name?"

Ed glanced up with the look Brett had seen on Bart before the wedding—total deer-in-the-headlights—so Brett guided him down the hall.

"She's going to be fine, Dad. I need to know, though, are they sure she's not having twins? I mean she's a tad early."

"No. No one mentioned twins." Then Ed's face grew pale. "Do you think..."

"It's not out of the realm of possibility, but I'm sure someone would have said something about it by now if you were." Brett handed Ed a pair of scrubs and took a set for himself. After he changed, he made a quick call to Belinda to get her phoning Alma's OB/GYN.

By then, Ed had donned hospital garb and added his tux to Brett's locker.

"So, Dad, are you ready to meet your son or daughter?"

Chapter 15
Sunday, October 29, 1972

Rose tapped her foot to the organ's pre-service music. Ever since Brett rushed off with Alma and Ed, it was like he'd gone radio silent. The church bulletin in her hand protested her concern as she crunched it in her fist while making a slow turn, sort of like she was stretching her neck. Not like she searched for Brett.

"He isn't here, dear." Mrs. Whitehead patted Rose's arm. She hadn't been as surreptitious as she thought.

"Oh, I realize he's been busy. I just hoped." Rose settled the abused bulletin on her lap, smoothing out the wrinkles. If Brett didn't get here soon, he wouldn't beat the organist to her first note. What about his fifteen minutes early or he was late rule? He was coming, right? After last evening, he'd attend this service, wouldn't he?

She sighed. It had been so strange and quick last evening. Stormy had whispered to Teri and Bart, and their expressions told Rose what happened before Teri shared the information with everyone.

Rose couldn't help but feel sorry for Bart. His family was gone at the height of the celebration. And worst of all, his brother couldn't be there to give the toast for them. John, the other groomsman, did a pretty good job for being put on the spot. Apparently John had some great stories from working with Bart at the legal firm, and this was his perfect forum to share them. Funny, but no way was it the same as had been planned.

Besides, what could Bart really say about it? His sister was having a baby—twins as it turned out. And they came as a surprise and earlier than expected. There was no way to know what all happened at the hospital at that moment, but still, Rose felt bad for Bart.

Which led her to more thoughts of his twin. She tried peeking for Brett again.

"Delivering babies can take a lot of time and energy. When you factor in twins, and that they were a little early, that probably required his whole focus, and now he's finally getting some sleep."

"True." Actually, Rose's prayers had been for Alma, who had a bit of a rough time. Teri called before she left on her honeymoon to fill her in that Alma was responding well to treatment, and the baby boy and girl, though small, seemed to be doing fine too. Her friend wouldn't have taken off without the assurance that her new sister-in-law would be okay. Rose hung on to that information, thanking God for His provision. She couldn't imagine what it had been like for Brett having this all be happening to his family. Rose had asked Teri if Brett ended up delivering the twins.

"Oh, good heavens no. As soon as the on-call doctor arrived, he took over. Brett turned Alma over to him and focused on Ed. Brett told Bart the man was a wreck, and that handling Alma would've been a piece of cake in comparison." Rose smiled, remembering Teri's words. Her friend had added that Alma's doctor arrived an hour after the babies.

But that was last night.

Maybe Mrs. Whitehead was right. He'd been up with that so late that he crashed at home and had to miss church.

Would he call her then once the service let out?

Rose was afraid to hope. Instead, she stood for the first hymn and threw her heart and soul into it.

After the benediction, while Rose walked with Mrs. Whitehead to the car, anxiety attacked again. Now that she understood what Brett had been juggling, and she wanted to find a way to work things out, did he change his mind?

Her keys jingled in her hand to the beat of the question. Where was Brett?

Mrs. Whitehead squeezed Rose's arm. "You're going to worry yourself to death. Just relax. I've got an idea. Why don't I bring lunch over to your house?"

The voice and touch pulled her back to the present. "Um, I like that in theory, but I'm concerned about you carrying things down and up the porch steps to me. You are doing so well, I don't want you to have any setbacks."

"And I don't want you to miss any phone calls. What do we do?" Her neighbor peered at Rose, expecting an answer.

"I've no clue. I guess I can come over to help carry things. We only need the food. I have plates and utensils. What all did you make?" That could have a bearing on the whole transfer situation.

"I made a small pan of manicotti and a salad."

"That shouldn't be too difficult. And I have lemonade in my refrigerator. Thank you, Mrs. Whitehead. For lunch and for getting me to think of other things."

The woman smiled and climbed into the car.

Soon they were home, and the food transport was a success. They sat at Rose's kitchen table while Mrs. Whitehead shared tales of the neighborhood. Rose hadn't realized she'd lived in that house over forty years. She'd seen so many people come and go. "The Tubervilles were a fun family. Seven children, each looking like each other. When you saw one, you knew they were a Tuberville. On Sunday, their mother got them all ready, and they marched in a line to the old Methodist church downtown, the youngest holding hands between the parents and the rest two by two behind. Those kids grew up to do some important work."

Of course, Rose realized her neighbor was only trying to keep her mind off Brett. She appreciated the effort, but with each pause in the conversation, he pressed his way to the forefront of her thoughts.

After they'd washed the dishes, Rose walked Mrs. Whitehead back with her leftovers. "I know he didn't call yet, but don't give up. I've got a feeling you're going to hear from your young man."

Rose hoped so, but the wait was driving her insane. Maybe if she grabbed a Sunday afternoon nap. Anything to make time pass until he tried to reach her.

She turned on the TV for background sound, finding an old favorite Marx Brothers movie, *Duck Soup*, to keep her company. Did Brett like the Marx Brothers? What would he think if he knew that was her secret special treat?

At least there was more room on the couch when she didn't have to share it. Rose closed her eyes, and soon the silly antics played in her brain. Only in the middle of it all, Dudley Do-Right rushed in. Groucho shook his cigar in the Mountie's face, claiming he had no sense of humor. Chico added that Dudley lacked timing too. Harpo kept making faces and squeezing his horn at the poor guy.

Then Dudley removed his hat, and he wasn't the famous Mountie anymore. He was Dr. Brett Shoffner, looking sad and tired, repeating over and over, "You don't understand. You don't understand."

Harpo continued to squeeze his horn, time after time, until the sound morphed into a ringing.

A telephone?

Rose rubbed her eyes as most of the characters returned to the TV set. The phone!

She jumped, ran to the kitchen, and swiped the handset from the wall. "Hello? Hello?"

Only to be greeted by the buzz of an empty line.

Lord, if that was Brett, please have him try again.

Of course, she could call him. Rose was a liberated woman. It was okay for women to call men in this day and age. But what if he was in the middle of something? What if he'd been called back to the hospital? Or he was taking care of his mother, who probably felt traumatized thinking she almost lost her daughter? Especially with what she went through after the tornado.

What if he still wanted an old-fashioned girl?

Ack! Who was this timid woman? She'd made it through school and all the challenges thrown at her by being assertive. By taking charge.

Only this wasn't something she should bulldoze her way through.

She needed someone to talk to. Someone who understood her, who could guide her.

Teri was out. There was no way Rose would attempt to contact her when she was on her honeymoon, even if she knew how. Sure, they'd gone to French Lick, but there was more than one place to stay there. How many honeymooners would she have to bother to locate Mr. and Mrs. Bart Shoffner? Rose imagined roaming from door to door, knocking while calling, "Teri!"

Now she was getting ridiculous.

The person she really wanted to talk to was her mother. They hadn't done much but say hello yesterday at the wedding, and because of the drive, Mom and Howard left early. Had she heard about Alma's twins? That made the perfect excuse to call. And hopefully Howard wouldn't answer the phone.

Only he did. Mom was out, he was home alone.

"Howard, would you please give Mom a message for me?"

"Yes, what is it?" He sounded deflated, for lack of a better word.

"Alma had twins. It got a little tricky, but mother and babies are doing well." That should cover it.

"Good. I'm glad to hear it. There's a reason they discourage doctors from working on their families, but this was a special instance. I would have been happy to assist, but I wasn't aware of what happened until after they left." Did Howard feel overlooked?

"I'm sure they weren't thinking that far in advance. Brett was at their table and the quickest help." She paused. Perhaps it was time to extend that olive branch. "If they'd have thought about it though, you would have been a great help."

Howard cleared his throat. "Thank you, Rose. Okay, then. I'll let your mother know. She stepped out to visit Mrs. Hanrahan. Took her some lunch because the woman sprained her ankle."

"I'm so sorry. Mom's probably cleaning her house or running errands for her. She's a dynamo at that."

"You've got that right. I... Never mind. I'll let her know. Thank you for calling, Rose."

Rose signed off and tried to analyze that conversation. It was the first time she could remember where it was only she and Howard speaking, and there were no fireworks. That had to be a God thing. Maybe there was hope for her family yet.

That still didn't give her anyone to talk to though.

She knew that was wrong the moment she thought it.

"God, I've no idea how to make things right. I'm not sure what to say to Brett or even if he wants to speak to me. There's a lot of need going on in this world that merits Your help more than this sad little mix-up. Alma and the babies, Mrs. Hanrahan's ankle, my patients, not to mention the war and the protests and the riots. In the scheme of it all, this probably isn't worth Your time. But if You have a moment, I'd appreciate a little guidance to resolve this mess with Brett."

She ended with thanking Him for what He had already done, especially for letting her have a normal conversation with Howard.

As she spoke her amen, the phone rang again. Rose wasted no time in answering, her pulse thumping.

"Dr. Crackinbush? This is Frank Brown." Definitely not who she hoped for. "I'm sorry to call you on Sunday afternoon. I learned that the person who was supposed to phone you only notified half of the list. So I'm trying to reach the others. We'll be announcing the medical team we've chosen to receive the bequest tomorrow at 2:00 p.m. We'd like to invite you to come."

Tomorrow? "Does that mean I'm part of the team?"

"Not necessarily. We invited everyone who showed interest and served on one of the project teams. We've tried to bring on board as many medical professionals as we could, thinking about the specific needs of the vets, but there's a limit to the funds, even as great as they are."

"Oh."

"But that doesn't mean you aren't on the list. It just means I'm not in a position to say at this point. The local commander wants to be the one to share the news."

"I see." She did. Rose most likely didn't make the team, but they invited her for the consolation cookie and coffee. Yay.

"So tomorrow at two."

"Got it. Thank you for calling, Mr. Brown."

This was turning out to be a humdinger of a day. Could the call she missed have been Mr. Brown? Most likely.

There had to be something she could do that wouldn't take her away from the phone. Just in case.

That sounded so pitiful even in her head.

No. She wasn't going to live her life just in case.

If she'd truly left things in God's hands, then she had to trust Him to work it out. There weren't many she could say she trusted. But God was the One she always could, even when life looked bleak. She just had to remind herself of that and stop sitting around waiting for the world to fly her way. God called her to a purpose. She would concentrate on the parts of it she was sure of and trust Him to handle any new adjustments needed.

Besides, the vets never got their brownies. That was something she could rectify.

Brett heard the phone before he unlocked his door and managed to swipe it up on the sixth ring. "Hello?"

"Dr. Shoffner, this is Frank Brown. I'm sorry for the late notice but needed you to know we'll be announcing the medical team tomorrow at 2:00 p.m and wanted to invite you to be there."

With everything that had gone on the past twenty-four hours, Brett hadn't thought about the VFW or the bequest once. It took him a minute to focus. "Sure. I'll be there." He started to end the call, but something had to be asked. "Have you invited Dr. Crackinbush?"

"Yes, I spoke with her personally."

"Good, then. She'll be on the team."

"Actually, I'm not supposed to tell anyone the results. But since you are her friend, some vets took Dr. Eilert's words as gospel, so she didn't make it. I probably shouldn't tell you but hoped you could be there for her?"

That stunned him, even though he'd been aware of the possibility. "Mr. Brown, would you give me a moment to speak to the members before you announce the team?"

"Of course. If you think that'll help."

"I don't know if it will. I'm not even sure what I'll say. But it's worth a try. Thank you. I'll see you there." Definitely worth it.

Then something the man said hit him. Mr. Brown spoke with Rose? Brett wanted—no—needed to call her. But he also ought to grab a shower before he did anything. He was growing a tad ripe.

Once Alma was stable and the babies in incubators, her regular doctor arrived and took over. Which left Brett to deal with Ed and Mom. Both were champs during the crisis but fell apart once things stabilized.

Seeing Mom that way gave him a glimpse of what it must have been like for her when Dad died and he was in traction. The empathy far outweighed any feelings of betrayal. Besides, if he had made a career in the military, he wouldn't have been there for Alma and the babies. Or any of his other patients.

It was as if God said, "I have a better plan," and worked things out in advance.

However, after changing back out of his scrubs, all he had to wear was the tux—that he took a nap in at his mother's house. Hopefully, whatever company the Weather Girls dealt with would be understanding about the wrinkled and smelly return.

Brett shook his head, peeled out of the mess, and headed for his shower. It had never felt so good.

Once clean and dressed, he toyed with the idea of just driving over to Rosie's. But when he had called her from Mom's earlier in the day, she hadn't answered. True, she could have been out somewhere. According to Frank Brown though, she was now home.

He hopped in his car and made it to Rose's in ten minutes.

Her Fairlane was in the driveway. Good sign.

Brett dashed up the steps, a nervous energy moving him forward. With a breath and a prayer, he pressed her doorbell and waited.

And waited.

And waited.

Nothing. Should he try again?

"You hoo! Dr. Shoffner." Mrs. Whitehead stood on her porch waving her hankie. "I know she's home. She didn't want to go anywhere. She was hoping for a phone call."

From whom? "Thank you." So he should give it another go?

Hmm. Maybe she waited for someone else to phone. Not him. Could be she got tired of waiting on him, even though it really hadn't been that long. Right?

Was she indisposed? Fine. He'd try once more. A little longer.

Still no response.

"Dr. Shoffner, I don't understand. I know she's home."

"That's okay, Mrs. Whitehead. I'll just catch her another time." Brett moved slower down the steps than he'd mounted them. There was no longer a rush. He climbed in his car and took a drive out to Russiaville. Not that he was going to see Mom again, but it was familiar ground. He could think better here.

He parked in the empty lot of a closed feed store, keeping his radio playing while he tried to make sense of things. Roberta Flack's "The First Time Ever I Saw Your Face" took him back to his brother's engagement party when he'd danced with Rosie, amazed it was possible to hold such beauty in his arms. The scent of her perfume, like a garden, still lingered in his memory.

"Oh, Girl" by the Chi-Lites spoke the words he was thinking. Not only would he be in trouble, he was already there, and he didn't know if she'd left him or not.

Though not answering the door if she knew it was him probably signaled it was over.

So what was he going to do? Tenacity had served him well in his healing and career, but at what point in a relationship do you let go?

Harry Nilsson answered with singing "Without You."

Despite the melodrama, Brett identified with Nilsson's emotions. Yes, he'd live without her in his life. He trusted God to work things out somehow. Still, God might be saying no.

Looking at the future with no hope that he and Rosie might find a way to make it brought on a whole lot of feeling lost.

There was nothing he could do at this point. However, tomorrow was another day. Guess Scarlett O'Hara was more sage-like than he'd given her credit for. The craziness of that thought tugged at the corner of his lip, and somehow he found a seed of hope. Tomorrow he'd see Rosie, and he'd do something to make things right. If after that she still wanted no part of him, then so be it. He'd toss that Hail Mary pass for the goalposts and leave the outcome in God's hands.

That brought a modicum of peace. At least enough to head back home, grab a bite, and watch some TV. It was a *MacMillan and Wife* night. Brett fell asleep on the couch while Susan Saint James's Sally MacMillan morphed into Rosie, and Mac no longer looked like Rock Hudson but had a scary resemblance to a certain Dr. Shoffner.

Brett woke with a start and dragged himself to bed only to fall back into the same dream. It made the morning come too soon.

After rounds, he headed to his office to find Belinda already hard at work. "How's the family, boss?"

"They're keeping Alma and the kids a couple more days at least. She was smiling and happy. Ed is wrapped every which way but loose around two of the tiniest little pinkies you've ever seen. And my mother? Whoa, she is totally in her element now that the crisis is behind us." He laughed. "Alma thought she'd covered all the bases, making her doctor check for twins and then surprise, surprise, surprise. But she's thrilled too."

Belinda chuckled. "Okay, Gomer Pyle. What names have they picked out?"

"Since they'd chosen one boy and one girl name, they get to use them both. Melissa Nicole and Jason Matthew."

"Those are beautiful." She handed him a stack of messages he'd missed already.

A quick peek said there was nothing from Rosie among them, but he told himself that was okay. He'd see her in a few hours. Just a few measly hours. "Oh, I need to duck out this afternoon. The VFW made their decision, and they're announcing it at two. I'll take a late lunch if you can rearrange things for me."

"No problem. Good luck, boss." She turned away to answer the phone, so Brett continued to his office, put on his white lab coat, and got his first file from Pam before seeing the patient in exam room two.

There was something good about being back in his routine. It kept his mind occupied on his patients, though any pause allowed Rosie to slip in there.

Around 1:40, Belinda caught him in the hall with a sandwich on a paper towel. "Know you won't have time to pick up something before the meeting, but you're good to go. No patients for the next two hours. Get some great news, boss."

"You are a godsend. Thank you, boss." He cocked an eyebrow as he squeezed her shoulder.

After leaving his lab coat in his office, he headed out the back door to his car and made the trip to the VFW, inhaling the PB and J sandwich at the lights.

Rosie's Fairlane was already parked in the lot. Good. Now to pull the words he'd practiced in his head since last night into a coherent message.

He double-checked his watch. No, he wasn't late. Apparently everyone was excited and arrived early. That caused his heart to pump a little faster.

Once in the conference room, he spotted Frank Brown and made his way past the trays of chocolate chip cookies and carafes of coffee toward where he sat on the stage.

Mr. Brown waved him up and whispered as Brett took the seat next to him, "You all set?"

"Hopefully."

Then the lawyer strode to the podium. "I want to welcome you all here today. I'm sure you are as excited as we are to finally get this team solidified. Murray Archer, the post commander, will read off the names, but first, we have a short word from one of the medical personnel who helped with our surveys. Dr. Shoffner? The microphone is yours."

Brett slid his hands over his pants and stood. It was go time. "Good afternoon, folks. I requested this chance to speak because I believe there's been a mistake and I hope to rectify it. During your deliberation period, someone who thought they were doing the right thing passed around some inaccurate information. However, this person was very mistaken. As a doctor and member of the AMA, I am limited on what I can explain on this subject, but let me say this. Chiropractic is a true medical field and offers important benefits. I have personal knowledge of this."

There were whispers in the room, and Brett finally spotted Rosie, her eyes large and glued to him. "So, I want to be clear, that if out of misplaced loyalty to a well-meaning friend, the members of this post decided to invite me but not Dr. Crackinbush to the medical team, then I will step aside and give my spot to her. You have multiple MDs to choose from in this gathering but only one chiropractor. Don't lose the opportunity of having Dr. Crackinbush part of this venture. Thank you."

Whew, he got the words out. But it wasn't until he sat next to Mr. Brown again that he heard the applause.

Then an older gentleman in the audience stood. "Commander, I move that the voting members meet for a few minutes to double check the results."

Another man joined him. "I second that."

The gentleman at the podium, Murray Archer, tapped the gavel. "All those in favor say aye."

The chorus was so deafening he didn't even call for the nays.

"Then we'll take a ten-minute break. All voting members meet me down in front."

Brett decided to get out of the way and left the stage. Before he could search for Rosie in the throng, someone grabbed his arm. He swung around to come face to lovely face with the person he most wanted to see. "Rosie."

"You stood up for me."

"Of course. I'm sorry you thought I wouldn't." He so wished he could explain.

"I get it. I do. No one has ever stood up for me like that."

He pulled her to a quiet alcove where they had some privacy. "I will always stand up for you. Will you give me a chance to prove it?"

Rosie slowly worked her hands up his chest to meet behind his neck, the action sending delightful chills running down his spine. Her touch did things to him that only she could do.

"Should I take that as a yes?"

She nodded.

There was nothing he desired more than to kiss her right now, right here. But would she let him? He drew his finger down her cheek to her bottom lip and traced it back and forth. "I'd like to—"

"Then do it." Only she rose on tiptoe and met his lips first.

Brett braced her against the wall, his fingers twining in her hair as he held her face, desire for her growing with her sweet chocolate and coffee taste and her garden scent enveloping him. Forget about old-fashioned girls. He could get used to a modern woman who knew what she wanted, who had such soft lips, who drove him out of his mind, who—

She broke it off. "Did you hear something?"

"Dr. Crackinbush?"

Oh, great, they were about to have an audience.

Rosie grabbed his arm and pulled him with her from the alcove while she stroked her hair back in place with her other hand.

"Oh, there you are." It was Frank Brown with Mr. Archer. They had to know what he and Rosie had been doing, but they were either clueless or gentlemen choosing to ignore the flush on Rosie's face. And most likely the same thing on his, from the heat radiating from his cheeks.

The second man held out his palm. "We'd like to offer you both positions on our medical team."

"Yes!" They said it at the same time. Rosie giggled, and both shook hands with the men. Mr. Archer moved on to another group.

"Looks as if you two are already working together." Brett caught the wink Frank Brown aimed his way. Guess the guy wasn't all that clueless.

Brett glanced down at Rosie. "Oh, we're just getting started. Trust me."

Rosie tightened the grip where their fingers tangled and met his gaze. "I do, Dr. Shoffner. I absolutely do trust you."

Epilogue
Sunday, December 24, 1972

R ose sat curled up next to Brett on his mother's couch. All his siblings, their spouses, and babies were there as well, basking in the glow of the Christmas lights and softly playing carols on the stereo. A sigh escaped. One of total satisfaction and pleasure. She could stay like this forever.

They'd be going to the midnight service at Wabash Community in a bit, that is all but Alma and Ed and their little ones. Then tomorrow it was Rose's side of the family's turn. They'd drive up to Lafayette and be with Mom and Howard and her brother.

But right now, leaning against the man who had proved himself trustworthy was more than enough. One day they'd probably take the next step, but she wasn't going to rush him. It would happen. He'd ask, and she was sure of her answer.

Teri, wearing her red fuzzy hat, played Santa and began passing out gifts. She handed a flat box to Rose designated for both her and Brett.

"What's this?" Rose couldn't imagine. No name or tag to say who had given the gift. She sat up.

"Why don't you open it?" Teri's grin hinted that she already knew. Hmm.

Brett swiped it. "Give it here. You're too slow."

"Now wait a minute. We can savor the moment."

Brett groaned but handed it back. "Savor away."

Rose giggled, tore the paper off, and opened the box. Inside was a frame. She turned it over to find a photo of her and Brett from Teri's wedding. They were under the sycamore where he'd dropped that kiss on her forehead. Windy had captured a flutter of red on the branch above. "Thank you, Teri."

"Oh, this isn't just from me. It's from Windy too. You know what that is, right?"

"It's Brett and me at your wedding."

Teri rolled her eyes. "It's more than that. You got a cardinal when he kissed you. And that means..." She motioned for them to finish her statement.

Brett shook his head while Rose stared at Teri. "No idea." Their unison responses were becoming legendary.

Teri sighed as if she was explaining to a toddler. "Oh, you two. When you kiss beneath that sycamore and a cardinal alights, you are meant to be together. Actually, Windy said it's the first time she's seen it where only one of the partners did the kissing, not both of you kissing each other."

"I could've told you we're meant to be." Brett drew her closer to him and kissed her forehead like in the photo.

"Thank you, Teri. And I'll thank Windy next time I run into her at church, probably tonight."

Brett stood and reached for something under the tree. Then he returned to her. "What if you're supposed to see her someplace else?"

"Like where?" What was Brett thinking?

"Maybe at Ferguson House? Because, Dr. Rose Anna Crackinbush DC, you drive me crazy in the best possible way. I love how you enjoy bringing tasty treats to others and showing compassion to those in need. You hope for the best and see the best in others and use your skill to accomplish it. You make me a better doctor and a better man. Don't change a thing. I love you with my whole heart, Cracklin' Rosie." Brett dropped to one knee.

Rose gasped. He was doing it.

"Will you marry me?" He extended a velvet box and flipped the top up.

This was real. Brett was asking her to share life with him. No giving up her career or pushing her into a mold that clashed with all her convictions. This man saw her, believed in her, loved her. "Yes, Brett. Oh, yes." She grabbed him in a bear hug and held on, whispering in his ear. "If you call me Cracklin' Rosie, I'm calling you Dudley Do-Right."

"You've got a deal."

Then he slid the ring on her finger, and they sealed it with a kiss.

* * *

Author Notes

D ear Reader, we've made it. Can you believe this is the nineteenth book I've published? I can't. It blows my mind.

This was a fun story even if it just about killed me to write it. To be honest, I didn't give myself enough grieving time after my mother passed, and trying to be creative when my brain wanted to hibernate, watch TV, and eat ice cream (or what really happened—do paper crafting and eat tacos) doesn't produce a lot of productivity. But God is faithful and He gently prodded me through to the end.

Then got me to rewrite the end.

Yeah, it wasn't easy (I can hear Ringo singing in my head, "You know it don't come easy").

But I learned a lot doing this book.

That part about getting kicked out of the AMA if a doctor got caught collaborating with a chiropractor? Totally true. Today the AMA doesn't hold the same power over doctors as it did in the early 70s. But back then, everything got tied to that organization because they had the money and could help fund hospitals and such. So they made the rules.

That is until a small group of chiropractors banded together and filed a suit. Wilk v. AMA.

It took a long time and a lot of tenacity. The case was filed in October of 1976. It was finally argued for the first time in December of 1988. And the final decision came down in February of 1990. You can learn more about it here: https://www.ncbi.nlm.nih.gov/pmc/articles/PMC8493 525/

By then the AMA had tried to loosen it's strangle hold in hopes of proving it wasn't such a bad guy. However, the chiropractors won. I'm of a mind that the real winners were, and still are the patients.

I became aware of this information from my friend Linda Larsen who is a chiropractor. She learned first hand what it was like before Wilk v. AMA as her father was also a chiropractor. I can't thank her enough for all the help to make this book accurate and true to life—for fiction, that is.

But now it's time to move on to book number twenty—***Ronnie***.

If you read ***Cheryl's Going Home***, you might remember the short appearance of her niece from Texas. That was Ronnie. I thought it might be fun to see if I could work a cowboy into this midwestern saga, and Ronnie seemed to be the best bet for doing it. Here's the blurb:

She's literally stuck in her engagement...

...He's trying to keep her there.

But when you take the couple out of Texas, is the romance lost too?

Ronnie Webb has broken her engagement to the love of her life, Carlos (Cal) Garcia, or would have if the stupid ring would come off her finger.

To find the space to get over him and the rest of what is going wrong in her life, she leaves her dad's Texas ranch to visit her aunt and family in Kokomo, Indiana.

But hanging out with the Weather Girls, especially with their cardinal in the sycamore legend sending out strong vibes, Ronnie's love life may not be as dead as she thinks.

Carlitos can't believe the letter Ronnie left him right before Christmas—his last one at home before his enlistment starts. However, his broken wrist might just be the break he needs to get Ronnie back before it's too late.

But what does this native Texan know about mid-western Hoosier romance?

And can he learn, or is this the end?

Ronnie: A Sweet, Quirky Romantic Yarn is book five in the *Weather Girls Wedding Shoppe and Venue* series. Inspired by *Frankie Valli and the Four Seasons'* 1960's song of the same name, this charming tale with a bit of western influence finishes off 1972 and brings you into the New Year in Kokomo, Indiana.

You will enjoy this sweet and wholesome romcom with a touch of western flavor because everyone dreams of their own cowboy romance.

To stay up to date on my progress, join our family of twice monthly newsletter readers. I send it out on the first and third Tuesdays of each month. Get to know me, my author friends, and there's often goodies offered. You can find us on my website jenniferlynncary.com

I'm hoping to have a February release—and I'd appreciate your prayers to help with that.

Anyway, keep reading to get a sneak peek at the first chapter of ***Ronnie***. Be sure to let me know how you like it. You can contact me at hello@jenniferlynncary.com

Until next time,

Abundant blessings,

Jenny

Sneak Peek at Ronnie: A Sweet, Quirky, Romantic Yarn
Chapter 1

Chapter 1

Tuesday, December 19, 1972

Kokomo, Indiana

"Pass the mashed potatoes, please?"

Ronnie Webb smiled at Windy, a cousin she barely knew. It probably looked more like a wince, and since her finger was throbbing, that made sense. She handed the ginormous bowl of spuds in her direction. The pre-Christmas meal Dad's side of the family had prepared threatened to bow the dining room table. Even with foregoing the meat centered dishes there was plenty on her plate. Just what she needed to be doing. Comfort eating to keep from bursting into tears. How had life become so twisted upside down?

Aunt Cheryl gasped, bringing her back to the present. "Oh, no, Ronnie, what happened to your finger?"

Oops. Ronnie's thoughts barrel raced through her brain. What could she say? "I think the ring got sized a little too small." Or maybe it's all the fast food from the trip?

"It's probably all the holiday sweets, shug." *Thanks, Mom.* Was she getting fat?

Shrugging in agreement, she added, "I'm just not used to it yet, I guess," before letting the amazing meal on her plate draw her eyes down. She'd known someone was bound to notice. After all the attempts to get the ring off, it was no wonder her finger was sore. But she'd hoped to put off explaining as long as possible, and maybe find success in removing the delicate solitaire from her stubborn digit before this. A mere hour after arriving in Kokomo, Indiana bordered on the abrupt.

"Hazel, do you mind if I make an ice pack for her?" Mom would have to do that. If only Ronnie could slide beneath the table. At least then, when everyone stared at her place, she wouldn't be able to see it.

"That's okay. I'll take care of it later, Mom." Only Hazel was already at the swinging door that led to the kitchen. Just swell. Pun intended. Later, after Christmas, Ronnie would explain to her parents, and by extension everyone else, that the ring was no longer hers. Nor was the man.

Her heart shuddered as a fresh pain stabbed her in the chest. It was taking everything she had to keep this news from her family until after the happy celebrations. The last thing she wanted was to ruin Christmas for everyone. If only her stupid finger didn't look like a mini-sausage.

The past two days had been horrendous. Riding in the family station wagon with her parents, keeping up the charade, eating every Stuckey's nut log she got her hands on all the way from Hood County, Texas. Ronnie stopped herself from shaking her head. She had only herself to blame for this moment. As much as she'd love to curl up and let Mom comfort her, it wasn't right. Not now, at least.

"I think what you need to do, sweetie, is hold your hand up in the air and let gravity do the work." This from her Aunt Cheryl who sat directly across from her.

That wouldn't look strange or anything.

"I think it's just sore from my playing with it so much." Hazel handed her the ice pack right then. "Thank you." She almost added "You shouldn't have," but the faster Ronnie could get this focus off her, the better.

Talk at the table ebbed, leaving too much quiet. As she raised her eyes, several glanced toward her left hand. Oh, they tried to hide it, but it was obvious. And with such a full table of guests—three cousins with their husbands and children, her Aunt Cheryl and Uncle Aaron, and then Aaron's mother, Hazel and her husband, Gene, not to mention Ronnie and her parents—there was no missing it.

This trip was supposed to be fun. After Aunt Cheryl, who was Dad's little sister, and Uncle Aaron came to Texas for Thanksgiving, there'd been no peace until another trip to Kokomo was planned to celebrate Christmas. At the time, Ronnie was excited even though Cal couldn't make it.

Cal. They'd promised to celebrate together once she got home again.

Another promise broken.

"I hear y'all have been working on a special Christmas program. Will we get to see it?" Ronnie hoped the change of subject would help as she rested her hand on the ice pack. *Brr.* Sure made the metal cold fast.

Aunt Cheryl's face lit up. "Oh, yes, Aaron's been working hard on it. Together with one of his prize pupils," she turned to her husband, "Mac MacKenzie, right hon?"

He nodded.

"Right, Mac. Anyway, they've written original music and the two of them have a guitar duet that will bring tears to your eyes, it's so good."

Uncle Aaron's cheeks got a little rosy and he patted his wife's hand before shoving his glasses back up his nose. "Thanks, hon."

"I'm just telling the truth. I heard some of their rehearsals. It's all scheduled for Christmas Eve."

Ronnie's uncle grinned. "Well, if you're going to share that, you should also mention that you and the girls have a quartet presentation. I would have loved to have given all the parts to my women, but we've got some talented folks in our church, and they deserve a chance too." He followed up with a wink at his wife.

"Now, Dad, we're happy to help, but singing all the songs? That's a lot of responsibility and a ton more than we could do." Sunny, Ronnie's eldest cousin on this side of the family, spoke for her sisters as well as herself as she rubbed her swollen belly.

"I guess you're right. But I'm pretty excited about how this is turning out. Can't wait for you all to see it."

"Anything with my talented little sis has got to be good." Dad beamed with pride over at Aunt Cheryl who at one time had been a movie star.

At least this conversation took the focus off her. Ronnie wanted to sigh but held it in just in case it put her back in the spotlight. This little bit of plans and the happiness they brought for while they were there proved she was right for not sharing her life-is-never-going-to-be-the-same news.

"Ronnie, you're not eating any of the roast. Oh, sorry, I forgot." Now Aunt Cheryl blushed.

"It's okay. I'm sure it tastes great, but I don't do meat anymore." Another hush around the table. How long before someone called *Ripley's Believe It or Not*?

"I should have remembered. Sorry."

"No worries." Ronnie forced a smile and took her final forkful of potatoes. Without gravy. She stared at the boat holding the mashed potato topping. Would that make the ring slide any better? At least she wouldn't be taking in internally. They'd probably question her sanity if she plopped her hand in the goop.

Hazel scooted back from the table and stood. "I have dessert. Sugar cream pie. There's more than enough. But do you want it now or later? I also have coffee ready."

The consensus was to wait. Gene captured Hazel's hand. "This was a grand meal, sweetheart, but we need a little time to make some room."

"Well, then, you men all go hang out in the den while we women get the clean-up done. Make yourselves useful and take the little ones with you." That drew a chuckle. There were only two. Heather, Cousin

Windy's daughter, had just had her second birthday in October, and Cousin Stormy's little Bobby was just a bit over a year old and trying to walk to keep up with Heather. They were definitely cute, and made Ronnie want to cry. The chances of her having one as adorable seemed slim to none right now. Another stab to her battered heart.

Stormy draped her arm over Hazel's shoulders. "Gramma, you always end up cleaning after every meal. Why don't you put your feet up and let us do it? We've got more than enough help, and you know we know where things go."

"On one condition. Sunny, you have to sit it out with me. I can see your ankles swelling from here now and if you overdo, you'll not make it to your due date."

Sunny shrugged. "I'm too tired to argue. Sure, I'll make the sacrifice. You all have fun without me." She winked and led her grandmother out of the kitchen to groans and chuckles from her sisters and mother.

"Let's shake it, ladies." Stormy turned on the faucet and soon had a sink full of hot water, suds and dirty dishes.

Ronnie glanced at her mother and volunteered to wash. "I don't know where things go, and the water might help my finger."

No one argued so she took Stormy's place and started scrubbing.

Mom headed toward the dining room with Aunt Cheryl for the rest of the dishes.

"Oh." Windy's tender gaze landed on her as she polished a willow patterned plate dry. What had she figured out? "We heard about your cousin, Sophie. We're so sorry."

Stormy nodded in solidarity.

The lasso around Ronnie's heart tightened, squeezing away all response.

Mom must have returned in time to hear. She reached out and tucked a lock of hair behind Ronnie's ear before she responded. "Sophie's my sister's daughter. Our girls were very close. She had that special spark, ya know? Just had to be helpful, do what she could. Seems unnatural that she's not with us anymore."

Had to be helpful was right. It was her kindness and sense of duty that got her killed. A stew of anger and despair warred for the upper hand whenever Ronnie allowed herself to remember that her best friend and confidant no longer lived. She scrubbed the next plate with gusto.

Windy and Stormy continued drying and putting away in silence. Ronnie didn't know if she could make words form yet. Instead a black cloud tinted her vision.

Mom leaned in close. "Many hands make light work."

Ronnie had to nod in agreement. But once the work was done, what other hidden trip mines would get uncovered?

Not even five minutes later, the kitchen was put back to rights, the sink drained, and the towels hung back on the rack. "Let's go find Hazel and Sunny." Aunt Cheryl led the way to the living room where Sunny was stretched out with her feet in Hazel's lap.

"Oh, let me move so there's plenty of room."

"No, hon, you stay put." Aunt Cheryl gently restrained her very pregnant daughter. "You work way too hard, and I'm concerned you'll make this baby come faster than he or she needs to. There's plenty of places to sit, especially if we bring in chairs from the dining room."

Stormy and Windy were on it before their mom stopped talking.

Mom took one of the two winged fireside chairs and Ronnie dropped to the floor, just like at home, criss cross. Maybe down here she'd be less visible.

"So Sunny, when is the big day supposed to be? Your parents didn't say a word about this when they were down last month." Mom would get all the details.

Sunny twisted around so she could make eye contact. "We made a deal. If you could come up for Christmas, they wouldn't let the cat out of the bag. But if you couldn't, they were allowed to share. We really wanted to surprise you so I'm glad it worked out. Please don't blame Mom and Dad, they were only doing what we asked."

"What about a shower? Have you had one yet?"

"We've been so busy with the holidays, there hasn't been time. I know Mom and Gramma want to plan something. The baby isn't due until January 20th, so I said we could do it while you're here."

Ronnie glanced up to see the smile on her mom's face. Mom loved this kind of thing. She was going to be disappointed not to plan something for Ronnie.

"I'm sure I can go shopping while we're here, but I'm fixin' to crochet y'all something once I get home and get it in the mail as fast as I can."

"Thank you, Aunt Alice."

"Actually, I never got to send anything to your sisters either."

"Don't worry about that. Windy has an announcement of her own." Sunny grinned as all the women turned in her sister's direction.

"Hey. Kris and I just found out last week. We've got a long way to go. Stormy could end up pregnant again before this new one arrives."

Which put Stormy in the spotlight.

"Don't look at me. If it happens, it happens. Bobby may end up with a brother or sister or have to learn to be satisfied with a whole lot of cousins." That had everyone chuckling. Almost everyone.

Ronnie tried to at least smile. No one seemed to notice so that was good.

Conversation centered around catching up with goings-on in Kokomo. Aunt Cheryl planned to go out for another play after the first of the year. Maybe. She was concerned about that pulling her away from Sunny if she went into labor. But then Sunny pointed out that they would only be in preliminary rehearsal at that time so there was no conflict.

"What happened to Bridget?" Ronnie blurted the question the moment it occurred to her. Last year when Bridget, who'd been closer to Ronnie's age, and she hung out, they'd had some fun conversations.

Aunt Cheryl sort of smiled. "She's in Hollywood, working on a new film. We were just there in October when Aaron was working on the Christmas specials. She's doing great and is loving her life. My old agent took her on and is a bit of a mother hen so that helps."

Ronnie nodded. She'd hoped to break her news to Bridget first, since she was so easy to talk to. The practice might have helped. But now, she'd have to wing it.

Another loss.

Losing Sophe had been hard. It still was. And it should have been enough loss for any one person to endure. But no. Bridget was gone too, though at least she was still living.

Hardest of all, she'd lost Cal. And she couldn't say a word about it. That knife that had been stabbing her heart now gutted her.

Tuesday, December 21, 1972
Lazy W Ranch, Hood County, Texas

Carlitos Garcia parked his truck next to the house and stared at his plaster-covered wrist one more time. He shouldn't even be home yet, but now he had to make a phone call and pray the answer wasn't as awful as he feared.

As he opened the truck's cab door, Lobo, Ronnie's German shepherd greeted him. "Sorry, buddy, but she's not with me. You miss her too, doncha?" He scratched between the dog's ears before climbing out. "Ma's gonna be all over me for not being careful, boy. Want to go with me and distract her a little?" He laughed at the thought of his mother allowing Lobo inside her house, and stooped down in front of the shepherd. "I'll be out to check on you in a bit. Why don't you go find Dex while you're waiting?" Carlitos gave the dog one more pet before heading to the back porch.

He did not look forward to this. Not one little bit. In fact, the only person who would remotely be okay with it was Ronnie. Would she think he did it on purpose?

Well, he didn't. And he wouldn't.

"Mijo, what are you doing here?" Ma nearly collided into him—and his broken wrist—on her way to see what was going on outside. He knew her. She heard something and had to investigate.

"Careful, Ma."

"Ay! Carlitos, what did you do?" Now she had her arm around him to lead him into the kitchen where she pushed him onto a chair. "Start talking."

"It's nothing. Really."

She stared him down.

"Okay, it's broken—"

"Ay, mijo, what can I do for you? Do you need ice?" She was at the freezer door before she finished speaking.

"No, Ma. I'm good. Maybe some Excedrin later."

So she pulled up a chair to face him and grabbed the bottle of Excedrin from behind the napkin holder, plunking it down in front of him.

"Thanks." He paused to see if he could get out of more of the story, but her stare confirmed she was having none of his evasive tactics. He sighed. "Fine. It's so stupid. It wasn't even my ride. I was helping Miggy Alvarez. He was set to ride Thunder Clap—"

"Oh, that dangerous bull?" Her hands covered her mouth.

"Yeah. But I wasn't riding. Remember? Only Thunder Clap was getting squirrelly and bounced the gate onto my wrist on his way out. Like I said, it was stupid. I just was in the wrong place."

Ma seemed to accept that as she chewed at her bottom lip. Then a light glowed in her eyes and her spine straightened. "What does this mean for January 4th?"

Maybe Ronnie wouldn't be the only one hoping. "I have to call them tomorrow. I doubt they want me showing up with a fractured wrist, but I don't know what the policy is."

"Maybe they'll say they don't want you anymore." Yeah, she was hoping right along with Ronnie.

"I don't think it works that way. They'll probably give me time to heal and a new appointment date. Most likely I'll have to bring in something from my doctor to say I'm now fit." *Wonder how long they'll give me?*

Ma popped back up and started making him a dinner plate. "Anything that keeps you here is fine by me."

"You want me to be hurt?"

She turned to him with big eyes. "Ah, no, mijo. No. But I don't want you going into the army. Not while the war still goes on."

"Ma. I was going to have to go anyway. My number was up. This way—"

"And you told no one. I can't believe you kept that to yourself." The way she dropped the dish of *refritos* and bowl of *pozole* in front of him, she was still upset about that. "Here." She handed him one of her homemade tortillas.

"I know, Ma. I'm sorry. I just didn't need you all fixin' to worry yourselves crazy. That's why I enlisted. That way I have a better chance of getting stationed somewhere else." She'd made the red pozole, his favorite. Someone else must be running late since she still had the soup and beans warming on the stove.

"*Por supuesto?* You're positive?"

"Ma, nothing is for sure. It's just a better chance. Hey, where's Pop?" A different topic would be welcomed about now.

"He's with Dex. My Lady is foaling and with Jack gone, he thought he ought to be there in case Dex needed help." She returned to her seat.

"So that's why dinner is still waiting. Guess I lucked out. I'll go down and help when I'm done here. If I'd known, I'd have headed there first." Of course that meant no seconds on the pozole now. Maybe Ma would save him some more. "So what's been going on while I was gone?"

Ma brushed some crumbs from her plastic table cloth into her hand before pulling a napkin from the holder in the center of the table and handing it to him. No words necessary.

"Not much. Jack and Alice pulled out about six yesterday morning. Saw Ronnie climb into the backseat like she was going to go back to sleep." That made Ma chuckle. "Oh, that reminds me. She came by and asked to leave you something. I told her to put it on your dresser."

Carlitos smiled. They'd agreed to exchange gifts when she got back since they were both supposed to be gone over Christmas. Guess she wanted to one-up him. No biggie. The gift he had for her was too large to wrap anyway. He hadn't decided until right before Thunder Clap did his damage whether he give it to her as a Christmas present or as a wedding gift. But he was too excited to wait so he was settling for belated Christmas/New Year.

He'd never tried anything this big. But he'd saved since he first could draw a paycheck for anything. This dream was one of the three goals of his life—this, marry Ronnie, and work the rodeo until he could start his own ranch. But Ronnie was the main goal. He'd fallen in love with her the moment his three-year-old eyes had seen her in that little sun suit with the ruffles on her butt. They might say there's no such thing as love at first sight, and even then, those how accept the possibility would most likely argue that a three-year-old didn't have the ability to do more than have a puppy love crush.

But then, they'd never met Ronnie.

She was his reason for getting up in the morning, for working until he was dead tired, and saving every cent he could. She was why he didn't tell anyone about his draft number. He knew she wouldn't be able to handle it.

So he'd waited until he met with the recruiter and had a plan. Then he explained, or tried to, that this was a safer bet. Still a bet, but with better chances.

She hadn't bought it.

He could still picture her, wide eyed and panicked, trying to get out of his truck so she didn't have to hear more. But the more she missed was what she needed to hear. He could only hope she'd be calmed down once she got home from Indiana.

Carlitos gathered up his dishes and put them in the sink before kissing his mother's cheek. "Thanks, Ma. I'll go send Pop in for his dinner."

She wrapped him in a hug. "I'm glad you're home, mijo."

"Me too, Ma." He squeezed her back and headed out to the horse barn where My Lady waited. The beautiful Appaloosa belonged to Becky, Ronnie's sister. But since she'd moved into town to work for the Hood County News, she only got to ride her horse on the weekends she could get away. Therefore everyone on the ranch stepped up to show My Lady some love. Dex had convinced Becky to let him breed the horse. But now, if something went wrong with the birth, Dex could be up the creek with his sister.

Carlitos could hear the men's whispers before he found them at a stall in the back of the barn. They didn't sound too upset so maybe things were okay. He could only hope.

Waiting until he was close to say anything to keep from startling the mother-to-be, he let his footfalls on the straw announce his approach.

His father looked up first from the stall next to My Lady's and gave him a hug while speaking soft and low. "Mijo, thought we wouldn't see you until after Christmas."

Carlitos held up his plastered hand. "It's not as bad as it looks."

"Looks like something's broke." Dex grinned at him.

"Okay, then it looks as bad as it is. Broke my wrist thanks to Thunder Clap."

"You tried to ride him?" Pop looked like he wondered where Carlitos left his brain.

"Nah. I know my limits. This was from helping Miggy Alvarez."

Dex and Pop shared a glanced and nodded in unison.

"So how's it going out here? She fixin' to be a mama or make ya'll wait all night?"

"I don't know if she knows. We've been waiting a good couple hours and I'm almost ready to call Doc Ford."

If Dex was thinking of calling the vet, there might be reason to worry.

"Maybe she's just feeling shy." Carlitos paused to watch My Lady who acted like she didn't know or care there were men here to help her. Then he remembered why he came out. "I told Ma I'd spell you, Pop, so she could feed you. She's got plenty, Dex, if you want to go too."

"Nah, I'll stay here. But Pedro, you go on. No need for you to go hungry."

Pop rubbed his belly. "No one's gonna accuse me of missing too many meals." He chuckled and turned to Carlitos. "Did you see Carmelita or Raul at the house?"

"Nope." Funny, he never even thought to ask Ma about his younger siblings. "Wonder where they are?"

"Probably not back from the church youth trip. More'n likely they're fixin' to be here soon. Let me go check in with Elena and I'll be back." Pop squeezed Carlitos's shoulder as he turned to leave.

Carlitos stooped next to Dex. "What are ya thinking?"

"She doesn't seem distressed. And up to about twenty minutes ago I figured it was all going like clockwork. Now, I don't know."

As if she heard Dex's words, the Appaloosa mare lifted her head, looked him in the eyes, and snorted. She'd been laying down but now pushed herself to her feet.

After about three steps, she crouched and her waters broke.

"It's time." They whispered at the same time and moved back into the neighboring stall to help ease things for the mare.

She lowered again and rolled to her side. Since this was her first foal, Carlitos knew it would take longer, up to an hour. He got comfortable on a hay bale to watch the show through the openings between the slats in the stall wall.

My Lady's hard labor lasted around fifty-five minutes when she expelled a miniature of herself, right down to the spots on the foal's flanks. Now the new mother needed time to recover. This was the only thing stopping him and Dex from coming around the corner to check. She might try to stand before it was safe for her. But given the time and space, she'd know when she was ready to clean and nuzzle her baby to stand.

Carlitos stayed long enough to see My Lady begin her licking process. Then he patted Dex on the shoulder and motioned with his head toward the house.

Dex nodded and Carlitos left.

Back in his Ma's kitchen, Pop wiped his bowl clean with his tortilla. "I should have come back out, but I didn't want to leave your mama alone." He winked.

Ma swatted his shoulder. "You better be grateful, mijo. I saved you some pozole before your papa could finish it off." She chuckled.

"Thanks, Ma. I'll be out in a minute to have some more. I just want to see what Ronnie left for me. I can't wait for Christmas."

"You better. You don't want to ruin her surprise." Ma's voice floated up the stairs to him.

He'd be happy to show her surprise, but he'd waited just as long as he could stand.

A white envelope sat on his dresser, his name written in her big, loopy writing. It made him smile.

Tucking a finger under the corner of where she'd sealed it, he tore it open to a folded piece of paper.

Cal,

I can't do this.

I'll return the ring when I get back.

Ronnie

Acknowledgements:

Abba Father, this was our most difficult one to write to date, but with Your faithfulness, it is finished. Thank You. I cannot do anything without You.

To my wonderful P.I.T. crew who prays me through each story keeping me accountable—Annie, Deb, Lori D., Julie, Alyssa, and Dorothy—I needed to rely on you all more than I did. Lesson learned. Thank you for praying even when I didn't keep you all apprised.

Thank you to my cover artist, Stephanie with Alt 19 Creative. I feel like we're a real team and I look forward to seeing how your genius captures my imagination with future covers.

My Beta Readers and Street Team, you are such a huge support. Thank you! And extra thanks to Katherine Karrol, Diana Lesire Brandmeyer, and Jennifer Crosswhite who all spoke the truth that made this book better..

To Liz Tolsma, my editor and friend, who took this with her while she did on-site research in Poland and while taking a family trip. That it dedication. Thank you for your wonderful edits and encouragement. You are amazing, kiddo. Hugs!

To Linda Larsen—who back in sixth grade made a statement that had a far-reaching effect on my life's career—you've now had a hand in my second career. I thank you for the chance to reconnect and all the help you gave with this book. It means a lot.

To my classmates at KHS—Yay Class of '74—who are generous to answer questions about things I can't quite remember. And especially Lisa Rink, thank you for coming up with the names for restaurants in Kokomo that I'd forgotten. Next year it's the 50/100—50th Class Reunion of the 100th Graduating Class. Can't wait to see you all!

My extraordinary family is so encouraging—Phil, Jaime, Jonathan, Alyssa, Juan, Natalia, Meg, Mat, Owen, Kami, Amy, Rick, Rusty, Sandi, Aunt Kay, Sheilia, Dardie, Vicki, Jo, Suzy, Linda, and all my extended loved ones. I couldn't do this without you all.

And, Mom and E.B. I miss you.

About the Author

Historical Christian Romance author, Jennifer Lynn Cary, likes to say you can take the girl out of Indiana, but you can't take the Hoosier out of the girl. Now transplanted to the Arizona desert, this direct descendant of Davy Crockett and her husband of forty plus years enjoy time with family where she shares tales of her small-town heritage and family legacies with their grandchildren.

You can contact Jennifer via her website www.jenniferlynncary.comOr use this QR code.

Also By Jennifer Lynn Cary

The Crockett Chronicles Series:

The Patriarch: : Book 1

The Sojourners: Book 2

The Prodigal: Book 3

Tales of the Hob Nob Annex Café

The Relentless Series:

Relentless Heart: Book 1

Wedding Bell Blues: Book 2

Relentless Joy: Book 3

Silver Bell Christmas: Book 4

The Traveling Prayer Shawl

The Weather Girls Trilogy:

Sunny

Stormy

Windy

The Forgotten Gratitude Journal

Cheryl's Going Home (A Weather Girls Novel)

The Weather Girls Wedding Shoppe and Venue Series:

Judy in Disguise (Book One)

Sylvia's Mother (Book Two)

Runaround Sue (Book Three)

Nonfiction:

When God Holds Your Hand

Or use this:

QR code for Amazon Author page

Made in the USA
Las Vegas, NV
03 January 2024

83846003R00194